MARK
of the
SYLPH

DEMONS OF INFERNUM

The Demons of Infernum series

Blood of the Demon

Mark of the Sylph

Touch of the Angel

Heart of the Incubus (novella)

MARK
of the
SYLPH

DEMONS OF INFERNUM

ROSALIE LARIO

Entangled Publishing, LLC
2614 South Timberline Road
Suite 109
Fort Collins, CO 80525
Visit our website at www.entangledpublishing.com.

Edited by Libby Murphy and Heather Howland
Cover design by Heather Howland

Print ISBN   978-1-62061-217-0
Ebook ISBN   978-1-62061-218-7

Manufactured in the United States of America

Second Edition March 2013

To my son David,
In many ways I feel as if I was reborn on the day of your birth.
You've changed my life so completely. Every day with you is one
of joy and discovery.
I hope I can one day inspire you as you did me.

CHAPTER ONE

Taeg was a man on a mission. Too bad he didn't quite know what it was.

For the third time this week, he stood in this old, stuffy library—the largest in New York City—a place no man in his right mind would ever be. He'd much rather be at a bar right now. Better yet, at the apartment of that bendy exotic dancer he'd met a couple nights ago.

If anyone had asked him last week, he would've known exactly what he was supposed to be doing here. But the librarian at the front counter distracted the hell out of him. Not because she was smoking hot—which, admittedly, she was—but no, it was something else.

There was something *off* about her.

From a distance, he watched her smile at the man on the opposite side of her counter, her lips forming the words, "Can I help you?"

It was far different from the way she'd treated him when she first saw him. The initial flare of recognition in her eyes

ROSALIE LARIO

had given way to revulsion and disdain. She'd treated him like gum on the bottom of her shoe. He would have understood her contempt if she had been one of the chicks he'd boned and never called back. But he was pretty damned sure he'd never slept with her.

He would have remembered her.

Her customer left and she bent over, searching for something under the counter. Damn, but she had a backside on her. From what he could see it was luscious, round and plump, the perfect match for her more-than-generous breasts. But that train of thought was way too dangerous, as his rapidly growing erection reminded him. Something told him she'd be none too pleased if he walked up to her sporting a semi.

Adjusting himself, he adopted a cheeky grin and sauntered over. "Good afternoon, sunshine."

She stiffened and straightened, shooting him a glare so blistering it would have made the toughest of demons cringe. Even coming from such a little slip of a thing—she couldn't be more than a couple inches over five feet—her stare was intimidating. "Here again, Mr…?"

"Meyers. Taeg Meyers," he supplied, using the last name he'd taken since making the move to this dimension six months ago. He'd bet his ass she remembered his name. She seemed to hate him too much to forget. He gave her a flirtatious wink. "Couldn't stay away."

The woman gritted her teeth. "What do you want?"

Yup, still hated him. He didn't get it. He was a good-looking guy. Plenty of women had told him so. Why did she look at him like he had a third eyeball growing out of his forehead?

He handed her the scrap of paper he'd scribbled his book requests on. She briefly glanced at it before raking him once again with her contemptuous glower. "More research on the Arthurian legend?"

"What can I say? I'm a sucker for the oldies."

Her gaze traveled down his body and all the way back again, the cold derision in her eyes so at odds with what he was used to getting from women when they checked him out. "You don't seem like the type to care about ancient myths."

Yeah, she told him that every freaking time. Taeg rubbed his chin, scruffy from three days without shaving, and glanced down at his tattered jeans and T-shirt emblazoned with the words NEED A JOB... WILL WORK FOR ORGASMS before giving her an innocent look. "What do you mean?"

She opened her mouth to reply, but anything she might have said was drowned out by the familiar pulse of energy that indicated someone was approaching. Someone who wasn't human.

A demon.

Taeg whirled around to see a creature sauntering toward them. He wore the guise of a scholarly old man, with white hair and glasses set askew on his large nose. Based on his genial smile and the fact he was in a library of all places, Taeg was willing to bet he was a nagora. They were harmless demons who, with their tiny bodies, green flesh, and pointy ears, resembled something of a cross between Yoda and a gremlin. The ultimate scholars, they would be at home in a place like this. Unlike him.

The demon gave him a curious glance and nodded his head respectfully. Taeg relaxed, returning the nod before turning back to face the woman. He froze at what he saw.

She stared at the nagora, the look of disgust on her face similar to the one she reserved for him. But wait... she wasn't staring in the right place. She appeared to be looking at the space where the nagora's head really *would* be. Not that Taeg could see it through the nagora's glamour.

What. The. Fuck?

She schooled her features into an expressionless mask and forced her eyes up as the nagora stopped in front of her desk.

"Good afternoon, miss," the nagora said to her. "Perhaps you could assist me?"

Her mouth tightened and her focus dropped once more before shooting back up. "What?" she snapped at the nagora, no less rudely than she'd addressed Taeg.

Taeg's breath caught in his throat. *No, it can't be.*

Books forgotten, he turned and stumbled off before he could give himself away. He forced his feet to move, one in front of the other, until he'd strode out of the large set of double doors and into the hall. Leaning his back against the wall, he took a deep breath and pondered the implications of what had just happened.

It seemed impossible. He'd never heard of anything like this before.

Taeg straightened and glanced into the research room. The nagora still talked to the librarian. She kept her whole body tense and her attention rooted in front of her, like she was forcing herself to stand in her spot and not look down.

"Son of a bitch," he muttered, ignoring the reproachful glance he received from a man walking into the research room. Impossible as it might be, it seemed pretty clear—the woman was a magic-sensitive. And not just any magic-sensitive.

She could see through glamours.

How rare was that? He'd heard of magic-sensitives before—humans who could sense the presence of magic or Otherworldly beings—but he'd never heard of one who could actually see through glamours.

"Well, what do you know?" Taeg let out a long, soft laugh. It appeared today was his lucky day. The saucy little librarian with her lethal glares had just become his number-one priority. Because, wouldn't you know…she happened to have the one thing he needed the most right now.

The woman obviously hated him—and probably all demons, from the looks of it—but she would help him. Whether she wanted to or not.

Taeg composed himself and strolled down the hallway. When he felt the urge to hum a rousing rendition of "Whistle While You Work," he gave in to it. Not even the angry hisses and boos of his fellow library patrons would get him down today.

He'd hunt himself down a member of the staff and learn all there possibly was to know about his bad-tempered librarian.

Like it or not, she was about to get to know him a *whole* lot better.

৯৽৻

Maya Flores anxiously counted down the minutes until closing time. When it came and went with no sign of the irritating Mr. Meyers, she let out a huge sigh. He'd left without getting his books, and she'd spent the rest of the day fearing he would return for them.

She grabbed a stack of reference materials and sorted through them. He disgusted her, masquerading as a human, when she knew perfectly well what he really was—one of the most vile creatures in existence. A demon.

Worse, he was one of the few demons she'd seen who appeared almost entirely human. Well, except for those fiery red eyes whose pupils swirled in a shade of plum, and that faint golden glow, as if he were an angel. *Ha.* Far from it.

Before he'd walked into her research room earlier this week, she hadn't known a demon could look like that. So carelessly masculine, with his lean, muscular physique, olive-toned skin, and dark, tousled hair. He would have had top male model potential…that was, if he weren't made of hellfire.

Even if no one else could tell, she knew he was a demon. He made her skin crawl. Made her want to puke. Made her ache to sever his head from his body, something she knew from experience killed all demons.

So if he was the evil and disgusting creature she knew he was, why did seeing him make her thighs tingle and her panties wet? Why did the flash of his perfect white teeth make her heart skip a beat?

"Why am I even thinking about him?"

He must be an incubus. That had to be it. There was no way she could ever be attracted to a demon. No way in hell.

Not after what she'd lived through.

"Shit." She slammed a book onto the counter, furious at the direction her thoughts had taken her. "I hate demons."

"Sorry?" a familiar voice said.

Maya whirled around, flushing as Alice, the head

librarian, walked up behind her. "Oh…um, just got some shelving to do."

"You're not staying late, are you?" Alice's eyes, round and large as an owl's behind her tortoiseshell glasses, stared at her in frank assessment.

"No." She let out a nervous laugh. "I'll be out of here soon."

"Mm-hm." Alice gave her a look that said she didn't believe it, but thankfully didn't question her. "When are you working next?'

"Not until Friday."

"Five days off, hmm?"

"Yeah, I need to concentrate on school," Maya replied, although really, that was the least of her concerns.

"Have a good evening, then." Alice reached underneath the counter for her purse. "See you on Friday."

"Bye." Maya ambled about the room, taking her time shelving the books. She forced herself to wait for about half an hour after Alice left, making sure the building had emptied. Now that the library was vacant, her real work began, the reason she'd taken this part-time position to begin with.

Tossing her backpack over one shoulder, she walked out of the research room and down the long hallway. Her thick heels made a rhythmic click on the marble floors, echoing loudly in the empty space as if pointing out how alone she was in this huge building. She passed several doors, coming to a stop at the room that contained the collection of ancient Bibles. After another paranoid peek around to confirm she was alone, she walked inside and selected one, then sat down to work.

෨ඁ෯

Where was she?

Taeg leaned against the wall of the building across from the library and checked his watch for the fifth time in an hour. Night had fallen a couple of hours ago, and the place had already cleared out.

Earlier, after he'd left his cantankerous little magic-sensitive, he'd managed to catch another staff member alone, an older woman. It had been the perfect opportunity to use his ability to charm her into spilling everything she knew about the librarian.

Maya. Even her name was sexy.

Thanks to the staff member, he now knew Maya was a part-timer, as well as a graduate student, who apparently liked to stay late after work. What the woman had failed to mention was how late Maya stayed.

What could she be doing alone in there for this long? Just thinking about it made him antsy. Too bad he couldn't flash in there. Not with the security cameras he'd spotted throughout the ground floor. He'd learned the hard way to check for those after an unfortunate incident shortly after he'd moved to this dimension, when he'd tried to avoid the line at a strip club. Thankfully, he'd been able to use his charm on the bouncers to make them forget what they'd seen. Pretty awesome gift he'd been blessed with, if he did say so himself.

For a second Taeg considered dissipating into air and gliding into the building to check on her. But no. Unlike flashing, his clothes didn't travel with him when he took his air form. They would fall to the ground and, knowing this city, be picked up by the bum lounging at the street corner in less than a minute. As much as the woman disliked him now, something gave him the feeling she'd have a real problem if he appeared in front of her buck-ass naked.

Just as he was about to glance at his watch again, a familiar figure came striding down the steps of the building.

"Finally." He pushed away from the wall and followed her at a safe distance. Once there weren't so many witnesses around, he'd pull her aside and use his charm to get what he needed out of her.

As he walked, he kept his sights glued on the round, lush curves of Maya's sweet little ass. Couldn't help himself. It was rounder and plumper than he'd suspected from his first brief glimpse of it. Some might even say it was too big, but if so they'd be idiots.

"Ain't nothing wrong with her." And no doubt, she knew it. Though her jeans and black shirt were respectable, they were tight enough that she obviously realized the appeal of her ripe curves. And those black knee-high boots she had her jeans tucked into? *Damn.*

He loved a woman with confidence, and her attire *screamed* confidence.

Taeg followed her for several blocks before losing sight of her at a red light. But he still smelled her, so he followed her scent. Little Maya's aroma was like honeysuckle and spice. Like an exotic, mouthwatering dessert. How hot was that?

He almost bypassed the dark alley, but his nose told him to stop. Turning to face it, he inhaled, ignoring the odor of garbage and rot.

What the hell?

Why would she have gone into a dark alley? Did the woman have a death wish?

With a muffled curse, he stepped into the alleyway, bypassing a sleeping drunk and several hungry-looking rats. Up ahead was a gap several feet wide. A crossroad of sorts, marking where one set of buildings ended and another began. A million spots for someone with dishonorable intentions to hide.

Seriously, was the chick nuts? Why would she have gone down an alley? This place gave *him* the creeps, and he was fairly sure he could take anyone or anything that might think to hide in here.

Taeg had taken several steps forward when a small figure whirled around the corner of the gap. Something came at his face. He had little time to jump back before a wicked blade sliced the air in front of him. It cut a shallow nick in his flesh. At least it hadn't lodged itself deep in his larynx, as it surely would have if he hadn't reacted quickly.

"What the fuck?" he choked out.

It was Maya. She whirled around and again aimed at his neck, her long hair slapping his chest and assaulting him with the muted scent of honeysuckle. He lifted his forearm, blocking the thrust with an outward jab that knocked her to the side. Before she could attack again, Taeg grabbed her wrist and slammed her against the nearest wall.

"What do you think you're doing?" he said.

"Fuck you, demon scum," she spat, struggling to free her hand.

O-k-a-a-a-y…that cleared up any niggling doubt that she could see past his glamour.

Taeg tightened his hold on her wrist until she dropped the dagger. He grabbed her other wrist and pinned it back. "Look at me."

Yeah, apparently she wasn't in an accommodating mood. Because instead of listening she jerked her knee up, catching him square in the junk.

"*Ooof.*" That freaking *hurt*.

He let go, hands automatically lowering to protect his goods, and she shoved hard on his chest. As he staggered several feet back, she spun and delivered a stunning roundhouse kick that almost had him admiring her form, right before it caught him in the side and sent him sprawling.

"What's the deal, lady?"

She grabbed the knife and flew at him faster than he would've expected from a human.

Taeg shoved off the ground and sidestepped her attack, and recaptured her wrist. He yanked her arm up behind her as he maneuvered behind her back.

"Shit," Maya cried. The knife clanged to the ground, and he loosened his hold a fraction.

"Stop. I don't want to hurt you."

"Yeah. Right." Her tone made it clear what she thought of that.

Pushing her to the nearest wall, Taeg turned her to face him. He kept one hand on her shoulder and the other on her chin, forcing her to meet his eyes.

"Calm down, Maya." The familiar hum of energy in his ears told him his charm was doing its thing. "I'm not going to hurt you. I only want to ask you a few questions."

Her scowl softened long enough for him to assume his power had worked. He let her go and backed up a few steps. "How do you know what I am? Can you see the real me?"

Rather than answering, she lifted a knee and slid one of her dainty hands into her boot. When she withdrew it, she clutched another dagger, a match to the one on the ground. Suddenly the reason for her boots became quite clear. The woman was a freakin' walking arsenal.

"Oh, shit."

She kicked off the wall and leapt into the air in a flying move that Jackie Chan would have envied, adjusting the grip on her dagger. Hand high in the air, she aimed for his neck. The woman was clearly determined to remove his head from the rest of his body. Taeg dropped his legs out from under him, hitting the ground hard.

Maya's legs struck his back as she flew over him. He untangled himself and whirled around, but *damn* she recovered fast. She tossed her dagger to the side to avoid jabbing herself as she tucked and rolled. Then she jumped to her feet and faced him with both fists up. Her face was almost expressionless, her heavy panting the only indicator she was battling to the death. Damned if his interest wasn't drawn to her ample chest beneath that tight black top.

She smiled, almost as if she were enjoying herself, and came at him with another kick.

He leapt back to avoid being hit. "Damn it, I'm trying to talk to you, lady."

Beyond frustrated now, Taeg closed his fingers around her arm and spun her toward the wall. She hit it hard, chest first, and he used his body to plaster her to it before she could attack him. Yanking her arms to her sides, he growled into her ear. "You've made it quite clear you don't like my kind, but can we stop fighting and talk now? Please?"

"Fuck you, demon." Maya rammed the back of her head against his chest in an effort to dislodge him. The woman was like a wildcat—she just wouldn't stop.

Taeg pushed in closer to her, and suddenly he had a whole different problem. All her frantic squirming and wriggling pushed her luscious ass into his front, and he was in no way immune to that. She couldn't possibly mistake his growing erection pressing to the small of her back.

Great. Now he looked like a would-be rapist. That wouldn't do.

"Can we just *talk* already?" he snapped, letting go of her and backing toward the wall behind him.

"I hope you burn in Hell." She spun and raced at him, her movements frenzied.

Fucking great. The last thing he wanted was to keep fighting her, but he wasn't about to walk away. Not when she hadn't responded to his charm. No, little Maya had now become more intriguing than he'd imagined.

He stepped to the side to avoid her attack, not realizing until he moved how close to the wall he was. She didn't, either. Her eyes widened a fraction of a second before she flew by him, colliding with the wall. Face first. Her head jerked back from the impact. She crumpled to the ground.

"Shit!"

Taeg raced toward her, crouching and turning her limp body so he could examine her face. An almond-sized lump formed high on her forehead, already turning purple from the force of the impact.

"Geez, lady."

It sucked that she'd knocked herself out because of him, but all he'd done the whole time was defend himself. The woman had more moves than a horny teenager on prom night. He studied her in the dim light. Long, dark hair with matching, slanted eyebrows. Mocha skin that suggested an ethnic heritage. And of course, the mouthwatering figure.

He touched his free hand to her bruised forehead. "What secrets are you hiding?"

Aw, crap. Looked like he had an unconscious, wannabe demon-slayer on his hands. What was he going to do with her? He couldn't very well carry her down the street, and he sure as hell couldn't flash home now, as he'd originally intended. Sighing, Taeg fished his cell phone out of his pocket and dialed his brother.

"Dagan, are you at home?"

"Yeah," his brother replied. "Why?"

"I need you to come pick me up. And hurry. It's sort of an emergency."

"What did you do this time?" Dagan drawled.

"Fill you in when you get here. Just move it along." Taeg gave him directions and hung up before his little brother could question him further. Hoisting Maya into his arms, he settled down to wait.

One thing was for sure: Dagan would never let him live this one down.

CHAPTER TWO

"What, you have to knock them out now to get 'em to go home with you?"

"Ha-ha, very funny," Taeg said to Dagan. "For your information, she knocked herself out."

Dagan chuckled from behind the wheel of the fancy 6-Series convertible he'd bought after his last two bounty gigs.

"What's up with the car, bro?" Taeg grumbled from the backseat, where he had a still-unconscious Maya laid across his lap. "Overcompensate much?"

"For what?" Dagan snickered. "I'm not lacking anything."

"Yeah, except humility."

Much as he loved to mess with his brother, Taeg was glad Dagan had taken so well to Earth since they had moved here. The circumstances leading up to that move hadn't been easy on him. On any of them.

Dagan snuck a look at Maya from the rearview mirror, narrowly missing a collision with another car. The other driver laid on his horn.

"Eyes on the road, Chuck."

"Sorry, man, can't help it." Dagan's attention darted back to Maya. "That chick is smokin'."

Taeg snuck his own glance. He couldn't disagree.

"Remind me again why you're taking an unconscious babe home with you? I mean, it'd be one thing if I was picking you up after a four-hour pub crawl, but—"

"I told you, she knew what I was." Taeg took a breath, trying to quell his impatience. If the tables were turned and it was Dagan in the backseat with a passed-out babe in his lap, he'd sure as hell be curious, too.

On second thought, maybe that wouldn't be so surprising, considering it was Dagan.

"Yeah, and on top of that, when I tried to charm her it didn't take," Taeg added.

"You mean *The Gaze* didn't work?" Dagan whistled. "That must have burned your ass."

Now that he mentioned it…that *had* been a major pain. No one had ever failed to respond to him before. Fought it, yes, but failing to respond altogether? "There's something unusual about her."

"I'll say. She's *stacked*. Smells good, too. Like flowers and…cinnamon or something," Dagan said.

Now Dagan was starting to irritate him. Yeah, that's what the tightening in his gut was—irritation. Not jealousy. Couldn't be that. He wasn't all caveman about women like his big brother, Keegan.

Dagan must have sensed what Taeg was thinking. "So you decided to kidnap your own woman, huh? After all, it worked out so well for Keegan."

"Bite me."

But Dagan had a point. When Keegan had kidnapped Brynn six months ago to keep their evil father from using her to raise an army of zombies, none of them could have imagined he'd end up married to her. And now Taeg had inadvertently conducted a kidnapping of his own. The irony wasn't lost on him. But it was for Keegan and Brynn that he was doing this. They were his family, and he owed them. If Maya had a gift that would help him find what he searched for, he would take advantage of that.

"What are you going to do with her?" Dagan asked.

Good question. Taeg studied Maya. She seemed so innocent in sleep with her head tilted to the side, her lips parted. "I'll wait for her to wake up, then find out if she can see through *all* forms of glamours. If so—"

"You think she'll help you find the sword." Dagan's words were more statement than question.

"Yup. She'll help me, like it or not." Taeg would make sure of it.

"Waking up in a strange place won't endear her to you."

"She hates demons, bro. Short of cutting off my own head, I have a feeling nothing I do could endear her to me. Besides, you didn't see her fight. She can take care of herself." Taeg was walking proof of that. He might've been at least ten times stronger than her, but she'd still managed to land some good hits. Thank the devil he healed fast, or he'd be dripping blood all over the inside of his brother's new car.

Just when Taeg was beginning to question his brother's uncharacteristic silence, Dagan asked, "Do you really think the sword can destroy the book?"

"I think it's the best chance we've got. I need to take a crack at it." When Dagan nodded, Taeg added, "Don't tell

Keegan, okay? I don't want to say anything until we know for sure it'll work."

"Yeah, especially considering how dangerous it is," Dagan muttered. "Seems like every Otherworlder on this planet knows about the book's powers and wants to get their hands on it. If you destroy it, you'll be putting a price on your own head."

"True." Taeg thought about it, then shrugged. "But since everyone I know wants to kill me already, what freaking difference does it make?"

"Good point." Dagan let out a snort as he pulled up to the front of Taeg's Lower East Side apartment, which he'd rented from Brynn after she married Keegan and moved in with him.

"Hey, bro, I need to borrow your car. Find somewhere around here to park it."

"Fuck you." Dagan turned to face him, a deep scowl on his face. "I just got this thing, and you want me to park it on the street? Plus, you've never really driven before."

"If an imbecile like you is doing it, how hard can it be?" Taeg nodded toward Maya's sleeping form. "I'll need the car to transport her."

"I can't believe this." Dagan muttered a defeated curse as he turned to face the front.

"Thanks, bro. Walk the keys up when you're done parking." Shifting Maya forward on his lap so he could reach the car door, Taeg turned the handle and slid out with her in his arms.

"Remember, not a word."

"Yeah, yeah."

At the building's entrance, Taeg fumbled in his pocket

for the key. Maya was light by his standards, but it was still difficult to maneuver her. Finally, he tossed her over his shoulder and opened the door. With his shitty luck, he half-expected one of his nosy neighbors to pop out to see what was up, but he got all the way to his third floor apartment without seeing another soul. Unfortunately, the way he carried Maya put her curvaceous rear on display.

Ignore it. Just ignore it.

Easier said than done.

He unlocked his front door and entered the apartment. What now? He couldn't just put her down. She'd probably karate chop his ass out the window the minute she regained consciousness. With a muffled curse, he carried her into his bedroom and laid her on the bed. He had to tie her up. No doubt that would piss her off even more once she awoke, but he couldn't think of a better option.

He rummaged through his closet and dug out some silk ties his friend Cresso had jokingly bought for him when he'd first made the move to Earth. After he'd tied Maya's arms to the ornate metal headboard he stepped back and admired his handiwork. She didn't budge. He touched the top of her forehead where a bruise had already formed. Too bad he couldn't heal others like his brothers, Keegan and Ronin. She would probably have a major headache when she woke up.

He didn't realize he was standing there watching her until a knock sounded on his door. Dagan, no doubt, with the keys to his car. After one last lingering glance, Taeg left the bedroom, closing the door behind him.

No, she definitely wasn't going to be happy when she woke up.

Awareness returned slowly, melding with the remnants of old memories and all-too-familiar nightmares.

Clomp... Clomp... Clomp.

The man's booted feet thumped across the wooden floor. From her hiding spot, she clamped her lips shut so she wouldn't scream. Could he see her? Did he know where she was?

She inched her bare feet farther back into the dark, terrified he'd be able to spot them. That he'd find her.

An amused, gravelly voice called out to her. "Donde estas, niñita?" Where are you, little girl?

He sounded human, so very human, but he wasn't. Por Dios, *she knew he wasn't.*

Maya's eyes flew open. Her breath puffed out in harsh gasps that made her fear she would hyperventilate. She tried to sit up but she couldn't move. "What the—?"

Her vision finally cleared. She was in a bedroom. A small bedroom decorated in warm, masculine colors. And she was *tied to the freaking bed.*

Her last memories came back in a blinding rush. She'd been walking home when she felt someone following her. Squeezing in with a small group of pedestrians, she'd snuck a quick peek behind her. It was the demon from the library— Taeg, he'd called himself. He'd probably decided she was his next meal. So she'd squeezed into the first dark alley she could find and snatched one of the daggers from her boot. Then she'd waited.

Oh God, she'd gotten cocky. Had thought she could use the element of surprise to take him. She knew demons were strong, much stronger than humans, but he wouldn't be the first demon she'd taken down.

The others hadn't seen it coming. But somehow, he had.

She'd underestimated his strength and speed. And now she was tied to his bed with her head propped up on two fluffy pillows.

"No." This couldn't be happening.

From the other side of the closed door came the soft thumping of someone walking across a room. She fought a burst of pain and the nausea that arose when she turned her head toward the door. Memories engulfed her, threatening to take over once again.

Clomp... Clomp... Clomp.

His boots stomped on the floor. So loud, but even still she was afraid the sound would be drowned out by the fierce pumping of her own heart. Could he hear it?

They were dead. They were all dead. She'd heard the screams.

The monsters had come here for her. Because of her.

And now everyone was dead. It was all her fault.

As if he could sense her fear, he laughed. "Donde estas, niñita? Te encontraré." I'll find you.

"No," Maya gasped, forcing her mind away from the memories she couldn't help but relive. Things had changed. She was much stronger now. No longer a frightened little girl who didn't understand the concept of true evil.

She would survive this.

Maya forced herself to close off her emotions, and braced for a fight. At least the sick bastard had neglected to tie down her legs. She still had some measure of control. All he had to do was get close enough to her.

The door swung open and the light came on. She winced as it temporarily blinded her.

"You're awake," the monster said, as if they were meeting somewhere for tea rather than in his bedroom with her tied to his bed.

"You'll regret this, demon." She tensed and the silk straps restraining her to the bed tightened. At least the material didn't cause her any pain.

He leaned against the doorjamb, looking confident and carelessly masculine in his T-shirt and worn jeans. Even she would admit that his playboy looks could make any woman drool. Any woman who couldn't see the real him, that was.

Those eyes, those evil red eyes.

"You're the one who wanted to turn our conversation into a Bruce Lee flick," he said to her. "I just wanted to *talk*."

"Yeah, 'cause all demons ever want to do is *talk*," she deadpanned.

He scoffed at her words. "You sure have a low opinion of demons. Someone did a real number on you, huh?"

"A what?" she sputtered. The nerve of him, to act like she was the crazy one. "You…you *suck*."

"How do you know what I am?" He cocked his head to the side in a manner that showcased the strong bent of his jaw underneath his scruffy growth of facial hair.

Again with that question. What did he care *how* she knew? "Eat shit and die, hell spawn."

The demon let out a disbelieving laugh, though if Maya didn't know better, she would have thought he almost appeared hurt at her words. "I'm in for one hell of a hard time, aren't I?"

"You'd better believe it." If she was in an apartment, he

had to have neighbors. Taking a deep breath, she screamed, "Someone help me. I've been kidnapped. Help!"

He chuckled and shook his head. He started toward her, the soles of his scuffed shoes rapping on the hardwood floor. "The walls in my apartment are soundproof."

Clomp… Clomp… Clomp.

"*Donde estas, niñita?*"

"No," she whispered, shaking her head in an effort to clear those unwanted memories.

He froze in place, a strange look crossing his face. Slowly lifting his hands up, he backed away a few paces. "I'm not going to hurt you. I swear on my mother's life."

Oh, shit. Despite her best attempts to hide her fear, he'd seen it. Maybe she wasn't as strong as she thought.

No. She was strong.

She squared her shoulders and made her voice hard as steel. "Yeah, right, like demons have mothers."

"Of course we do." He gave her a puzzled look. "Did a demon hurt you?"

Maya fought to keep her mouth from dropping open. Why was he asking her this? Why hadn't he attacked her already? And why on earth was he trying to reassure her, of all things? "Mind your own business."

He shook his head and actually had the nerve to look exasperated. "I would never hurt a woman."

"Yeah, why don't I believe that? Maybe 'cause I'm tied to your bed." The dull throb heightened to a sharp ache every time she lifted her head to look at him.

"Hey, all I did back there was defend myself, sweetheart. If you'll recall, I tried reasoning with you."

Reasoning? She let out a snort. "Like demons can reason.

And don't call me sweetheart."

Something about his frown almost made her feel guilty. That pissed her off.

"You are an amazingly difficult woman to talk to, you know that?"

"What do you want with me?" By some miracle, she managed to keep her voice even.

"Look"—he raked a hand through his hair before looking her in the eye—"I couldn't help but notice back at the library that you could tell what I was, what the other man—"

"*Demon*," she said. "He was not a *man*."

"I want to know more about what you can do," he continued, ignoring her outburst.

Maya stared at him in disbelief. This wasn't at all going how she'd imagined. Why hadn't he attacked her yet? What was he waiting for? That he'd tied her to the bed while she was unconscious told her he liked to play with his prey. But now she was beginning to suspect he liked to talk them to death first. "Why would you care about what I can do?"

"I have my reasons." His bit his lip and turned away, as if he were nervous. Hiding something, was more like it.

"Let me get this straight. You kidnapped me because you want to know more about me, not because you have any plans to hurt me? Because of course, you would never do that." Maya made sure her tone left no doubt as to what she really thought about him.

He lifted one perfect brow. "That's right, sugar."

Grrr. Gritting her teeth at his casual endearment, she said, "Excuse me if I don't believe you. Something about being *tied up*." She rattled her wrists for emphasis.

Her point must have struck home, because he tilted his

head and narrowed his eyes, as if considering the wisdom of her words. "If I untie you, do you promise to hear me out?"

Maya stilled. Did he mean that? Even if he didn't, if he could only get close enough to her...

She looked him straight in the eye. "Yes."

He nodded and started toward her. She held her breath and focused on him, rather than on the nightstand she'd spotted next to the bed. It held a lamp that looked heavy enough to do some damage. Better yet, a glass picture frame, with a photo of him laughing as he casually reclined on a couch with three other men. Three other gorgeous men who looked quite similar to him. Funny how the demon qualities didn't capture on film. He looked normal. Human.

"Listen, I'm sorry about your head." He reached the side of the bed and leaned over to untie her wrist. "I'd heal it if I could."

"Heal?" Anything else Maya might have said died away as she breathed in his scent. Lord, it was positively sinful, like chocolate and sex. And his fingers seared where they touched her flesh, body heat rising off him in palpable waves. Despite herself, she felt an answering twinge between her thighs and fought back a flush of shame.

Incubus. He had to be.

She couldn't tell if she was more shocked or confused when he actually did as he said and released her wrist. She tensed, prepared to fight, but forced herself to lie still when he moved around to the opposite side of the bed and went to work on the knot restraining her other wrist.

"There." He gave her a quick smile and rose off the bed. "All done—"

Before he could finish his sentence, she swung her leg

around and kicked him square in the jaw with the heel of her boot.

He dropped to the ground, flat on his back.

Perfect.

That should give her enough time.

Twirling her body back toward the nightstand, she slapped the picture frame down, shattering the glass, and grabbed the biggest sliver. Then, ignoring the prick to her finger, she launched herself over the bed.

"Shit," he grunted when she landed hard on him, jabbing her knee into his gut. His hard-as-steel gut. Not that she noticed.

She aimed the glass at his throat, but he blocked her with his forearm to her wrist. *Damn it.* He used her shock to his advantage and flipped her onto her back, covered her body with his, and knocked the glass away.

"I didn't figure you one for breaking your promises." His eyes flashed a brilliant, dark red, showing her just how angry her betrayal made him, as he dragged her wrists above her head.

Damn, he was too strong. She couldn't get leverage on him. Blinking away the sudden sting of hot tears, she focused on causing maximum damage. If he was going to take her down, she'd at least make sure it hurt.

"Promises made to a demon don't count, incubus."

That gave him pause. He shot her a lopsided grin. "You think I'm an incubus?"

Oops, she hadn't meant to say that aloud.

"Go back to Hell." She punctuated her words with a head butt that caught him on the chin. Stars flared in her vision and her head pounded.

"Ow!" He pushed his upper body off the floor, leaving a few inches of space between them. "Give the jaw a rest, will ya?"

She took advantage of the gap and bent her knees, popping her pelvis to the side and using his hands around her wrists as leverage to flip him onto his back. She straddled him, trying to twist her wrists free from his grasp. "Let go of me."

"So you can gouge my eyes out with your nails? I don't fucking think so, lady."

He almost sounded amused by this whole scene, damn him. Growling deep in her throat, Maya slammed her forehead down toward his, but he anticipated it this time and shifted so she only caught his shoulder.

Crap. She tried to lurch back but he clamped his forearms around her legs at his sides, while keeping her wrists enclosed in his hands. He'd managed to trap her as effectively as a hogtied animal, even though she was the one on top. She tried to shimmy off.

"I wouldn't do that if I were you," he said. "I'm afraid you won't like the consequences."

Maya froze when her ass met with the very consequence she was certain he referred to. *He* might not like her squirming, but his body apparently didn't agree. Mortified, she chanced looking him in the eye.

The insolent demon actually had the nerve to wink at her.

"Then again," he drawled, "if you think I'm an incubus, maybe that's exactly what you're looking for." He injected a good dose of humor in his innuendo, as if he wanted to make sure she knew he was only kidding.

All her fight fled her in a defeated rush. He was obviously far stronger than she was. He could have killed her a dozen times over by now. Instead, he cracked jokes with her. What kind of demon would do such a thing?

"I...I don't understand."

He sobered as he replied evenly. "You might, if you stop trying to kill me for one second and just talk to me."

She stared at him, certain her utter confusion read on her face. What could he possibly have to say to her? Why was he acting so reasonable? And why oh why, knowing what he was, could she not help but notice the searing heat of his body pressing against her thighs, or the hard ridges of his muscles beneath her?

"Okay," she said, all too aware that she sounded beaten. "Let me up, and I'll listen to what you have to say. I promise."

"All right." His grip on her wrists tightened. "But you have to tell me one thing first."

She gave him a suspicious glare. "What?"

"No fucking around. Can you see through glamours?"

The unexpected straightforwardness of that question startled her into aggression. "Screw you."

She tried lifting up again but his forearms pressed tighter into her thighs. There was another hard poke against her ass and this time he laughed. "I already know the answer. Just admit it."

"Bite me."

"Careful what you say around here. For all you know, I'd gladly do that."

"You're such an ass." Maya tried to twist away again, but gave up when the hardness against her rear noticeably grew.

"Fine," she snapped.

He raised his brows. "Fine what?"

"I can see through glamours," she admitted.

Although he must have expected her to say it, his surprise was clear. A calculating expression came over his face. He let her go with an easy grin. "This is going to be interesting."

Chapter Three

Tonight was a nice night for a walk. Not that Dagan wasn't pissed about Taeg ganking his car, but if he had to take the subway home at least the weather was good.

Dagan gave the doorman an easy nod as he strolled inside his building. He rode the elevator up to the huge apartment he shared with Keegan, Brynn, and Ronin, wondering all the while what Taeg was up to with his new find. He had all the luck, snatching up a little hellcat like that.

Would she make love as passionately as Taeg had told him she'd fought? An interesting thought, but he didn't hold out any hope he'd find out. Demon-hater or not, if she was going to spend any amount of time with Taeg, there was no doubt in his mind whose bed she'd end up in. Even without his ability to charm.

He unlocked the front door, nodded at Reiver, one of the guards Keegan had hired to watch over Brynn and the apartment, and hollered, "I'm home. Miss me?"

Dagan strolled into the kitchen and pulled a beer out of

the fridge. The soft pad of footsteps alerted him to someone's presence. Keegan—shirtless, his shaggy hair dripping wet, as if he'd just gotten out of the shower.

"Want a beer?" He tossed Keegan his beer without waiting for a response and opened the fridge for another. "Ronin around?"

"He's out on a job. What are you doing home so early?"

Dagan shrugged and started toward the living room. "Thought I'd hang out for a while, watch the tube."

Keegan followed close behind him. "Something's up," he said. "Where's Taeg?"

Dagan hid a smile. Keegan knew them too well. He was adept at reading their body language. And Dagan couldn't resist fucking around with him. That's what brothers were for, after all. "He was at home last time I saw him. I imagine he'll still be there."

"What is it?" Keegan asked flatly.

"What do you mean?" Dagan threw himself back onto the couch and plunked his feet on the coffee table. He picked up the remote and was about to turn on the television when Keegan snatched it out of his hand, carelessly dropping it on the floor.

"Dagan, what are you not telling me?"

"Taeg needed to borrow my car. I'm just tired from the walk home."

"Bullshit. You could walk from here to Florida without getting tired." Keegan narrowed his eyes and pinned him with blatant suspicion. "Why did Taeg have to borrow your car?"

"He thinks he'll need it to transport the chick he kidnapped tonight."

"The *what?*"

This time Dagan didn't bother to hide his grin. "Yeah, Taeg went and got himself his very own prisoner. It's all the rage in our family, I hear."

Keegan's patience must have worn thin, because he reached down and grabbed a fistful of Dagan's shirt, spilling some of Dagan's beer as he lifted him a few inches off the couch. "What the fuck is going on?"

Dagan lifted his beer for a sip. "Maybe you should ask Taeg."

"Dagan," his brother said.

"What?" He sobered when it became clear Keegan wasn't going to give up. "I promised him I wouldn't tell. You'll have to talk to him about it."

Which was exactly what needed to happen, in Dagan's opinion. Taeg should've told Keegan months ago what he was up to. It was beyond him why Taeg hid it.

Keegan let go of him and turned around, muttering something about pain in the ass brothers as he strode out of the room. Searching for his phone, no doubt.

This was too much fun. He'd promised Taeg he wouldn't tell Keegan about the sword, but he'd made no such promises regarding the woman. Yeah, he'd admit it; he was still a little pissed about Taeg stealing his ride. But now they were even.

With a chuckle, Dagan picked the remote back up and clicked on the television.

∂∘∽

"Is it just demons you hate, or are you this cheery for everyone?"

Maya glared at Taeg from across the room, rubbing her

wrists with her back against the wall. But in the end, she said nothing. From the noticeable tension in her shoulders, she still had a lot of fight left in her.

Taeg grinned, even though he knew it would only piss her off further. He carelessly dropped onto his side on the bed, propping up his upper body with his elbow. She glanced at the door as if she was contemplating making a run for it, but she turned to glower at him instead.

He sighed. "Come on, Maya. I only—"

"How do you know my name?" She straightened and walked away from the wall, back in full warrior mode. This woman was wound so tightly it was a miracle she could breathe.

"I asked one of your coworkers. Relax for a second, will you?"

She pressed the fingers of one hand to the opposite palm, where she'd nicked herself with the glass. Taeg turned to the broken picture frame. "I really liked that picture, you know."

"Who are those men sitting with you?"

"My brothers."

Her mouth tightened. "More demons."

"Only half." Damn, she was like a dog with a bone, with all her demon-hating. "How long have you known about demons?"

She stilled before she made her admission. There was a story there, and no doubt it was what made her so prickly. "Since I was a little girl."

He put on his best psychiatrist voice. "What happened?"

Maya crossed her arms, putting her ample chest on display. No doubt she'd try to rake his eyeballs out if she knew that he'd noticed. "None of your business."

He dragged his attention to her face. "So you can see what I truly am?"

"Yes."

"You sound disgusted," he noted dryly. "Am I really that ugly to you?"

"Evil is always ugly."

Man, but she had a chip on her shoulder. He tried not to let it hurt his feelings, but yeah, it stung a little. No one had ever looked at him with such pure hatred. Save the exception of his former friend, Leviathos.

"Not all demons are evil, you know."

She laughed at that. "Yeah. Right."

He left it alone. For now. Sitting up, he asked her, "Is it only glamours you can see through?"

"What's it to you?"

"Come on, Maya," he said with forced patience. "You already told me that much. I let you go. Now keep up your end of the bargain and talk to me."

Maya fidgeted, hesitating for a fraction of a second. "Not just glamours. At least I don't think so. There are these... these *things* I see. I don't know what they are. They're hard to describe. Like shimmering spots of land hidden by a hazy, glowing blue veil. There's one in Central Park."

She was talking about the inter-dimensional portals, magical devices that allowed for travel between planes. Not only were the portals invisible to humans, but they contained repellant force fields to keep non-Otherworlders away. And if she could see through them, she could see through anything.

He leaned forward with his elbows on his knees. "When I questioned you back in the alley did you feel any compulsion to obey me?"

Maya gave him a challenging look. "This is the twenty-first century, buddy. I don't feel compelled to obey anybody."

He held back a weary sigh. "I meant my ability to charm."

Well, that got her attention. "You mean to tell me that demons can hypnotize people?"

"Not all demons. Just me."

"Gee, aren't you special?"

Her eyes narrowed in on him, telling him exactly how she felt about him. He had a feeling that to her, he was about five levels down from the piece of gum stuck to the bottom of her boot. Try as he might to ignore it, her contempt burned his ass.

"You know, if you took the time to get to know me, I think you'd realize I'm a halfway decent guy."

"Decent?" she said. "You're not decent. You're not even a guy."

Damn it all. This was just his luck. He'd managed to find a one-in-a-million chance to help him locate the sword, and she held what had to be the world's biggest grudge against demons. How was he going to convince her to help him? "Maya, I—"

His phone rang, startling him into silence. He looked at the caller ID. *Keegan.* A knot of dread settled in his gut. "Damn you, Dagan."

"What?" Maya asked from across the room.

He held up his hand to silence her and answered. "Hello?"

"What the fuck are you doing?" Keegan said without preamble.

"Well hello to you, too, bro."

"Don't mess with me. Dagan told me you kidnapped a woman."

"That little shit." Taeg let out a deep sigh. He should've known Dagan would blab. For some crazy-ass reason, Dagan didn't think he should keep any secrets from their big brother.

"Tell him I'm going to kill him next time I see him."

"Does this have something to do with Leviathos? Because I swear, Taeg, if it does—"

Taeg lowered his voice and said, "She can see through glamours, bro."

That shocked Keegan into momentary silence. "Really?"

"Yeah. People, portals. All types of glamours." Taeg cast a glance at Maya, who was inching toward the door. He hopped off the bed and strode over to it, blocking her way. She retreated to the far side of the room.

"Huh. I won't deny that's interesting," Keegan said, "but that's no reason to kidnap her."

"She can be useful to us," Taeg insisted, lowering his voice even further. If he could avoid Maya hearing this, all the better.

"How?"

"I…" Shit. He wasn't about to tell Keegan about the sword. Not yet.

From the other end of the line, Keegan let out a deep exhale. "You have to let her go. Charm her into forgetting this whole thing and put her back where you found her."

"I can't do that."

"Taeg, you—"

"It doesn't work on her."

There was another long moment of silence before Keegan said, "What?"

"Yeah. She's immune to my ability."

"You can't keep her."

"I know that. I'll treat her right, but first I want to see what she's capable of. And then I'll let her go."

"This *is* about Leviathos, isn't it?" Keegan finally asked. When Taeg didn't respond, he said, "Bring her here. We'll find out what she can do together."

Damn. He didn't want to involve his sister-in-law, Brynn, in all this. Didn't want to remind her of the threat she faced. She had enough to think about right now. He turned to face the doorway so Maya wouldn't hear. "Keegan, why don't—"

"Together," Keegan said, leaving no room for argument.

"Fine." Taeg breathed in deeply. "Tomorrow, okay? I need some time alone with her first."

"Okay. Tomorrow."

Keegan hung up without another word.

Great. Now he had his brother and sister-in-law to deal with, too. Jamming the phone back in his pocket, Taeg turned around to face Maya. "That was—"

He saw the base of the lamp a millisecond before it smashed square into his face.

๑∕

Maya watched Taeg slump to the ground. She'd hit him so hard her arms ached and her shoulders felt like they'd been jerked out of their sockets. But that should keep him down for a while. Maybe.

She dropped the lamp and tried to make her feet move. *Run. Go.*

But her body refused to obey. It wanted to stay here. Stare at the demon who resembled a man. Especially with his eyes closed. If she was smart she'd get out of here quickly, before he recovered. She probably didn't have much time. Rolling his body away from the door, she opened it and stepped out into a small, cozy-looking living room with dark green walls.

There. The front door. She was steps away from freedom. After taking a few uncertain steps forward, she paused.

Go, Maya. Go.

But her feet wouldn't listen.

It appeared she wasn't going to be smart today.

She slipped back into the room and stepped around the demon's unconscious form, heading toward the bed. Moving as quickly as she could, she loosened one of the silk ties from the headboard and knotted an end around the foot post. Then she grabbed his arm and, with a great deal of effort, dragged his solid weight toward it. She knelt on the floor next to him and tied the other end of the silk around his wrist in a thick knot. That would do for now.

Maya leaned back onto her haunches and examined the demon. Unconscious, he didn't appear evil. In fact, with his sharp, symmetrical features and golden glow, he was different from any other demon she'd ever seen. A demon who joked around. Who had family he seemed to care for. Who sounded believable when he assured her he wouldn't hurt her.

How wholly unexpected.

"What's your game?" With her fingertips, she tentatively touched his lips. Soft and full.

What an elaborate ruse to make her believe he wasn't an evil fiend. She wasn't buying it, though.

Then why are you still here, Maya?

Good question. She allowed her fingers to trail down to his chest, which felt like molten steel beneath her fingertips.

She knew from experience that demons ran hot, but she'd never wondered about it before. They came from Hell, after all.

He groaned and shifted, the big lump on his head already beginning to recede. She yanked her hand back. When he settled down without regaining consciousness, she returned her fingers to his stomach. Not an ounce of flab on him, as far as she could tell.

The memory of his hard length pressed against her penetrated her mind, and a rush of warmth coursed through her. He'd seemed surprised when she called him an incubus, but what else could he be?

Without warning, a hand seized her wrist. Before she could react, he flipped her onto her back and buried his face in her hair. His weight pressed down on her. *Oh, fuck!*

"You sure like to play rough, don't you?" he said in a sleepy voice.

For one long moment she lay there, too caught off-guard to answer. She pushed against his chest. "Get *off*, demon."

Taeg lifted his head and curved his lips into a wicked smile. "Is that an invitation, sweetheart? Cause I'd sure as hell love to."

Apparently. The proof of that dug hard and hot against her. Much to Maya's embarrassment, another flare of heat unfurled low in her belly, warming her from the loins up.

"Get off *me*, you idiot."

As if he read her shame, he frowned and raised himself off her. "Sorry, I thought…you had your hands on me."

Maya scrambled to her feet and ran across the room, grabbing the sliver of glass she'd dropped earlier. She fought back a fierce flush as she turned to face him again. "I was…I was checking you for weapons."

"Weapons?" He pushed off the floor with the hand that wasn't tied to the foot post and sat up awkwardly. Doubt written across his face, he muttered, "Well, you found one."

Oh God. Could a person possibly die of mortification?

"If you try to untie that knot, I swear I'll slit your throat. Understood?"

"Loud and clear." He leaned against the bed, somehow managing to appear calm and in control. "So now the tables are turned and I'm the one tied to the bed. Now what?"

Maya lifted herself to her full height. "Now you're going to answer some of my questions."

That was it. That was why she'd stayed when she could have fled. She wanted some answers. Yeah, right. She *almost* believed that.

His eyes shone with obvious amusement. "What do you want to know?"

Man, where did she start? She asked the first thing that came to mind. "Why do you glow? Most other demons don't."

His lips curled into a smile, as if he liked that she was thinking about him. "It's a trait I inherited from my mother."

"Demons actually have mothers?" She'd sort of assumed they were created from hellfire or something. Imagining him with a mother didn't seem possible.

He cocked his head to the side, throwing her an unreadable look. "Everyone has a mother. And mine wasn't a demon."

Huh? "You mean she was *human*?"

A soft sound escaped his lips. "You don't know a damn thing about the Otherworlds, do you?"

"Otherworlds?"

"Never mind. That's a topic for another day."

Okay. Whatever. "What do you want with me?"

He sighed, bringing one of his knees up and casually folding his free arm around it.

"Do you realize how rare your gift is?"

"I…" She toyed with the shard of glass between her fingers. "As far as I know, no one else can see them. Demons, I mean."

"That's right. It makes you very valuable."

"Valuable?" Why did that sound so threatening? She glared at him. "How so?"

"I'm searching for something that's protected by a glamour. But you can see through them, so I thought…"

What he didn't say was loud and clear: he wanted to use her to find this hidden object. As if she'd ever agree to help a demon. But her curiosity got the best of her. "What is it that you're looking for?"

"A sword."

"A sword?" Maya leaned against the wall and crossed her arms. That's why he went to all this trouble? To find a *sword*? "Offhand, I can think of a million places you can find one."

"Right. But this one is special."

"Yeah? How?"

He rubbed his free hand over his eyes, the gesture betraying a level of weariness that surprised her. Did demons get tired?

"Someone I know is linked to something very dangerous," he told her. "An object that can't be destroyed. But I think that maybe, quite possibly, this sword has the ability to do it."

Indestructible objects. Special swords. Sounded like he was talking about magic. But that wasn't possible. Magic didn't exist. Did it?

Well, demons existed…

She started with the obvious question. "Why would I ever help you?"

"Finding it could mean the difference between life and death for someone I care deeply about."

That was a laugh. "I'm not interested in helping out your demon buddies."

He frowned, his brows creasing. "She's not a demon, Maya. She's a human. Like you. And you *are* going to help me, so you might as well get used to it."

Yeah, sure she was. "That's an easy thing for you to say. Especially when you're tied to the bed."

"Enough games." Eyes blazing, he tugged on the silk tie, and it tore with a loud rip. Before she could process what'd happened, he shot up and moved forward until he stood mere inches from her.

She staggered back until she made contact with the wall.

His eyes softened. "I swear to you, Maya, you'll come to no harm by my hands."

The way he said it, she almost believed him.

"But I need your help," he continued, "and you're going to give it to me."

His body was so close she felt the heat emanating from him. She could barely think, much less fight. Her head fell against the wall and she met his level stare. "And if I don't agree to help you?"

"If you don't?" He gave her a feral grin that made her heart give a frightened leap in her chest, even as her limbs weakened from the intensity radiating from him. With deliberation, he lowered his head until his hot breath fanned her ear, sending a warm shiver throughout her body.

"If you don't," he said in a husky tone, "I'll just have to convince you otherwise."

Chapter Four

One thing could be said about spying on Taeg—it never grew boring.

Leviathos pushed away from the wall and stubbed out the cigarette in his hand. He didn't particularly enjoy smoking, but it made for good cover. Since coming to this dimension he'd noticed that lurking outside of a building with no discernable reason for being there tended to arouse others' suspicions. But holding a cigarette? Nobody questioned that.

He gave one last glance at the third-floor window of the building across the street. The light was still on, but he couldn't see anything past the curtain. Shoving his hat farther down his forehead, he walked away.

In the months he'd spied on Taeg, not once had he seen him bring a woman to his apartment. That he'd brought an unconscious one there now was beyond curious. This was no ordinary Friday night fuck. Something was up with that woman. And he intended to find out what.

Taeg must have realized Leviathos would learn the address where he now lived... And the fact that he'd chosen to live in the former apartment of Brynn Meyers, the woman who was the key to the spells contained in the book Leviathos sought, showed just how ballsy he was. He was practically flaunting his location, daring Leviathos to go after him. Apparently Taeg didn't think Leviathos would be able to recover the book.

He would prove him wrong on that one.

Trailing Taeg had led him to the building where Keegan now lived with Brynn. That was probably intentional on the demon's part, considering Brynn was heavily guarded everywhere she went. Taeg no doubt hoped Leviathos would try something stupid like kidnapping her, so he and his brothers could catch him.

Well, he'd show Taeg. And all of his brothers. He wasn't as stupid as they thought. If all went according to plan, in short time he'd have the *Book of the Dead* in his hands. Then he'd find a way to get to Brynn. And he'd finally be able to accomplish what their father had failed to do.

He would become the ruler of Earth.

Truth be told, that wasn't what appealed to him most, though it was certainly a bonus. But no. What he truly longed for was the opportunity to get his revenge on Taeg—the man he'd once loved as a brother.

The man who'd betrayed him.

After a brisk twenty-minute walk, he made it back to the building in which he'd rented an apartment a few months ago. It was a nice, though small, two-bedroom residence located adjacent to Gramercy Park, but that wasn't what he prized about the place. Rather, it was an easy walk to Taeg's apartment, without being close enough for him to worry about Taeg or his brothers inadvertently spotting him. Also, the building happened to house a fair number of demons. Their distinctive auras pulsed around him, oozing and swirling with their combined energy. It was a perfect place to disguise his own presence—right in the thick of the crowd.

Leviathos unlocked his door and stepped inside. Re-locking it, he walked the short corridor leading into his living room…and froze.

A figure stood in the center of his sparsely decorated room, his image shimmering as he peeked out the large window.

"Belpheg," he rasped out, his body going cold as a wave of energy shot through the room, crackling his skin with static electricity.

The man turned to him and smiled. Power shot off his tall, thin frame, sparking an involuntary shiver. Nothing new. Leviathos had come to expect that in the months since they'd become associated.

For not the first time, Leviathos wondered how powerful Belpheg truly was. He'd learned shortly after the man had introduced himself that it wasn't his actual body he was seeing. No, Belpheg wasn't even here. Rather, he was back in his home dimension of Faelan and merely projecting an image of himself onto Earth…one that he'd glamoured into human form. As Leviathos now knew, he was some sort of fae.

An amazing one, clearly.

Belpheg's use of astral projection to transcend dimensions spoke to a level of power that would have cowed Leviathos, had he not known how limited the fae was in this form. No, as it was, he was nothing more than a 3D image. Nothing to fear there…even if his aura did emit a level of electricity that raised all the hairs on the back of Leviathos's neck.

The fact that Belpheg used astral projection rather than traveling to Earth told Leviathos one thing: he was a fugitive from the Council. Interesting to note, but not a real concern. Not as long as Belpheg continued to provide him with the resources he needed to recover the *Book of the Dead.*

"I believe I've found someone who can aid you in recovering the book," Belpheg said, his aura crackling with power.

"Excellent." Leviathos didn't really know how Belpheg found the resources he did, especially in that limited form, but he didn't care. As long as it benefited him.

Belpheg recited the number of his contact, a man named Horster, and then turned back to the window, his shoulders stiff with tension. "We need to recover the book, and soon. I must avail myself of its powers. Time grows short."

The last sentence he muttered so softly that Leviathos barely heard him.

Leviathos held back an amused chuckle. In return for his assistance, Belpheg had requested Leviathos's aid and temporary use of the book once they recovered it. Though Leviathos had agreed, he had his own plans. After all, the fae didn't even have a body in this dimension. Powerful as he might be back on Faelan, how much harm could he possibly cause here on Earth?

"I saw something unusual tonight," Leviathos said as he casually took a seat on his brown leather couch. "Mammon's son, Taeg, carrying a woman back to his apartment. An unconscious woman."

Belpheg's figure floated around to face him, one eyebrow cocked. "And this is abnormal behavior for him?"

Leviathos nodded.

Stroking his chin, Belpheg said, "Then look into her. She might become useful to us."

"No shit," Leviathos said acidly. Belpheg might be right, but that didn't mean he got to treat Leviathos like a mindless minion.

Something dark flashed in Belpheg's eyes, but he refrained from commenting on Leviathos's tone. "I'll check back with you tomorrow."

With those words, Belpheg disappeared.

The crackling of static electricity that accompanied Belpheg's presence faded, leaving Leviathos alone with his thoughts.

Yes, he would explore whether the woman Taeg had brought home could be of use to him. If so, he wouldn't hesitate for one second to exploit her. As Taeg hadn't hesitated to betray him.

He would take the woman, and he would delight in doing so.

ॐ∽

Belpheg broke the link anchoring his essence to Earth, and his spirit sucked back into his body with a painful *slap*. He groaned and clutched his chest, heaving for breath as his weakening heart stuttered before resuming its normal beat.

Damn this body. Little had he known when he'd set out to attain increased power so many years ago that his physical form would be too weak to hold it all. The dark fae were the most gifted of the species, and his clan had been the strongest of them all. The ability of his people to manipulate energy had been unsurpassed…though that still hadn't stopped them from being tricked. From being decimated by the very people who were supposed to protect every species.

The Elden Council.

Members of the Council had learned that their clan leader planned to incite change within the group. He'd felt the members were too powerful. Corrupt. And clearly he'd been right.

They'd wiped out his clan in the span of minutes, casting a spell to stifle the dark fae's powers and razing the entire village. Only he, a boy of twelve years old, had managed to escape, taking with him just a few of the clan scrolls holding the wisdom of his people.

Ever since that night, he'd studied the spells and knowledge laid out in the scrolls. Made himself stronger than he'd ever imagined. Prepared for the day when he would get his revenge.

But he'd never have guessed that strengthening his power would weaken his body so. Which was why, when he'd learned of the *Book of the Dead* and the fact that the man who'd helped him escape the Council, Mammon, was searching for it, he'd sought him out. Thanks to Belpheg's desire to spy on the Council, he'd perfected the ability to astrally project throughout dimensions, and he'd used it to find Mammon.

Arriving too late to stop Mammon from being captured by his sons, he'd sought help from Leviathos. Second best, yes, but he would have to do, since Belpheg didn't have the ability to travel the dimensions and recover the book himself. But once he had the book, once he used the regeneration spell to absorb the energy from the reanimated corpses—as he'd learned he could do from his clan scrolls—he would be strong again.

He would be invincible.

Belpheg had only to pray that Leviathos wouldn't somehow fuck it all up.

CHAPTER FIVE

For what seemed like the millionth time that day Maya found herself imprisoned in Taeg's arms as he dragged her toward the bed. Not only was she afraid, but he also confused the hell out of her. Instinct told her he would hurt her, but so far his actions hadn't proved her right. What was happening here?

"Let me go," she said.

Something that looked like pity flashed in his eyes. "Are you agreeing to help me, then?"

"Help a demon? I don't think so."

"Then I'm afraid I can't let you go. I'm sorry, but I can't." He tossed her onto the soft mattress and straddled her to immobilize her legs. Then, ignoring her attempts to buck him off, he wound the silk tie still attached to the headboard around her wrist.

"You can't keep me here forever," she bit out.

He straightened, keeping a tight hold of her free wrist. The look in his eyes was a cross between exasperation and amusement. "Then I'm going to have to figure something out real fast, aren't I?"

She tried to strike out with her fist, but he easily kept hold of her hand. Her confusion gave way to desperation. "Why don't you let me go? We'll forget any of this ever happened."

"Right." He let out a disbelieving laugh. "Like you wouldn't hunt me down and chop off my head first chance you got."

Reaching down with his free hand, he grabbed the hem of his shirt and started to lift it.

"No," she whispered, horror and dread building up inside her. Was he going to show his evil side now? Would she survive it?

He paused, his lips curving into a wry smile. "Usually the women are dying for me to take my clothes off."

"Don't."

"I already told you, I'm not going to hurt you." With those words, he drew his shirt over his head.

Maya gasped, screwing her eyes shut as he transferred his hold on her wrist to his other hand to yank his shirt off. Already she feared the image of his naked chest would be burned into her memory for all eternity. Tan and smooth, with pronounced muscles, his torso was a masterpiece any artist would kill to sketch. How inappropriate that she noticed how well-defined it was, when he might be about to kill her. Or worse.

"I'll have you know this is my favorite shirt," he muttered.

Maya peeked as he grabbed an end with his teeth and tore off a long strip. He bent over her, using the fabric to tie her other wrist to the metal headboard. The heat from his chest drifted toward her, enveloping her with his sex-and-

chocolate scent. She moistened lips that had gone dry. "You...
you said you weren't an incubus."

He leaned back with a half grin. But then he must have
sensed how serious she was, because his expression sobered.
"Avaritia. Greed demon."

"Greed?" That certainly didn't sound good.

"Don't worry." He winked at her, but with none of
his usual cockiness. Almost as if he was going through the
motions of flirting with her. "None of that transferred from my
father to me."

Taeg rose off the bed and grabbed the heel of one of her
boots and slid it off her foot.

"What are you doing?"

"Checking for more hidden knives. Should've done that
while you were unconscious." He peered inside her boot, then
let it fall to the floor before he removed the other one.

"You're not going to find any more."

Without responding, he ran his hands up the sides of her
body, then over her breasts.

"Wha—what the hell are you doing?"

"I told you." He quickly and efficiently cupped the
undersides of her breasts. "Checking for hidden weapons.
Believe me—I don't enjoy feeling up unwilling chicks."

But a quick glance at his jeans revealed he wasn't being so
honest about that.

She rode the sudden burst of anger that exploded inside
her. "I already told you I don't have any."

He ignored her, sweeping his hands down her jeans,
running two fingers along the crease at the juncture of her
thighs.

Maya tensed and bit her cheek to hold back a careless

whimper.

Finally, he drew away with a muffled curse. The muscles in his back clenched when he turned away. "Look, I don't like this any more than you. I don't *want* to be in this position, and I sure as hell don't enjoy being treated like a murdering rapist."

His words unsettled her. What kind of demon was this? He'd had every opportunity to hurt her, but instead he explained himself to her over and over. Not sure how to respond, Maya did what she did best. She hid behind her prickly tone. "It sure looked to me like you enjoyed it."

Taeg turned to face her again, his expression pained. "If it were for any other reason, I'd let you go. Terrorizing women is not my idea of a fun pastime."

She wanted to respond, to reassure him that he wasn't. She bit her lip to keep quiet. He *was* terrorizing her. If not with his insistence to keep her and use her for his friend, then it was definitely the fact that he sat on top of her—shirtless—and touched her.

"I *need* your help, Maya. Someone who can do what you do is one in a million, if that. Right now you're the best chance I've got at protecting my friend."

When she didn't say anything, he let out a deep sigh. "Tell you what. Tomorrow I'll explain to you what's going on. If, after that, you still won't agree to help me, I'll let you go. No strings attached."

Maya stared at him, well aware that her suspicions showed on her face. He couldn't be serious. He really expected her to believe he would let her go? But crazily enough, his words sounded like truth. "Why can't you just explain it to me now and let me decide?"

He sat next to her on the bed. "Because there's someone you need to meet first. She can help me explain it better than I ever could."

What should she do? Should she kick him and try to get away again? He'd already proven he wasn't like the demons she knew. He wasn't like those monsters who'd taken her entire world away so many years ago. Of course that didn't necessarily mean he *wasn't* evil. Perhaps evil was a relative term.

"If I agree, are you going to untie me?"

He moved his palm to her cheek and lightly stroked her face. His lips twisted into a smile. "That doesn't seem like a wise idea if I'm keen on keeping my head attached to my shoulders. Which I am."

Maya fought to take calm, even breaths that didn't betray her body's reaction to his touch. Incubus or no, there was no denying her base attraction to him. "What are you going to do with me until then?" she asked, her voice tart. "Feed me like a baby? Bathe me?"

He snickered. "Now that sounds like the best evening I've had in a long, long time."

Taeg shifted on the couch, trying to find a comfortable spot. *Restful* was not the word he'd use to describe the kind of sleep he was getting. Not by a long shot. Whether that was due the broken spring that dug into his lower back, or the knowledge that his exasperating little librarian slept in *his* bed, was anybody's guess.

Earlier, when he'd regained consciousness and found her

hand on his stomach, it had been like a wet dream come true. For a second he'd thought she was someone who got off on fighting and then fucking. Hell, he would have gone along with that in a heartbeat. Now he saw the truth.

Maya was attracted to him. Of that he could be reasonably sure. But she was also ashamed of it. She thought all demons were evil, and it burned her ass that her body responded to him.

A whisper of a sound drifted from the other room, almost like a sigh. His body lifted off the couch without him moving a muscle. He felt a million times lighter than normal, like he floated on a cloud. Looking back, he saw his physical body still sound asleep on the couch.

Son of a bitch. He was dreamscaping.

Demons had an ability to communicate telepathically with humans through their dreams, a process his father had discovered. Taeg and his brothers had only learned of it a few months ago. He had personally never dreamscaped before, but in his current state he feared what would happen. He found Maya far too attractive, and here, in the dream realm, he didn't know if he could fight it. But he should. Something bad had obviously happened to her, and a demon was to blame. He wouldn't endear himself to her by jumping her in her dreams, and he wanted her to like him. He *needed* her.

"Go back to bed," he admonished himself. Ah, but he'd always been a cantankerous asshole. He wouldn't even listen to himself.

Turning, he floated across the room and through the doorway, to where Maya lay in his bed, trussed up like a freaking Christmas goose. If he was smart he'd turn his ass around and get back into his body before she noticed him.

But he could no more walk away right now than let Maya go if she refused to help him. While part of him felt guilty as hell that he'd deceived her into believing otherwise, she was too important for him to allow her to walk away.

"Maya," he whispered as he sat next to her on the bed.

She moaned and shifted her head, her eyes creeping open. They narrowed when she saw him. "I told you, get out of my dreams."

She'd been dreaming about him already? Well, all *fucking* right.

Taeg gave her a cocky grin. "Come on, baby, it's your fantasy. You know you want to, so do it." He spread his arms wide. "Use me."

She snorted, pinning him with a derisive scowl. "Even in my fantasies you're annoying."

"That must mean you secretly like it."

Maya's mouth tightened in denial, but then she let out a defeated sigh. "Maybe. Are you going to touch me now?"

All thoughts of humor fled. Because damn, did he ever want to touch her. "Where?"

"Everywhere." She sounded as if the words had involuntarily torn themselves out of her.

He wouldn't joke about that. Not at a time like this. His fingertips crept to her stomach, which was soft and rounded the way a woman should be. Then up her body, until they closed over her breasts much like they had done earlier when he'd checked her for weapons. Yeah, he'd noticed how full they were, her ripe globes spilling over in his hands. But he'd been ashamed of noticing it back then. Now there was no shame. Nothing but pleasure.

She left out a little gasp and arched into his palms.

"You like this?" He didn't actually expect a response when the answer was obvious. Good thing, too, because she didn't give him one. His hands trailed down to the hem of her shirt, and this time he lifted it up to her underarms.

"Demon." The softly spoken word sounded like a caress this time, rather than a curse. Her wrists tightened against the strips of fabric restraining her.

Taeg breathed in deep as he took in Maya's form. Her breasts were encased in a strip of black lace that made his mouth water even as he ached to remove it. He fumbled underneath her, looking for the bra clasp.

"It closes in the front," she said.

Smooth, Chuck. Real smooth. He found the clasp and released it, freeing her from the confines of the fabric.

"Sweet devil, but you're exquisite." Her breasts were round with dark little pearls in the center. Perfect. He ached to close his mouth around one of them.

So he did.

She moaned as he rolled his tongue around the hard bud. She tasted like she smelled—flowers and spice, the perfect combination of tart and sweet. He worked the other nipple with his thumb.

"That's…that's…so good," she said.

Sitting up, he gazed down at her. With her eyes half-closed in ecstasy and her taut buds arching up toward him, she looked like every man's fantasy come to life.

"Demon," she whispered, her voice seductive.

"What do you want?" His voice came out gruff with desire.

"I…" She opened her eyes to give him an annoyed glare. "What?"

She didn't want to admit she desired him. But he didn't care if she wanted to. No, deep down, he wanted her to *beg* him to do it.

"Just tell me." He trailed his thumb along the crease of her lips. She parted them and sucked his thumb into her mouth, eliciting a deep groan from him. His cock strained against his boxers, eager to come out and play. It didn't give a shit whether she admitted she wanted him or not.

Yeah, his cock could be a real dick sometimes.

"What do you want?" he repeated.

"You," she admitted, her mouth tight. "I want *you*."

"Yeah?" *Hell yeah.*

He shifted his trembling hands to her zipper. Just then, a glimmer of light streamed in from behind the window shade, momentarily blinding him. Was it morning already? No. Not yet. *Not freaking yet.*

He fumbled with the button before undoing it and unzipping her jeans.

She moaned and arched her hips. "I can't believe I'm dreaming about doing this with a dem—"

A clock chimed somewhere in the background and she flinched, her eyes darting to the side. Her eyes widened and her mouth dropped open in obvious terror.

"What?" He looked behind him and, without explanation, the scene morphed into something else. He no longer sat on his bed. Hell, he wasn't even in his apartment anymore. Taeg stood in the hallway of a dark, unfamiliar house. Although quiet, the house was tinged with fear. The walls practically breathed terror. Something bad was coming.

He heard the *swish* of fabric and turned his head to see a small girl creeping down the hallway. Her facial features were unmistakable. Maya, but as a child. She bypassed him as if she didn't see him, and continued down the hall. With a sinking heart, he followed her.

Taeg stepped into a small living room, and the scene changed. He now stood next to the girl, who stuffed her tiny body into a shadow behind a potted plant. She pressed her knees to her chest and wound her arms around them, shivering in fear.

Down the hall, a chorus of ear-piercing shrieks echoed. Then silence, followed by the piteous, agonized screams of what sounded like another little girl. The horrific sound made his skin crawl and his stomach turn.

"Maya, no—" He jolted awake on the couch. "*Son of a bitch.*"

What the fuck had that dream turned into? Beyond horrific, it had made every one of his pores tingle with fear, and he'd seen some real scary shit in his time. He sat up, rubbing his hands over his face.

This was what she lived with?

What the hell had happened to her?

Oh devil, why had he dreamscaped with her? He didn't need to know this about her. Now he wanted to comfort her. To make her pain go away. But he couldn't. He couldn't afford to become involved with her. Not emotionally. His duty was to Keegan and to Brynn. He'd failed them once before and he wouldn't fail them again. And instinct told him involvement with the woman he needed to use in order to save Brynn could become dangerous indeed.

No, he'd be better off keeping his emotional distance. The stuff she'd gone through, it obviously sucked. But it had nothing to do with the present. He couldn't help Maya bury her ghosts, but Brynn he could help. And he wasn't about to let her down.

So what to do about Maya?

Focus on finding what he needed her for, and forget all about her hot little body and her fucked-as-hell past.

Now he had to figure out how to pretend he'd never gotten a glimpse into her memories.

Just keep your cool, Taeg. Flirt and joke like you always do.

Yeah. Easier said than done. But what other options did he have?

CHAPTER SIX

By the time Taeg wandered into the bedroom the next morning, Maya had already managed to rationalize all her crazed sex dreams from the night before. Just because she'd spent half the night fantasizing about doing him didn't mean she had the hots for him. No, he was still firmly in her *People Who Must Die* category.

Remembering that would have been so much easier if he hadn't managed to look so damn sexy this morning. He wore a Harley T-shirt over a pair of cotton boxers, and his hair stood on end, as if he'd been pulling on it. On top of that, red eyes aside, his bleary expression made it clear he'd gotten about as restful a sleep as she had.

What would he have said if he'd known she'd dreamt about him?

The thought alone was enough to spike her body temperature a few degrees. Then she remembered what that dream had turned into. An old, familiar nightmare. That was more than enough to cool her down fast.

"Good morning, sweetheart," he drawled as he approached the bed with a plate in his hands. He stopped a few feet away and gave her a knowing look. "How'd you sleep?"

"Shitty." She hoisted herself into a sitting position. "I can't feel my arms."

Taeg smirked. "I'll let you loose for a bit after breakfast."

"How am I supposed to eat with my hands tied?"

"Easy. I'll feed you."

"I don't think so. I can feed myself."

"And deny me the pleasure?" He sat on the bed next to her and grasped a chunk of delicious-looking watermelon between his fingers. Then, brows raised in challenge, he held it out to her.

Part of her wanted to decline just to be difficult, but the melon looked so good and the rumbling in her stomach reminded her how hungry she was. With a glacial glare, she closed her lips around the melon.

"Good girl," he said, not bothering to hide the amusement in his voice. "For a second I thought you were going to refuse to spite me."

Readjusting her grip on the melon, she bit down hard on his fingers.

He broke out into a grin. "How did you know I like it rough?"

Maya's heart rate shot up to triple speed. For one long moment they stared at each other as something heavy passed between them. But then she blinked and broke eye contact and the heaviness in the air dissipated. She concentrated on chewing her melon, on the sweet taste of the juice dribbling down her throat. Anything not to think about him and the way he looked. Like he'd be ready to go a round or ten if she but said the word.

"What do you plan on doing with me?" she asked when she trusted herself to speak again.

Taeg chuckled, the sound promising and foreboding all at once. "I know what I'd like to be doing."

She gave him a sharp look. "What's that supposed to mean?"

He sobered and fed her another slice of melon. "You're a big girl. Figure it out."

How the hell was she supposed to respond to that? Casual joking she could deal with. Cruelty wouldn't be unexpected. But straight-up innuendo? Even worse, right now he seemed as put out by this whole deal as she was. Could it be that, like her, he felt the attraction, yet didn't want to?

For what must be the tenth time in the last day, Maya wondered how much she truly knew about demons. So far, Taeg's actions had been a total surprise. And when had she stopped thinking of him as just another demon and started thinking of him by name?

"When are we going to go see your friend?" she asked him once he'd fed her all the fruit on the plate.

"Couple hours. Should give you enough time to freshen up."

"Do I stink?" She fought the urge to take a self-conscious sniff. She'd not only battled him in a dark, dank alley, but she'd managed to knock herself out in one, too. No surprise if she smelled bad.

"Yeah right. You stink like freaking flowers and candy," he deadpanned. "Your only problem is you smell *too* good, little slayer."

A rush of heat warmed her cheeks. "Oh."

Taeg set the empty plate down on the bedside table and lifted a hand to her chin, tilting her face up. "How's the head?"

"Better." She winced when he touched the spot. "Pounding headache's gone at least."

"I'm just now beginning to realize how strong you are." He grimaced and dropped his hands. "Sorry you got hurt. Maybe one of my brothers can take care of it."

Brothers? Maya took a shaky breath. "We're going to see your brothers?"

"You've got a busy day ahead of you." He leaned over and untied her wrists.

Maya swallowed a pained groan when she moved her stiff arms down to her front. Taeg surprised her by taking hold of one of her arms and applying pressure along the wrist to increase the blood flow, then repeating the action with the other arm. She bit her lip, uncertain what she should say or do.

What was she doing here? This was crazy. A demon had kidnapped her. She should be trying to kick his face in right now. Instead, she was letting him give her a mini-rubdown and sneaking peeks at his boxer shorts.

"I've lost my mind," she muttered.

Taeg's fingers worked their magic on her wrist and palm. "I usually find that's when all the best stuff happens."

"I don't understand." Maya tugged her hand back. "You're evil. I should be trying to kill you right now. You should be trying to kill *me*."

Taeg smirked and shook his head. "You've got a lot to learn about demons, sweetheart."

"Don't call me sweetheart." But even she recognized the distinct lack of heat behind her words. She was seriously losing it.

"Come on, I'll give you first dibs on the shower." Taeg rose off the bed, giving her a lazy grin that made her stomach spin a little cartwheel. "Tell you what, demon-slayer—if it makes you feel better you can torture me by using up all the hot water."

⤜⤛

A few hours later Maya was cleaner, but no less mystified when it came to her demon captor. The man was an enigma. He'd kidnapped her, yet treated her like an honored, if well-guarded, guest. He'd insisted on standing outside the bathroom while she showered, but had allowed her to lock the door. Of course that might have been because there were no windows in there and he knew she couldn't escape. Still…

So far, this experience had been as different from that one horrible night so many years ago as night and day. It almost made her believe Taeg when he assured her not all demons were evil.

But no. She knew what demons were capable of. She'd witnessed it firsthand when she was a mere child. He might be better at hiding his true colors than other demons, but she still knew what he was. And she'd do well to remember.

Now, showered and dressed in her day-old clothes, Maya stood in Taeg's tiny living room and waited for him to find the car keys.

"I swear I left them over here somewhere," he said as he rummaged through an avalanche of paper on the small dining table.

She stood no more than a few feet from the door. But even if she was quick enough to unlock it and race out, she held no illusions of getting away. Taeg was stronger and faster than her. Maybe she'd be able to alert a neighbor before he caught her again, but maybe not. No, she would go along with him for now. There would be plenty of opportunity for her to escape later.

"Aha, found 'em." He snatched up a set of keys from underneath a stack of mail and turned her way so she could make out the words emblazoned on his T-shirt: *Real Men Don't Follow Directions.*

She swallowed the laugh that threatened to force its way out.

When he strode toward her, she fought the instinctive urge to edge away. But whether that was fear or anticipation unfurling in her belly, even she couldn't tell. Oh damn, she felt naked without her daggers hidden in her boots.

Taeg unlocked the door and opened it, taking a step back to allow her to exit first. She slid past him and he grabbed one of her hands, holding tight while he locked the door then led her down the stairs.

Cool, fall air blasted her as they descended the steps outside the apartment. Falling leaves rustled in the breeze, their muted autumn hues adding depth and color to the neighborhood. Though the street was relatively empty by normal city standards, small crowds of people walked by.

Maya tensed at the sight of the passersby. Should she run? Surely he wouldn't try to chase her down with so many witnesses around.

"Don't even think about it," Taeg said in a pleasant tone, his hand clenching hers tighter. "I'll pick you up and carry you to the car if I have to."

"I don't doubt it." She shot him a dirty look. For one

second she considered breaking free just to be difficult, but what was the point? There would be a better opportunity to escape. And if she had to be honest, she was more than a little curious about the woman Taeg wanted her to meet. Yeah, maybe he'd lied about the whole sword thing and was leading her to her death or to some weird sort of demon ritual, but the odds were slim. If she'd managed to live through one night in his apartment, he probably didn't plan on killing her anytime soon.

He led her to a fancy-looking sports car, a steel gray BMW with leather seats and a convertible top. The car practically screamed *I've Got Too Much Money*.

"*This* is your car?"

"My brother's, actually." He opened the passenger-side door and gave her a gentle push inside. "He's probably still pissed as hell about me borrowing it. He'll be lucky if I don't put a dent in it."

Taeg waited until she sat before slamming her door shut and walking around the car to slide into the driver's seat. Then he held the keys up with a blank look on his face. "Where do these go again?"

"Ha-ha." But when he didn't laugh, Maya furrowed her brows. "Goes right there, in the ignition."

"Oh. Makes sense." After a few fumbling tries, he shoved the key in and started the car.

Her confusion gave way to jaw-dropping amazement. "You do know how to drive, don't you?"

"Course. I did it once before." He gave her a rakish grin and threw the car into gear, taking off so fast the tires squealed.

Maya clutched her stomach, which felt like she'd left it a block behind.

Taeg whistled casually while they sped down the street, headed uptown. He played with the pedals, then the wiper blades and air-conditioner, until it became clear he truly didn't have much driving experience.

Maya maintained a death-grip on the passenger-side handle while Taeg turned the stereo knob, stopping at a classic rock station. She suddenly wished she'd learned how to drive, but living in the city, she'd never found the need. "Maybe you'd better concentrate on the road."

"Loosen up. I'll get us there."

"Yeah, but in what condition?"

He screeched to a stop at a red light, neighboring cars halting all around and beside them. Maya tensed. There might never be a better moment to get away. Sure, she'd be leaving with a bunch of unanswered questions, but she'd be alive.

As if he sensed her thoughts, Taeg reached out and closed his hand around hers. The light turned green, and she forced herself to relax. The truth was, her fingers felt good closed inside his. This felt right. And wasn't that just wrong?

She snatched her hand back. "I'd rather not get demon DNA on me, thank you very much."

Taeg let out a snort and gripped the steering wheel. "I'll show you demon DNA."

Her cheeks flaming, Maya turned her head to stare out the window and tried to concentrate on where they were going. He hadn't even bothered blindfolding her. Was that a good thing or not? "Is your friend expecting us?"

"You could say that," Taeg replied.

"And you'll let me go if I still refuse to help after this?"

There was a moment of silence before Taeg let out a soft laugh.

Maya turned. "What?"

"You pretend like you're so hard, but I have a hunch about you, little slayer." He gave her a glance so heated that she felt far too warm beneath her jeans and shirt. "I'm betting you're not as hard as you think. By tonight, I bet you'll be willing to help me."

"That's a bet you'll lose, demon."

"Oh yeah? Then let's make it interesting, shall we? If I win, I get a prize." The challenge in his voice dared her to refuse.

"What kind of prize?" she grudgingly asked.

He arched a brow. "A kiss."

"A *kiss?* You must be crazy." Maya took a deep breath, forcing herself to calm down. This bet would only be too easy to win. All she had to do was refuse to help him. "And if you lose?"

Taeg laughed and shrugged. "Then you can kiss me."

"That's not what I meant—"

He took a hard right onto a side street and pulled into the parking garage of one of the swankiest buildings in New York.

"Your friend lives *here*?"

"Yup. Surprised I'd know someone who lives in a place like this?"

"Everything about you surprises me."

She answered with such brutal honesty that his attention whipped toward her, eyes widening, and he almost drove straight into a post.

"Eyes on the road," she squeaked, tightening her grip on the handle.

He corrected and headed toward a valet station, where

a uniformed man awaited them. "Careful, sweetheart," he murmured, "you might just be the death of us."

The valet opened the door and waited for Maya to slide out before heading to Taeg's side of the car. "Good day, Mr. Meyers, sir."

Taeg clapped the man on the back in greeting, then walked over to Maya. He slid an arm around her, guiding her toward the door leading into the lobby of the building. She tried her best to ignore the heat emanating off his body and the promise of indulgent sin oozing from his pores. Impossible.

Inside the lush lobby, a security guard sat behind a marble desk, checking in a visitor. Taeg's arm tightened around Maya and he leaned down to whisper in her ear. "I hope you're not thinking about trying to run away or asking the security guard for help, 'cause he knows exactly what I am and he'll only assume you're another captured demon fugitive."

"Another *what*?"

"Good afternoon, Mr. Meyers," the guard called.

"Hey, Winslow, how's it hanging?" Taeg breezed by him and toward the elevator.

"Did you just say fugitive—?"

"Later," Taeg interrupted. The doors opened, and he pushed her into the elevator.

She broke free of his grasp and rounded on him, barely paying attention as he pressed a button. "What do you mean, a captured demon fugitive?"

"We'll talk about it some other time."

Like hell. "You can't expect me to keep my mouth shut like you never mentioned a thing about some sort of fugitive."

He leaned forward with a soft laugh, and she instinctively retreated until her back hit the elevator door. He took advantage of that by pressing his arms to either side of her, effectively imprisoning her with his body. "Sweetheart, I wouldn't expect anything less from you than defiance and general kick-assitude."

Maya said nothing, just held her breath while he lifted one palm to her cheek, caressing it. He regarded her like she was some yummy dessert he wanted to devour. She didn't know how to respond to a demon who wasn't trying to kill or harm her. Much less one who was openly admiring of her. This was beyond her level of expertise.

"You are so…weird," she finally said.

He laughed. "You don't know the half of it."

Her mind barely registered the *ding* of the elevator when it arrived on their floor. The door slid open so quickly she would have fallen flat on her ass if Taeg hadn't caught her by the shoulders and steadied her. He flashed her a brilliant smile. "Come on, let's go."

Maya followed him down a long hallway. At last he stopped. Rather than knocking as she'd expected, he took a set of keys from of his pocket and unlocked the door.

"Knock, knock. It's me. Hope everyone's dressed," he said as he nudged the door open.

She followed him inside and froze. They were in a luxuriously appointed foyer the size of Taeg's entire bedroom. A leather chair and end table had been set up in one corner, and a burly man sat there, watching a tiny television set on top of the table. He wasn't human. His outline was hazy and jagged, as if he was about to bust out of his skin.

"How's it going, Taeg?" the man asked conversationally.

"Good. Brought a friend. Her name is Maya."

The man smiled and rose, starting toward her. When she backed away, Taeg stopped him with an upheld hand. "If you don't mind, buddy, she's got a thing about people getting too close to her."

Maya blinked and looked over at Taeg. If he only knew how close to the truth his words were...

"No problem," the man replied. He nodded at her and sat back down with a smile. "My name is Bram. Nice to meet you, Maya."

"I...uh...me too." Because what was she supposed to say? *I hate you, demon scum*?

"Bram's a family friend and a personal bodyguard," Taeg said.

A demon bodyguard. "How nice."

Taeg shook his head, clearly amused. "Come on."

He grabbed her hand and led her into an expansive living room that had a wall of windows with what could possibly be the most amazing view in the entire city.

"Oh my God. This is incredible."

"Isn't it?"

Maya staggered to the windows and drank in the view. This building was taller than the surrounding ones, dwarfing the rooftops surrounding it. Below, a long row of cars snaked along the street. Off to the side was a stunning and very large terrace. What would the view from that terrace look like at night, when the neighboring structures and streetlights were all lit?

"There you are," a feminine voice said.

She whirled to see a willowy woman stroll into the living room. Her lack of glamour gave her away as human, though she had a peculiar sort of energy flowing from her that most humans didn't have. She had long, honey-brown hair and the body of a dancer. And while Maya was dressed in yesterday's shirt and jeans, the woman was outfitted in light-gray wool slacks and a cream-colored silk blouse.

Immediately, Maya became all too aware of how short and squat she would look standing next to her, and she winced inwardly at the unfavorable comparison. It was like comparing silk to burlap.

The woman gave Maya a thorough once-over before she turned her attention to Taeg. Her gaze raked across his T-shirt and a glint came to her eyes. "Isn't that the truth?"

Taeg let out a short bark of laughter. "Hi, Brynn."

To Maya's shock, his expression lit up with pure joy at the sight of Brynn. He crossed the room in three long strides and enveloped her in his arms. She couldn't help the small gasp that escaped her when he pressed his lips to Brynn's cheek.

It wasn't that she was jealous. No, of course not. But how could he flirt so callously with her and then bring her to a girlfriend's house? Did he really think this was going to make her want to help him?

Taeg pulled away from Brynn. "How's the baby?"

What? She was having his *baby*? How dare he act the way he did when he had a woman and a child on the way? How sick. And who even knew that demons and humans could mate?

"Good. Hasn't been giving me so much trouble lately."

Taeg turned to her. "Maya, I'd like to introduce you to Brynn Meyers. She's my sister-in-law."

"Your...your..." For the first time, Maya noticed a picture hanging on the wall. It was of Taeg and his brothers, a twin to the one in his room. "Oh."

This time there was no denying the relief that rushed through her veins, easing the tight pressure in her chest. *Oh God.* She'd actually been jealous. Over a *demon*. No, how could she feel that way about him? How was it even possible? Just the thought of it made her feel sick to her stomach. She pressed her hand to the spot to calm the sudden roiling in her gut.

Affecting a calm she didn't feel, Maya turned to Brynn. "Can I use your restroom?"

CHAPTER SEVEN

"I like her."

Taeg tore his eyes from the corridor where Maya had disappeared and speared his sister-in-law with a questioning glance. "I'm sorry, what?"

Brynn grinned, no doubt amused by his inability to focus. "I said I like her. She's got spunk."

"Oh yeah," he responded. "If there's anything Maya has in abundant supply, it's spunk." And man, was it a turn-on. She would never be one to stand by quietly and put up with someone's crap.

Still, her reaction to Brynn had surprised him. For one moment she had actually looked jealous. And no doubt she'd realized it. Why else would she be hiding out in the bathroom?

"Where did you meet her?" Brynn asked.

Taeg fought back a shameful wince. Keegan hadn't told her? "Uh, long story."

"I have time," she said, effectively putting him on the

spot. Damn, she knew him too well.

"Well...I sort of noticed yesterday that she has the ability to see through glamours."

Brynn stared at him for several long seconds. He could practically see the wheels in her head spinning. "And...?"

Taeg fought the urge to fidget. "And I thought her gift might come in handy."

"What aren't you telling me?"

"Nothing."

Her eyes narrowed in on him. "Taeg."

This time he did wince. Brynn was going to make an excellent mother. She already had the scolding bit down pat.

"I, uh...accidentally...kidnapped her," he mumbled.

"I can't hear you."

"I kidnapped her, okay?"

"Taeg!" She crossed her arms and shot him a disapproving glare.

"What? I didn't mean to. I tried to talk to her, but she kept on attacking me. She even knocked herself out trying to kill me. Taking her home was the only way I could get her to listen. What? Would you rather I left her to the bums in the alley?"

Brynn let out an exasperated sigh and shook her head. "This has something to do with Leviathos, doesn't it? That's all you've been focused on for the past few months."

"I—"

The front door opened, saving Taeg from further explanation.

"I'm home," Keegan called. After a second, he appeared in the room.

As always, Taeg felt that familiar tug of guilt upon the

sight of his brother. He'd failed him in so many ways. And he owed him so much. Though Keegan was only a couple of years older than him, he was more of a father figure to him than their own dad had ever been.

Keegan spotted Taeg and let out a snort. "Welcome home, idiot."

"Good to see you, too, shithead."

Keegan snatched Brynn into his arms and gave her a kiss so long and heated that Taeg finally had to clear his throat.

"How's our little one?" Keegan asked, breaking away to place his hand on Brynn's stomach.

"Good." Brynn smiled up at him. "No contractions today."

Children of demons and humans were quite rare. At less than three months along, Brynn's pregnancy had so far been difficult. There had been a few scares, and now Keegan tried to stay by her side as much as possible. One of the main reasons Taeg was so damn eager to take care of Leviathos; she didn't need him hanging over her head. Then there was the whole fact that it was his fault Brynn was in danger. Leviathos had major beef with him, and he would go to any lengths to punish him. Even hurt the ones he loved.

Keegan straightened and looked around the room. "Have you come to your senses and let the woman go, then?"

"She's in the bathroom."

Brynn turned to scowl at Keegan. "You knew about this?"

Keegan winced, making Taeg laugh. Seeing his big brother in trouble was always a fun little side bonus.

But then Keegan put the heat back on him. "What's all this about?"

Aw, crap. He tried sidestepping the question. "Are Ronin and Dagan here?"

"Ronin's in his room, and Dagan will be here soon," Brynn said. "We're having an early dinner. And don't try to avoid answering."

"All right, I'll tell you," he grumbled. "When everyone's here. Don't want to have to repeat myself."

"Fine." Keegan turned to Brynn. "I'm gonna go have a word with Ronin."

He strode out of the room, leaving Taeg alone with Brynn.

She didn't waste any time. "I know you're focused on tracking down Leviathos out of some weird sense of guilt over him being your childhood friend."

Not just because of that. No, there was much more behind it. Like the fact that Taeg had betrayed a friend. Let down his big brother. Made too many mistakes to name.

"Brynn, I—"

"I'm not scolding," she continued softly. "You're doing it to protect us, and I love you for it. But you need to think long and hard about involving that girl, because you're putting her in danger, too, and that doesn't seem very fair to me. Just think about it, okay?"

"Okay," he said, mainly to appease her.

With a small nod, she left the room. He turned to stare out the window, barely noticing the striking view. A niggling sense of doubt wormed its way through his head. Brynn was right. He could be putting Maya in danger by involving her. Prickly as she was, she seemed like a decent-enough person. From what he'd seen in her dream, she might even be a little broken. He couldn't offer her anything other than danger and the possibility of getting more broken. Or dead.

Maybe keeping her around wasn't such a good idea after all.

"Shit."

Taeg stared blindly down at the street. Why couldn't this be easier? Why did he have to feel so damn guilty? No matter what, he couldn't stop now. What were the odds of him finding someone like Maya, someone who was uniquely qualified to help? He wasn't about to turn his back on that just because it might be dangerous for her.

Family was the most important thing to him right now. He couldn't lose sight of that. Keegan, Brynn, his unborn niece or nephew—they were the ones he needed to concentrate on. To protect.

As for the tempting little Maya…

Too bad for her.

He sighed. If only he truly meant it.

ॐ∽ॐ

Maybe if Maya was lucky they'd forget she was in here. She could wait for the appropriate moment, then slink out the front door.

Not freaking likely.

How could she have felt jealous back there? Over *Taeg*?

She gripped the countertop and stared into the large, ornate mirror. "He's a demon, Maya. A demon. How could you forget that, even for a minute?"

Maybe because he had seemed so human when he had looked at Brynn with love in his eyes. There was no mistaking that emotion. Demons could love. Who knew?

A knock at the door brought her back to reality. She turned away from the mirror with a loud sigh. No doubt it was Taeg, eager to confuse the hell out of her some more.

"Remember that he's the enemy," she whispered as she walked to the door. Pasting a frown on her face, she jerked the door open. "What do you want now?"

Brynn, not Taeg, greeted her at the door.

"Oh, sorry."

The corners of Brynn's lips twitched as if she fought to keep from smiling. "It's okay. I thought we could talk for a moment."

"Um…sure." Maya shuffled backward when Brynn took that as an invitation to enter the bathroom.

Brynn shut the door and strolled over to the large jet tub, taking a seat on its wide ledge. She motioned toward the closed toilet lid, a few feet in front of her. "Have a seat."

Throwing her a puzzled look, Maya obeyed.

"I heard about how Taeg…came to be with you. Sorry about that." Brynn's expression was warm and open. "He can be a real tool sometimes, but he has a heart of gold. That I can vouch for."

"Heart of gold? He's a demon."

"What?" Brynn's brow creased, then a look of understanding crossed her face. "Ah, I see." She leaned forward with a sigh. "How can I put this?"

"I don't—"

"Not all demons are evil."

All of Maya's breath escaped her body in one single *whoosh.* "I…but they're *demons.*"

Brynn shook her head. "Not in the sense you're thinking of."

"I don't understand. I mean, I've *seen* them. I've witnessed their evil."

"Oh, I'm not saying they're all good. Just that they're

not all evil. You'll get the good and the bad, same as with humans."

Maya felt her mouth open and close. Demons weren't all evil? Her eyes narrowed as she examined Brynn. Was there something there she couldn't see? "You're not a demon, are you?"

"No," Brynn replied with a little laugh. "At least, not mostly."

"What do you mean?"

"I didn't know what to believe when I first met Keegan and his brothers," Brynn said. "But after seeing them all risk their lives to save my mine, I'll tell you one thing. They're more decent than half the human men you'll see out there. Despite the foolish, half-assed ways in which they like to do things, they're good people."

"I...I can't believe that." But then, she didn't know what to believe anymore. She was so confused.

"You'll see." Brynn curled her hand around Maya's. "You don't know me from Adam, so I don't expect you to believe me, but all I'm saying is maybe give Taeg a chance. You might find more of him to like than you could possibly expect."

Maya flushed at the innuendo behind Brynn's words. "It's not as if we're dating or anything. He only thinks I could be useful to him. Like a I'm a...a human metal detector of sorts."

Brynn snorted while she worked her thumb around the ring on Maya's finger. "Yeah, right. Let me tell you, whether you're useful or not, if Taeg brought you here it's because—"

She cut off suddenly, letting out a soft gasp as her eyes fluttered shut.

"Are you okay?" Maya tugged her hand back and grabbed

Brynn's arms. Just when she was about to call out for help, Brynn's eyes opened.

"I'm fine. Sorry about that." Her cheeks turned pink. "Things are a bit loopy ever since the pregnancy."

Maya let go of her. "Are you sure you're okay?"

"Yes." Brynn's focused her attention on Maya's hand. "That's a pretty ring. Is it old?"

"Oh. Yes it is." Maya smiled down at the delicate gold band on her finger. It had little monetary value, but to her it was priceless. "It was my mother's."

Recovered off what was left of her corpse.

A glimmer of understanding flickered in Brynn's eyes. She nodded and cast a slight frown at Maya's leg. "Oh no, you have a tear in your jeans."

"What?" Maya bent down to examine it. "Damn it, Taeg, these were my favorite jeans."

"Taeg did that?" Brynn asked, lifting her brow.

"Yeah. Uh, long story." She wasn't sure whether Brynn would appreciate hearing how she'd tried to kill Taeg numerous times last night.

Brynn nodded. "You don't have any clothes to change into, do you?"

Maya smiled. "How'd you guess?"

"Just thought back to when I was first kidnapped by Keegan."

"*What?*"

"I'll have to fill you in on that some other time." Brynn rose with a laugh and looked Maya up and down. "I'd offer to lend you some clothes, but I'm afraid mine won't fit." She sighed dramatically. "God, how I envy your curves."

"Really?" Maya shuffled to her feet and looked down at

herself. "I was thinking I looked like a troll compared to you. I always wanted to be tall and thin."

"I guess we all want what we can't have." Brynn gave her a conspiratorial grin and Maya realized she liked this woman. And Brynn liked Taeg. So what did that say about him?

"Come on, the men are probably starving." Brynn grabbed her arm and headed toward the door. She opened it and started out. "Do you know, I—"

Brynn cut off when she saw Taeg leaning against the opposite wall. "Waiting for us?" she said to him.

The heat in his gaze speared Maya, making her belly tingle. The man looked dangerous even doing something as innocuous as leaning against the wall. "I want to talk to Maya."

Brynn crossed her arms. "Do you promise to behave yourself?"

"No," he replied bluntly.

"Good." Brynn grinned as she turned and retreated down the hallway.

Maya recalled Brynn's words: *He can be a real tool sometimes, but he has a heart of gold.*

Taeg pushed off the wall and stalked toward her. "You okay?"

"I'm fine." Although the way he looked at her made her nervous. So she did what she always did when she was nervous—she hid her emotions behind a layer of bristle. "Do you mind respecting my personal space?"

"Personal space?" He let out a snort and kept coming, mere inches away now. "Yeah, 'cause you were so worried about personal space last night when you were trying to kill me."

"I said back off." Her fist shot out and caught him in the chest. His hand closed around her wrist, dragging her with him when he stumbled backward. Her front made contact with his chest at the same time his back hit the wall, and his arms closed tight around her, flooding her with the superheated warmth of his body.

"That's better," he said.

"Let me go."

"I don't think so." One of his arms traveled up her back while the other slid decidedly lower, in dangerous proximity to her bottom. "You didn't seem to hate me so much earlier. In fact, I'd almost say you were jealous."

"Jealous? Ha!" She struggled in his grasp, but all that managed to do was rub his body against hers. Ignoring the growing hardness pressing against her stomach was impossible.

"Uh-huh." Taeg flipped them around so her back was to the wall.

"You know what I think, little slayer?" His lips brushed against her ear. "I think maybe you like me more than you'd care to admit, and it scares you. Your mouth tells me you want to kill me, but your body says another thing entirely."

"You're crazy," she panted.

"Am I?"

If only. She was beginning to think she might be the crazy one. When she breathed in deep, his eyes dropped to the rise and fall of her chest, and stuck there. "Brynn told me demons aren't what I think they are. What does that mean? Is it true?"

"What if I told you it's true? That demons aren't evil beings from Hell, like you seem to think they are? Would that change things?"

"I…I don't know."

"Why doesn't that surprise me?" With those words, he lowered his head toward hers.

Her heart rate tripled, pounding to a loud, fierce rhythm he probably heard. *Say no. Head butt him. Knee him in the groin.* But she couldn't force her body to respond to her brain's commands. Of its own volition, her tongue wet her lips, all but inviting him to continue his downward descent.

Holy hell, a demon was going to kiss her. And she was going to *let* him.

Maya let out a gasp when, rather than touching his lips to hers, he shifted his head so they brushed along her cheek, down to her chin. Static electricity racked her body with an involuntary shiver. He stopped at her ear, and she felt a light flick to her lobe. Was that…was that his *tongue?*

This time Maya couldn't hold back the moan bubbling in her throat.

"Come on, little slayer," he whispered in her ear. "They're waiting for us."

With those words, Taeg released her and pushed away. Before she could respond, he turned on his heel and disappeared down the same corridor as Brynn.

Maya kept her back against the wall, bracing herself on legs that seemed too shaky to provide any real support. What had just happened? She'd known Taeg less than a day. She knew he was a demon. And she'd been about to let him kiss her?

Maybe she was mistaken about his powers not working on her. Maybe he had charmed her after all, and that was why she responded to him the way she did. Yeah, and maybe pigs could fly. As much as she'd like to deny it, she had to face the truth: she had the hots for a demon.

"Madre, perdona me." *Mother, forgive me.*

Shame coursed through her body as she walked down the corridor behind Taeg. How could she be so fickle? How could she forget, even for one second, what had happened to her family? What *demons* had done to them?

Maya reached the entrance to a small dining room and stopped dead, her shame all but forgotten. A large, rectangular table filled most of the room. And seated in the chairs were more demons than she'd ever seen in one place.

"Oh, shit."

All eyes turned to her, and her courage deserted her. She backed up slowly, going on pure instinct as her brain screamed one thing to her body, over and over again.

Run.

Chapter Eight

Leviathos spoke into his cell phone while he walked down the busy street. "What kind of tracker are you? Shouldn't you have some information on her already?"

"I track scents. I'm not a detective," Garin replied in his nasal voice. "You'll need to give me more than a few hours, especially with the shoddy description you gave me. It hasn't even been twenty-four hours yet, so it's not like I can check the missing persons reports."

Leviathos tried his best to quell his impatience. This was the problem with working with just one goon—it was almost impossible to accomplish things at the speed he desired. Still, the fewer people who knew about his mission, the better the likelihood of accomplishing it. If his former mentor, Mammon, had believed that, he might very well have succeeded in raising his undead army without the Elden Council being any wiser for it.

Leviathos was so unlike Mammon in that way. He'd never let pride stop him from acquiring his ultimate goal.

"I'll try tracking her scent from the address you gave me, see if I can trace it back to her apartment," Garin continued. "But for obvious reasons I have to wait until dark."

Garin was a wolf-shifter, a skilled tracker in wolf form. But that did have clear limitations in a city like this. Not too many wolves roaming the streets. So his business was best conducted in the deepest part of night, when he had less chance of someone spotting him. Although in a city that never slept, there was always a chance.

"Just do it as quickly as you can." Leviathos hung up and ground to a stop in front of his destination. The nondescript building didn't have any sign to indicate that a public establishment lay within. Of course Eros was specifically designed to keep out as many humans as possible. Located in the Lower East Side, not far from Taeg's apartment, it catered to all classes of Otherworlders.

Due to the early hour, the entrance lacked its customary security guard. Leviathos opened the door and descended the narrow stairs. Taking up a good portion of the basement, Eros had a marble-stained concrete floor and a tiled bar that matched the beige walls. On its own, it might have resembled a subway station, but the dim lighting, candles, and red leather stools lent it an aura of sophistication.

This part of the bar was empty, save a tired-looking bartender behind the counter. Leviathos gave her a curt nod and moved farther back, where a separate room contained a couple of secluded seating areas. With the exception of the contact Belpheg had set him up with, who sat in a booth sipping a dark liquid from a tumbler, there was no one else here. Eros never filled up during daylight hours, one of the reasons he preferred to conduct business here during the day.

"Do you have it?" he asked without preamble, sliding into the red leather seat across from Horster.

Horster lifted a brow, his countenance somewhat unsteady. "How's your master?"

"He's not my master," Leviathos snapped. Belpheg wasn't even on this dimension; he was stuck somewhere else. And Leviathos was his own master.

"Whatever." Horster rubbed one of his bleary eyes. "Do you have what I need?"

Leviathos stifled a smile and reached into his jacket pocket. He pulled out an envelope. Horster was a font of information for everything supernatural. As Belpheg had informed him, Horster was also addicted to *score*, a drug made from ground unicorn horns. Easy enough to buy on this dimension, but the habit could get quite expensive. Lucky for Leviathos, he had access to the fortunes Mammon had amassed on Earth. Once Mammon had been captured by Taeg and his brothers, Leviathos had seen no harm in claiming the money as his own.

Horster's eyes glazed over and he reached for the envelope. Probably already imagining how much *score* he'd buy with this. Leviathos waited until his fingers almost reached the envelope before tugging it back. "Not so fast. Where's my information?"

"Here it is." Sweat beaded on Horster's forehead as he reached a shaky hand into his pocket and withdrew a small notebook. He ripped out a page and handed it to him. "I followed the leads your mast—uh, partner gave me. They led me to what you were searching for."

Examining it, Leviathos allowed himself a smile. Just what he needed. Once again Belpheg's resources had come through for him. He'd doubted it once or twice in the time since he'd agreed to partner up with Belpheg, but it seemed like he'd made the right choice in bringing the fae on.

Yeah, but at what price?

Belpheg said he only wanted to use the book once, but what man in his right mind, after getting a taste of such power, would willingly give it up?

Of course, once Leviathos got ahold of the book, he could always refuse to comply. What harm could Belpheg cause in his incorporeal form?

But with this information Horster's giving you, Belpheg has the ability to cross into this dimension.

That wasn't something Leviathos was sure he should allow.

Well, he might simply have to withhold this information from Belpheg. The man trusted him. He would be none the wiser. And even if Belpheg managed to get his body to this dimension after Leviathos procured the book, it would be too late. Leviathos would be in command of the undead army by then. He'd be invincible.

"You know, Taeg and Keegan are serious about tracking you down," Horster said in an unsteady voice. "They've offered a serious amount of cash for your whereabouts."

Leviathos could practically see the dollar signs in Horster's eyes. Leviathos infused a healthy dose of menace into his expression. "You're not threatening me, are you?"

Horster let out a little shiver and averted his eyes. "N—no. Just sayin'."

"Say so again, and you might meet with an unfortunate accident."

Horster nodded his flustered agreement.

"It's been a pleasure." Leviathos handed the envelope to

Horster and rose to leave.

A pleasure indeed.

❧❧

Demons. There were so many demons here. Blurry outlines. Glowing flesh. Red eyes. All watching her. Maya's heart dropped to the pit of her stomach, dread choking off her air supply. She inched back on wooden legs, barely registering Taeg's movements as he pushed away from the table and stood.

"Maya, are you okay?"

There was no way she could take this many. Not without her weapons. She was a good fighter, but she was no match for five—no, *six*—demons.

"Maya," Taeg said, wearing a concerned look on his face. "Are you okay?"

"I… " Her throat closed up on her.

He approached her and placed his hands on her arms, backing her out of the dining room. "Are you okay?" he repeated, his voice hushed.

She focused in on his face. "I…yes. It's just…" Now that she couldn't see them anymore, she was kind of embarrassed by her reaction. It wasn't like they had all charged her, or even looked at her in a threatening way. "I'm all right."

"It's a lot to deal with. Believe me, I know. But no one in there will hurt you. I promise." The honesty in his eyes convinced her she would be fine.

Come on, Maya. Get your act together. They're not going to eat you. She took a breath and firmed her resolve. "Okay. I'm good."

"All right." Taeg examined her face. Whatever he saw there must have satisfied him. Turning, he enclosed one of her hands in his and led her back into the dining room.

The expressions on everyone's faces would have been comical if they hadn't been demons. They all wore broad, exaggerated smiles, as if they were trying to be as non-threatening as possible. While Maya appreciated the effort, it wasn't working. Not when half of them had red eyes.

The demons she recognized as Taeg's brothers were just as big, if not bigger, than Taeg. And the other two demons, one of whom she recognized as Bram, were massive, at least six-and-a-half-feet if she had to guess.

Taeg kept a tight grip on her hand, lending her support while he guided her into the chair next to his and sat down. He motioned toward the head of the table. "Maya, I'd like you to meet my older brother, Keegan. He's married to Brynn. The ugly guy next to him is my younger brother, Ronin."

"Screw you," Ronin said to him before he gave her a welcoming grin. But he didn't sound offended and it was easy to see why. With a long, lean body, shaggy hair that hung to about chin-length, and features that resembled Taeg's, there was no way anyone could ever consider him ugly.

"And that's Dagan, the baby of the family," Taeg continued without missing a beat.

"Baby, my ass," Dagan muttered.

Yeah, he definitely wasn't. If she had to guess, he was in his mid-twenties, which made him close to her age. He had the most beautiful voice she'd ever heard on a man—deep and smooth as silk. The kind of voice that could talk a girl's panties off without her realizing it. He also seemed to share Taeg's proclivity for T-shirts with slogans. The one he wore now had the words *Envy Me* written on it. Guess he didn't lack for ego.

"Nice to meet you guys," Maya offered. She raised her hand into a little wave before thinking better of it and dropping her hand limply to the side.

Despite their similarities, the brothers had many differences. Not in their facial features or body shapes. No, those were quite similar. Even their eyes were identical—a hypnotic, swirling red. But while Taeg had a soft glow about him, Ronin's flesh was almost opalescent, and Dagan's was so eerily perfect he might have been constructed from marble. Keegan had a general haziness about his form that she couldn't place.

Maya turned to Taeg. "Are you full brothers?"

He gave her a little smile, as if he found her question funny. "Half. We each have a different mother. What do you see when you look at us?"

"I…" The numerous sets of eyes on her made her feel self-conscious. "I don't know."

Taeg raised a brow but he didn't challenge her. He motioned to the two demons sitting on the far end of the table. "You met Bram earlier, and that's Reiver."

Reiver's form resembled Bram's and Keegan's—fuzzy, like something fought to rip out of his flesh.

"Don't worry," Taeg continued, "they might look tough, but they're as sweet and harmless as kittens."

Maya couldn't help but laugh when the two giants mumbled protests. They seemed to take great offense at being called kittens.

Taeg addressed everyone. "You're all probably wondering why Maya is here."

"Yeah," was Keegan's brief response.

"I already know." Dagan crossed his arms and leaned back in his chair with a wide, satisfied smile.

Taeg gave him a warning glance before continuing. "As I was lucky enough to discover yesterday, Maya is a magic-sensitive. She can see through glamours."

There was a moment of shocked silence as everyone turned back to Maya. She sucked in her breath and her stomach clenched. What if demons saw that ability as a threat? Would they let her leave here alive?

"That's a very rare gift," Ronin said.

Taeg must have noticed her tense up, because he tugged on her hand and leaned toward her. "It's okay," he whispered.

His reassuring words prompted the stiffness in her muscles to loosen. Wait, she was *trusting* him now? He was a demon, for God's sake. But she couldn't help herself. For some reason, he made her feel safe.

"That isn't all," Taeg continued. "I wasn't able to charm her."

"*What?*" Ronin asked.

Again with the surprised looks. What was the big deal?

"She's an immune," Reiver finally said.

"Can't be," Bram said. "I've only ever heard of one other immune in existence, and that was hundreds of years ago."

Keegan gave her a thorough, appraising glance. "One way to test that theory." He motioned to Ronin, who nodded and stood, starting toward her.

"What are you doing?" Maya squeaked.

She tried to stand but Taeg kept a tight grip on her hand. "It's okay, sweetheart. He won't hurt you."

She kept her eyes locked on Ronin, who raised a brow at

Taeg's casual endearment. But he said nothing, just came to a stop in front of her and knelt down. She flinched when his hand slowly reached for her face. Hot fingertips seared the knot on her forehead, and she could feel Ronin's body heat, even from a few feet away. Clearly, his temperature ran as hot as Taeg's.

Ronin held his fingers there for a few moments before lifting his hand and examining the spot. "Huh. Nothing."

Over the shocked murmurs, Maya turned to Taeg and asked, "What was supposed to happen?"

With his free hand he touched his palm to her cheek. The movement was soothing, erotic.

Her breath hitched in her throat when his touch ignited a sharp pang deep in her belly.

"Ronin can heal others, but he couldn't heal you," he said. "You're immune to magic."

Her words came out a near whisper. "And that's truly rare?"

"Truly," he whispered back, a husky undertone in his voice.

How long they stayed frozen in that position she couldn't say, but finally someone's throat cleared. Taeg gave a slight start and dropped his hand.

"Okay, so we know Maya is an immune." Keegan leaned back as he scrutinized first Maya, then Taeg. "That's interesting, but what does this have to do with you, uh—"

"Kidnapping her?" Dagan finished helpfully.

"Thanks for that, asswipe," Taeg said. "The kidnapping was unintentional. I just wanted to talk to her. Maya doesn't…have a good track record with demons."

"Track record?" She echoed in disbelief. Glaring at him,

she jerked her hand out of his. He had no freaking idea what she'd been through, or the horrors she'd witnessed. Demons had taken *everything* from her.

Taeg gave her an apologetic glance. "Let me start at the beginning. Six months ago, me and my brothers were sent here to stop our father, Mammon. He's the pure definition of evil demon. Mammon tried to take over Earth using an ancient book, the *Book of the Dead*, to resurrect an army of the undead. Zombies."

"Uh, zombies?" Maya echoed in disbelief.

Brynn let out a deep sigh. "I knew this was about Leviathos."

Keegan leaned over to rub Brynn's stomach, and her agitation melted away. The look she gave him was filled with love.

Love. Brynn loved a demon with all her heart. What did that mean?

"Go on," Keegan said to Taeg.

"The *Book of the Dead* was created by Brynn's ancestor. Within it was a spell allowing for the resurrection of zombies. But only Brynn, as the heir, had the power to activate the spell."

"There's actually a book that can create *zombies*?" Maya shook her head. This was crazy. Were vampires and werewolves real, too?

"We stopped Mammon and hid the book somewhere safe," Taeg continued. "But he had someone helping him, a demon named Leviathos. Someone who used to be my friend. He got away. The problem is, the book is indestructible. And as long as it exists, Leviathos will be plotting to find a way to retrieve it."

"And Brynn will never be safe," Ronin added.

Neither Brynn, nor the child she carried, would be safe, she realized. Maya bit her lip. She began to see the dilemma here. "This thing you're looking for, this sword, you think it can destroy the book?"

"I think there's a good chance." Taeg looked over at Keegan, his red eyes shining with unspoken emotion. When he spoke, his voice was quiet. "It's Excalibur."

Maya's gasp was drowned out by Brynn's.

"You mean the Excalibur from the Arthurian legend?" Brynn asked eagerly.

Keegan glanced at Brynn before asking Taeg, "Are you sure it really exists?"

"My research leads me to believe so," Taeg replied. "But from what I've managed to discover, Merlin hid the sword using a powerful invisibility spell. He wanted to keep it out of the wrong hands."

"But I can see through glamours," Maya said. And if everything they'd said was true, she was one of very few people—if not the only one—who could find the sword. Oh, hell, she didn't even know how to feel about this.

Taeg swiveled his head toward her and he gave her a slow nod. "Exactly. You have what I need."

The tone of his voice, layered in double meaning, sent shivers down her spine.

"Merlin was *real*?" Brynn asked. She obviously hadn't gotten over that big revelation. Not that Maya could blame her. It was a lot to take in.

"He was real," Taeg confirmed, "though obviously many of the legends about him are inaccurate. But he was a powerful mage."

There was another long moment of silence before Keegan

said, "You've done a lot of research on this, haven't you?"

Taeg nodded.

"Why didn't you say anything? We could have helped you."

Taeg shrugged. "I didn't want to get anyone's hopes up."

"Do you have any leads on where this sword is?" Ronin asked.

"That's what I've been working on. I've been going to the library." Taeg gave a fake shudder. "That place gives me the creeps."

All those trips to the library, researching Arthurian legends. Maya let out a grunt. "I knew you weren't the library type."

He snorted. "So what do you think, Maya?"

Her smile faded. She knew what he was asking. He wanted to know whether she would help him find the sword. Nothing like pressure.

"I…" Part of her wanted to say yes, for Brynn's sake, and for that of her child. But this was so much to take in all at once. Saying yes meant she would have to face these demons again.

Saying yes means you'll be working with Taeg. In close proximity, for who knew how long. The thought of that made her twitchy in ways she couldn't explain.

"This is a huge decision," Keegan said. "One she needs to think about, to examine the consequences. I don't think we can expect her to answer that today."

Maya gave Keegan a grateful glance. He must want her to do this more than anyone, if he truly believed it might work. After all, the purpose of the sword was to protect his wife and child. That he'd spoken up for her said a lot about what sort of man he was.

Not a man, Maya. A demon.

An honorable demon.

That feeling of uneasiness in her gut increased. She'd thought she had everything figured out, but did she really know anything? Those few demons she'd managed to kill throughout the years…had they been evil at all?

"Okay," Taeg finally responded, somewhat grudgingly.

After a moment of awkward silence, Brynn rose and said in a cheerful voice, "Well, I know you guys have a never-ending appetite, and let's face it, lately so do I. Let's eat."

Brynn and Keegan brought steaming plates of pasta out from the kitchen and everyone dug in as conversation reached a comfortable chatter. Maya picked at her food. She was far more interested in observing the banter between these demons. They appeared so…normal. They even ate normal food. She wasn't sure what she'd expected. Human brains, maybe?

While Brynn tried to engage her in conversation, Taeg kept giving Maya little reassuring glances. Her stomach warmed in a way that it shouldn't, and that was a problem. Everything about him was a problem.

"Some words of wisdom," she overheard Taeg quip to one of the giants. "Never boink a haknasa demon. Dagan was clever enough to figure that one out for us."

"Fuck you," Dagan snapped, and Maya hid a smile behind her hand.

Given half a chance, she was afraid she might grow to like these demons. Some of them more than others.

A sudden image of her mother's bloody remains flashed in Maya's vision. She dropped her fork to her plate with a loud clatter.

What would her mother say if she saw her here, casually sharing a meal with demons?

Forgive me, Mama. Forgive me.

ॐॐ

By the time Taeg led Maya out of Keegan's apartment, confusion was evident on her face. She absently followed him into the elevator and down to the garage, not even taking note of their surroundings. He'd challenged all of her conceptions about demons. Hell, that should make him happy. It had been his plan, after all. But instead he felt only empathy for her. She'd been through a hell of a lot in her short lifetime.

Come on, man. Don't forget what's important. Your family. Brynn. The baby.

He'd already failed them once. Twice if he counted letting Leviathos get away. He couldn't fail them again.

Taeg slid into Dagan's car while the valet opened her passenger-side door for her. He opened his mouth to press for a reply, for a promise to aid them. What came out was, "How was the food?"

Maya gave him a startled glance. "Fine."

Once outside the parking garage, they passed a row of trees changing into fall colors. Bright reds melded with deep orange hues and shades of brown. His first fall here on Earth, and man was it beautiful. He usually never stopped to notice things like that.

After a few minutes of silence, Maya turned to him. "You promised to let me go. So are you?"

Like hell he was. He ground his teeth together, but managed to keep his voice casual. "Where do you live?"

She fidgeted and didn't answer.

"Oh come on," he scoffed. "What do you think I'll do, slip in there in the middle of the night? If I haven't done anything to you yet, do you think I'll change my mind for no damned reason?"

After a moment's pause, she recited her Greenwich Village address. Not too far from where he lived. They drove the rest of the way without exchanging two words. Not until he pulled up into a spot a few blocks from his apartment did she notice where they were.

"I thought you were taking me home," she said, crossing her arms over her chest.

"Your backpack is in my apartment."

"Oh, that's right." She relaxed and followed him inside. Good. That would make things easier.

Opening the door to his apartment, he nodded toward his bedroom. "I put it under the bed. Why don't you go grab it?"

Her instincts were sharp. She frowned and gave him a nervous glance.

He kept the front door open. "I'll wait for you here."

Taeg waited until Maya nodded and retreated to the bedroom before closing and locking his door. Then he followed her into the room. Oh man, she was going to spit fire when she caught on, and he felt like shit about betraying the little amount of trust she'd managed to place in him. He didn't want to do her wrong. But he couldn't let her go. Not yet. Not until she'd agreed to help.

Don't forget you're doing this for Brynn and Keegan. For the baby.

He entered the room as Maya straightened, her brows

furrowed. "I don't see it under here—"

She cut off when he swung the door shut, imprisoning her inside the room.

"What are you doing?"

Something she wasn't going to like. Not in the slightest.

CHAPTER NINE

Taeg stalked toward Maya with single-minded purpose.

"What are you doing?" she repeated, but he didn't waste his time with a response.

She lunged for him just as he moved within striking distance. Her fist shot out, on a direct trajectory toward his jaw. And yeah, he couldn't help but grin as he sidestepped it. Fighting with her was fun. Like foreplay.

Maya whipped out her leg and kicked the side of his knee, sending him tumbling to the ground. In the precious seconds it took him to get back up, she was already at the door. He caught her before she could open it, whipped her around, and imprisoned her against his body.

"I knew I couldn't trust you," she spat. "*Demon.*"

Taeg swallowed back the snicker that threatened to escape his lips. He closed his hands around hers. "Relax, sweetheart. I'm not going to hurt you."

She struggled against his grip, but froze when he closed the gap between their bodies. She'd be smart to stop squirming. Because there was no doubt she could feel how much he liked it.

With her head against the wall, she tilted her chin up to rake him with a defiant glower. "You promised you would let me go."

"And I will. Once I know for sure you won't seek to harm any of my family."

A flicker of understanding crossed her face, and some of her anger faded. "I would never hurt Brynn."

"I believe you," he agreed. "But I can't say the same for my brothers. You've made your demon issues crystal clear. So until I know you aren't going to rain down on us like some sort of avenging angel, you're stuck with me."

Her mouth tightened, her lips pursing in a way that highlighted their fullness. "You can't just keep me. People will notice I'm missing. I've already missed a day of class. And my coworkers will call the cops when I don't show up to work."

Taeg grinned at her. "Who the hell keeps attendance in college? Nobody will notice. Also, when I charmed that lovely coworker of yours, I found out you don't have to be at work for four more days."

That made her blink. "You're such an ass."

"Guilty as charged." He dropped his eyes to her lips. Couldn't help it. "I also found out you don't have anyone waiting for you at home, little slayer, so I can do whatever I want with you for the next four days."

Much to his surprise, her eyes welled with unspoken emotion and she lowered her head.

Shit. He'd expected her to fight back when he said that, not be terrified. Releasing his grip, he stepped away from her. "Hey, I was kidding about that. I won't hurt you, I promise."

"It's not that," she whispered. She took a deep breath, visibly collecting herself.

"Well…" Taeg moved his hand to her jaw and forced her to meet his eyes. "What is it?"

"I…it's nothing." Maya didn't make any effort to move, just stood there with her back against the wall. "Why did you want to know my address if you're not going to take me home?" she finally asked, dropping that cool, collected mask onto her face once again.

"I planned on going to get some of your clothes."

"Really? And what did you plan on doing with me?" When he glanced at the bed, and the silk ties attached to it, she let out a derisive snort. "You've got to be kidding me."

"Sorry."

Much to his surprise, she didn't try to hit him. Didn't even move. What was it that had her so upset? He didn't like this Maya, the beaten one. What could he do to make her smile again? And why did he even care? He should be focused on one thing right now.

"Will you help Brynn?" he asked bluntly. "Help *us*?"

"I…don't know yet," she answered, closing her eyes. "Give me a few days to think about it."

"Okay." When she didn't say anything further, he got an idea. It might not make her smile but at least it was bound to elicit some sort of emotion from her. "What about my prize?"

"What are you talking about?"

He grinned at her. "Remember that bet we had earlier? Winner gets a kiss."

She blinked once. Twice. "But I didn't say I would help you."

"You didn't say no, either. In my book, that's a win."

Maya smiled and shook her head. "You're impossible."

"That's why you like me," he quipped. "Come on baby, pucker up."

Taeg braced a hand on either side of Maya's body and leaned forward with an exaggerated pout of his lips. Her eyes narrowed in on him. He saw her fist coming with enough time to prevent it, but hell, what would be the fun in that?

Her punch landed dead-center, sending sharp stabs of pain spiderwebbing across his face. He grabbed his nose and stumbled backward. "Ow."

Maya's glance was shrewd. "If I didn't know any better, I'd say you liked it."

"Coming from you, sweetheart, I'll take what I can get."

A soft blush erupted on her cheeks, lending her face a rosy glow. Yeah, that was better. Much better than her sadness.

"Come on, little slayer." He dropped his hands and adopted a fighter's stance, playfully angling toward her once more. "Show me what you've got."

ॐॐ

Ronin would never get over how peaceful it seemed up here.

He stood on the balcony of the apartment, leaning over the railing while he rolled the glass tumbler between his palms. The soft whistle of the blowing breeze muted the distant sounds of screaming traffic. This place was paradise compared to Infernum.

At least it would be, once they caught Leviathos and didn't have to constantly look over their shoulders. The situation had become even more dire since Brynn had gotten knocked up. She was vulnerable, and it terrified all of them.

He didn't bother to look back when the balcony door slid open. Didn't have to. He could sense his brothers from a mile away. That was one of the benefits of being half-angel, his hypersensitivity to other demons.

Keegan now stood beside him, wearing a T-shirt and a pair of jeans. He seemed oblivious to the cold air as he stared out into the horizon. "What do you think?"

Ronin didn't have to ask what Keegan meant by that. "I came across the research on Excalibur months ago, but I discounted it because Merlin's invisibility spell was rumored to be so powerful that it couldn't be undone."

"If Taeg's intriguing little find can see through glamours, then that doesn't matter," Keegan said.

"Yeah." Lucky break. In fact, given the circumstances, Ronin couldn't fault Taeg for holding her against her will.

"What are the risks?" Keegan asked.

He thought hard about that one. "I can't think of any, other than the possibility of wasting our time."

"Yeah, but let's face it." Dagan's voice sounded behind them as he strolled out to join them on the balcony. "We don't have any better ideas anyway."

"That's true," Ronin replied. The *Book of the Dead* was locked up somewhere safe, but that wasn't good enough. Leviathos was resourceful. Even if it was almost impossible for him to get his hands on it, he'd never stop trying.

"He's going to fall for her," Dagan commented. It didn't take too much thinking to figure out he meant Taeg and Maya.

"Good," Keegan said. "He could use something else to focus on. I want to find Leviathos more than anyone, believe me, but his determination borders on obsession. It's not healthy."

"He feels guilty," Ronin told him. "He thinks he betrayed you when he refused to help you save Brynn after the Council ordered her execution. I don't know if he'll ever forgive himself for that."

Keegan grimaced. "Yeah, that's what worries me."

They stood in silence, looking out onto the cityscape.

"Damn Taeg," Dagan finally said. "He's a lucky bastard."

Ronin thought about Maya's lush curves and her exotic features. Yup, Dagan had it right there.

"I'm gonna go check on Brynn," Keegan said. "She's feeling sick again."

Ronin couldn't help but feel a twinge of envy. Keegan was happily married, with a baby on the way. Taeg was occupied with Maya. Dagan had already screwed half the chicks in the city, and was on a mission to get the other half. He was living life just the way he liked it. But for him…life felt a little empty. He wanted… Shit. He didn't know what he wanted. But he did know one thing: marriage and babies weren't in the cards for him. Not after what he'd lived through. He knew how easily loved ones could be ripped away, like Mammon had taken him from his first family. And he could never risk loving a woman when he'd have to live with the fear of losing her. No, wasn't meant to be.

"You're sighing like a chick, dude." Dagan raised his brows. "What's up?"

"Nothing." Because he couldn't say what he truly felt. There were only so many feelings brothers could share.

ॐ≼

Well, damn. Twenty-four hours after being kidnapped by a demon and here she was, tied to the bed again. At least Taeg had tied her in a sitting position this time. He'd also turned on the television and left a remote within reach. After he'd let her spar with him and allowed her to land a few hits. She didn't hold any illusions about that one.

Maya let out a deep sigh. Was she totally insane, letting the demon tie her to the bed again? Not that "letting" was the right word, since Taeg was far stronger than her and wouldn't take no for an answer.

Crazy enough, she sort of understood why he was doing this. He'd taken a big risk bringing her to his brother's apartment, and he wanted to make sure they'd be safe, even if she chose not to help them. Made sense since he knew she loathed demons.

What would he say if she told him she had killed more than a handful of demons over the years? She'd gotten lucky, she now knew. Demons were strong. Fast. The only thing she'd had on her side was the element of surprise and a deep sense of vengeance that allowed her to switch her emotions off during a fight.

For the first time since meeting Taeg, she allowed that sliver of doubt buried deep in her mind to rise to the surface. Those demons she had destroyed, none of them had ever done anything to her. She'd killed them simply because of what they were. Because of her belief that they were evil, that they would hurt others if she didn't destroy them. But if demons weren't all evil, as Taeg and Brynn would have her think, did that mean she might have taken innocent lives?

Was she no better than those demons who had brutally murdered her family?

"No." Her breath came out in large gasps, and somewhere in the dim recesses of her mind, she recognized she was on the verge of hyperventilating. She concentrated on taking slow, even breaths.

No. She wasn't like those monsters. She wasn't evil.

She wasn't.

By the time she heard the footsteps outside the bedroom, signaling Taeg's return, Maya had managed to calm herself down. Right now she had to focus on herself, and what she was going to do about Brynn. And Taeg.

While she hadn't been able to save her own family, she might actually have a chance at helping Brynn and the baby. What kind of person would she be if she walked away from that?

Taeg entered the room with a suitcase she recognized as hers.

"I didn't hear you open the front door," she said. "I didn't hear you leave, either, for that matter. How do you do that?"

He smiled, though it lacked its characteristic cockiness. "I have my ways."

"What's wrong?"

"I got a call from a contact of mine," he replied with a frown. "He's got some information that may be helpful in locating the sword. I need to go meet with him."

"Tonight?"

He nodded.

"Where are you going?"

"To a bar not far from here." He set down her suitcase next to the bed.

Well, she wasn't about to stay behind. Besides, if there was a chance she was going to help him, she wanted to see more of his world. "I want to go, too."

That earned her a husky laugh. "I don't think so."

"Why not? You can't expect me to stay tied to this bed all night."

He gave her a smoldering look that was much more like him. "Sounds good to me."

"Come on," she pressed. "You want me to help you. So let me come with you."

Taeg's expression grew serious. "Does that mean you're agreeing to help?"

"I'm thinking about it," she answered honestly.

He stared at her for a long moment. Was he waiting for her to change her mind about wanting to go along? She wasn't going to. Finally he let out a sigh and strode over to sit on the bed next to her. "Maya, the place I'm going is a bar that caters to Otherworlders. I don't think you can handle that."

"Otherworlders?" Her mental warning system went on red alert. "What's that?"

He rubbed his chin. "Tell me what you think you know about demons."

"I…" She stiffened her spine. "Demons are evil creatures escaped from Hell, like it says in the Bible. At least…that's what I *thought*."

"Yeah, I had a feeling." He took hold of one of her hands and looked her in the eyes. "Did you notice that me and my brothers are different from each other?"

She gave him a slow nod. "Yes. I did find it strange. I mean, I know you have different mothers, but you share the same demon father, right?"

"Yes." He took a deep breath. "This may come as a shock

to you, but not every non-human you see is a demon."

"*What?*" Maya lurched forward so fast her wrists tugged against the binds, jerking her back a few inches. "What do you mean?"

"Demons aren't those evil beings from Hell that you read about in your Bible. We're actually a race from a different dimension."

"Different dimension," she echoed hollowly, barely hearing the sound of her own voice over the sharp ringing in her ears. "What do you mean?"

"There are many dimensions, each inhabited by separate races of beings," he continued, with more urgency this time. "Here on Earth, we refer to them as the Otherworlds. Most humans don't know this, but there's a way to travel between the dimensions. A portal. Many, in fact. They're policed by the Elden Council—a council of beings composed of different races."

"A council."

"It's how we came to Earth."

Maya stared at his unflinching face. A wellspring of emotion erupted within her, working its way up her throat. It came out as a laugh.

"I'm not joking."

She cut off abruptly. "You're telling me demons are another race of beings, one of many that walk around here on Earth?"

He nodded. "There's some reality to pretty much every one of your myths. Vampires, werewolves—they all exist."

"Vampires and werewolves." Oh God, this was like her worst nightmare come to life.

"Yes. Wolf-shifters to be more exact, but remember, they're not all evil creatures. Like humans, there are good ones and bad ones." Taeg reached out and gently squeezed her arm, as if he were trying to lend her his strength, to convince her he was telling the truth.

This was unbelievable.

"Untie me."

He lifted a brow but did as she asked.

Maya shrugged away from his grasp and bounded off the bed. She rubbed her wrists while she paced the room, trying to absorb what he'd told her. She turned back to where he sat, leaning forward with his elbows on his knees. "Okay, I'll bite. If you're only half-demon, what's the other half? Based on what you've told me, I'm guessing it's not human."

"You'd guess right. My mother came from a world called Faelan. She was an air sylph."

She gave him a disbelieving look. "A *faerie*?"

Taeg winced at her use of the word. "Yeah, I guess you could say that."

"You said you have the ability to compel others. To *charm*, I think you called it."

"Yup."

"Oh shit," she whispered. She'd studied enough mythology as an archaeology major to know that many cultures had stories of faeries and their ability to compel others to do their will. "I need to sit down."

Maya wobbled toward the bed on rubbery legs and slumped down next to Taeg. All the demons she had seen over the years—pale or colored flesh, grotesque features, pointed ears—a good portion of those were bound to be something other than demon. Which meant…

"Oh God."

"I know it's a lot to take in." Taeg leaned toward her and

placed his hand on her back, rubbing it much the way a parent would when consoling a crying child.

This was too much. And if this was true, it meant all her years of research, of studying the Bible and trying to find a way to banish demons back to Hell, they were all for nothing. She couldn't think about that right now. She simply couldn't.

"Your brothers? What are they?"

He took a deep breath. "Keegan's mother was a dragon-shifter."

She gulped. "Dragon?"

"Dagan's mom was a siren. Legged cousin to the mermaid. They can breathe underwater but don't grow tails."

"Okay…what about Ronin?"

"Ronin?" He let out a husky laugh. "Ronin's an angel."

She blinked at him.

"And before you say anything, no, I'm not referring to an angel from Heaven. They're another species from my world, Infernum. They can heal and have the ability to calm others with their presence. I guess you can say they're the equivalent of hippies in my dimension. Thankfully, Ronin is half-demon, so he's not too big a pansy-ass."

Maya stared down at her clasped hands. *Focus, just focus.* "The other two men who were at the apartment—Bram and Reiver?"

"Panther shifters."

"Shifters." *Oh Jesus.* That's why Keegan, Bram, and Reiver all looked like something fought to crawl out of their flesh—they were *shifters.* "This bar you're going to, it will have all these kinds of beings?"

"Yes."

Okay. She'd dealt with some pretty bizarre things before.

She could handle this.

"What should I wear?" Her voice came out far more even than she could have imagined.

Taeg cocked a brow, but he didn't try to argue with her. "Upscale casual. You should be able to find something among the clothes I brought you."

Maya concentrated on acting like she had her shit together. "All right, I'll be ready in twenty minutes."

Beside her, Taeg let out a defeated sigh. "Good times."

⮜⮞

It took far less time for her to get ready than Taeg would've thought, especially considering how good she looked. But then, his tempting little Maya would look good wrapped in a bedsheet. Especially with nothing else on.

Yeah, his cock liked this train of thought. She might not appreciate him walking around with a raging hard-on, though, so he needed to cool it.

"You look *good*," he told her.

"Did you purposely pick my skimpiest outfits?" She cast a wry glance down at her body, clad in skintight black jeans and a red halter-top that put her ample cleavage on display and billowed in loose layers below.

Fuck yeah, he had. Had she noticed her pajamas yet? He'd bypassed all the respectable pieces and gone straight for the slinky lingerie. Who knew? Maybe he'd get to see her in them.

Never hurt to be optimistic.

Taeg grinned at her. "I have no idea what you're talking about."

"I'm sure you don't." The corners of her mouth ticked upward and she peered down at her boots. "I feel naked without my daggers."

"Here." Taeg strode over to the wooden coffee table and lifted the top to reveal a hidden compartment. He retrieved the daggers Maya had used to attack him back in the alley and held them out to her, hilts first.

Her mouth dropped open. "You're going to give them back to me?"

"If there's a chance we're going to work together, we have to learn to trust each other." And after the glimpse he'd gotten of what she'd been through as a kid, if it would make her feel safer, he was all for it.

When she continued to stare at the daggers with wide eyes, he said, "Just promise you won't use them on me."

She looked at them but didn't reply, as if she actually debated stabbing him in the heart. But when she took them she slid them into their sheaths inside her boots without a word.

"Better?" he asked.

"It'll do. I usually have an iron dagger I strap to my stomach when I go out, but I left that one at home yesterday."

She had to be kidding. "Where did you leave it?"

Maya frowned. "Beneath my bed."

"I'll go get it."

"You'll have time to do that?"

"Sure. Be right back."

He opened up a fae path, the air shimmering in front of him. In the span of a heartbeat, he was at her apartment. Maya was no doubt shocked as hell, but he figured she'd learn about his ability to flash soon enough. Might as well show her now.

He grabbed the dagger and a holster from under her bed, then flashed back to his place.

She stood by the coffee table, right where he'd left her. Her mouth hung open in shock. "What *was* that?"

"I forgot to mention it," he said casually. "The fae can travel paths to get from one spot to another in an instant. It's called flashing. Only works within the boundaries of the dimension I'm in, though."

She plopped down onto the coffee table, her eyes glazed over as if she was stunned. "What else can you do that you haven't told me about?"

This was almost kind of fun. "I can dissipate into air form."

"Show me."

"I'd love to"—he gave her a wry smile—"but I can't take the clothes with me, so unless you'd care to see me in all my naked glory—"

"Let's skip that one." Standing now, she took the dagger and holster from him, and with shaky hands lifted her shirt far enough to strap them around her waist.

Taeg swallowed hard. He turned away before Maya could tell how much he liked getting a glimpse of her softly rounded, utterly feminine belly. Damn, she was like a walking wet dream.

"Ready," she said, and tossed on a light jacket he'd stuffed into her suitcase. "Are we going to flash to this bar?"

He wished. "No, I can't bring people with me. Just objects."

"Guess we'll have to get there the old-fashioned way, huh?"

Taeg chuckled and grabbed the keys. They left the apartment and walked downstairs. He couldn't help but like that she followed him willingly. Not even a hint that she thought to escape. Maybe she was beginning to trust him after all.

He hoped so, because if she tried anything funny on the way to or at the bar, he'd have to handle it. Now that he had her, he wasn't about to let her go. Not when she could lead him to the sword.

"Once we get to the bar, stay by my side," he told Maya on the steps of the building.

"Got it," she replied with a nod.

"One more thing." He looked pointedly at the spot where she'd hidden her dagger under her blouse. "Please, *please*, try not to stab anyone."

She must have found that funny, because she let out a silky laugh that reverberated all the way down to his bones. "I'll do my best."

Chapter Ten

What a perfect fall night in the city. Wearing her black denim jacket, Maya barely felt the light breeze that blew through the street, fluttering stray scraps of paper. They took the steps down, but instead of heading toward the car, Taeg turned in the opposite direction. For a moment, she stood still and admired the way his jeans hugged his perfect ass. Delicious. But then she realized he'd kept going, leaving her behind.

She hurried to catch up with him. "We're walking?"

He flashed his straight, white teeth at her. "Eros is only a few blocks away."

"Oh, that close, huh?" They passed a Chinese restaurant and a pizzeria whose combined aromas made her mouth water.

"Listen," Taeg said in a low tone, "when we get there, don't stare too much. I don't want anyone to know you can see through glamours."

"I'll try," she replied, since she didn't know if that was a promise she could keep.

By the time they strolled up to a nondescript building, Maya's nerves had built to a fiery crescendo that manifested as an unsettled stomach. Was she crazy? She'd spent the last fourteen years of her life destroying demons and searching for a way to banish them to Hell, and now she was going to walk willingly into a bar full of them? Not to mention the other creatures she hadn't known existed—faeries and shifters. Vampires and werewolves, for God's sake.

Taeg must have sensed her unease, because he paused and slung an arm around her shoulders. "It'll be okay. Promise."

She gave him a shaky nod.

He kept his arm around her as he sauntered over to the huge, burly man guarding the door. "Hey, Giorgio. How's it hanging, dude?"

"To the left." Giorgio's attention darted to Maya and his eyes narrowed.

"She's with me." Taeg pulled her so close that the heat pulsing off his body penetrated her layers of clothes, warming her instantly.

Giorgio nodded and opened the door to allow them inside. They stepped into a small space that contained nothing other than a narrow staircase leading down.

"Was he some sort of shifter?" Maya whispered as they made their way down the stairs. Giorgio had that same ragged aura as Keegan, Bram, and Reiver—like something inside him longed to tear its way out.

"Shush," Taeg replied.

Damn it, she had to know. But now wasn't the time. They reached the bottom of the stairs. In front of them a long, narrow room housed a bar, small stage, and dance floor. But the room wasn't nearly as interesting as its patrons. Short, squat men who looked like pigs, women with long, flowing hair and blue flesh, creatures with five eyes instead of two. There had to be at least thirty people in this part of the bar, and not one of them human. Not even the DJ, a beautiful woman with swirling amber and gray eyes who danced to the beat of her music behind her equipment on the small stage.

"Holy shit."

Taeg tightened his hold on her, as if warning her to keep her mouth shut. She wasn't about to blab, but man did her fingers itch to close around one of her daggers. He practically dragged her over to one corner of the bar.

"Hey, buddy"—he placed his hand on the shoulder of a guy who looked like a biker—"give the seat up for my girl, will you?"

The biker dude swiveled to face her and Maya stiffened, her fingers automatically moving to graze the hilt of her dagger over her shirt. But after giving her a once-over, he grinned and rose from the red leather barstool. "Sure, anything for a lady."

She took the seat and Taeg squeezed between her barstool and the neighboring one.

The bartender sidled over to them. She was beautiful, with hair the color of midnight falling to her waist and glowing white skin with a tinge of blue. "What can I get you?"

Much to Maya's surprise, Taeg barely spared her a glance. "I'll take a Corona." He turned to Maya. "You?"

"Gin and tonic, please." Not that she would drink much of it. Even if she were safe here, as Taeg reassured her, the place creeped her out. She had to stay on top of her game.

The bartender quickly returned with their drinks. Maya

waited until she left before leaning toward Taeg. "Did you charm that guy into giving up his seat?"

He rested his elbows on top of the bar and bent so that his mouth was close to her ear. "No. The use of powers inside the bar is strictly prohibited. People would be a lot less likely to cut loose if they had to worry about others using their abilities on them, so everyone's happy to obey that rule here."

"Wouldn't they know if someone was using their power on them?"

"With some things, yes. But I could charm someone into forgetting we ever spoke, for example. It would work just the same on an Otherworlder as it does on a human."

That was a pretty impressive gift he had there. "Don't you wish that worked on me?"

Taeg let out a low laugh. "You don't know the half of it."

"Let me guess. You would have forced me to help you, right?"

He surprised her by looking her straight in the eye when he answered. "Yes, but you can't deny it would be with good reason. Besides, you can rest assured knowing there's plenty of stuff I would have imagined charming you into doing but would never have acted on."

There he was, flirting again. But since he had broached the subject… "Have you ever…you know…with a girl?"

"Charmed her into digging me?" His eyes widened and he pulled back a little. "Do you think I would stoop so low?"

That was the thing. She didn't. He wouldn't have to. If she hadn't known what he was, she might have jumped his bones herself.

"No, I don't." She turned her focus to his fingers, which were closed around his beer bottle. They were long, the nails neatly trimmed. Artist's hands. Not a demon's. But that was what he was. Maya had the feeling Taeg would never stop astounding her, would never act according to her expectations. Much as she wanted to deny it, he wasn't like any demon she'd ever met.

Almost as if he'd read her mind, Taeg said, "You know, nothing's ever black and white, Maya. Not demons or humans. Not anyone."

"I'm beginning to realize that."

He studied her as if he was trying to see below the surface and into her soul. As if he could.

She held her breath when he lifted his hand to brush a loose strand of hair out of her face, tucking the piece behind her ear. And when he traced his forefinger down her jaw, her whole body broke out into a shiver that had nothing to do with being cold.

"Little slayer," he said, "when are you going to tell me what happened to you?"

She froze at the unexpected question. Damn him for asking like that. Damn him for being him, because it made her want to confide in him. And damn her for feeling weak. "I—"

"Am I interrupting you two lovebirds?" a shaky voice said beside them.

Taeg stiffened and dropped his hand. He turned toward a tall, gaunt man whose horns and mottled flesh betrayed him as a demon. At least, she *thought* he was a demon. For all she knew, he might be something else entirely.

"Shit, Horster," Taeg said. "You look like you got run over by a fucking Mack truck."

"I'm fine." But the way Horster's whole body trembled,

he didn't look fine. Not even close. "Ready to deal?"

Taeg nodded. "Let's find a table in the back."

Maya rose from her stool and Taeg laced his fingers through hers. He led her toward an arched doorway that split into two areas, one with booths and the other with tables. They followed the stumbling Horster toward one of the tables.

Taeg leaned down to whisper in her ear. "Horster's a lorne demon, the local go-to guy for information on Otherworldly stuff. Unfortunately, word on the street is he got himself addicted to *score*."

"*Score*?"

"A hallucinogenic. Deadly stuff."

Horster slid into a chair and fumbled inside his jacket, pulling out a linen handkerchief, which he used to mop his sweaty brow.

"Can you trust him to give you the right information?" Maya asked.

Taeg laughed. "I don't trust anyone, but I haven't got much of a choice here."

They made it to the table and Taeg pulled out a chair for her before taking his seat. "Horster, you don't look good, man," he said quietly. "I think you need some help. You're going to kill yourself one of these days."

Horster bristled at that. "I'm fi—fine. Now, you got the money?"

Taeg looked like he wanted to argue, but in the end he reached into the back pocket of his jeans and pulled out an envelope. "You got the list?"

Horster placed his sweat-stained handkerchief back in his jacket pocket and withdrew a folded scrap of paper from the same place. He handed it to Taeg. *Eww*. Couldn't he at least have put the handkerchief in a different pocket?

"That's the information my contact in Europe compiled," Horster said. "He's a professor, and he's studied this legend for close to a hundred years now. He assures me this will lead you to the right spot."

Taeg opened the paper and began perusing it. "Thanks."

Horster nodded. His leer wavered to Maya, then down to the envelope on the table. He snatched it up and stuck it in his jacket. "Until next time."

He rose and practically ran out of the place. As bad off as he looked, he was probably rushing out to buy his next fix.

"See ya," Taeg grumbled noncommittally.

Maya examined the paper, which contained a bunch of foreign words. "What does it say?"

"Don't know. It's Welsh. I have a friend who reads it."

"Are these potential locations for the sword?"

"Shit." Taeg banged his fist on the table and abruptly rose, stuffing the paper in his pocket. He held his hand out to her. "Come on."

She scrambled to her feet. "What's wrong?"

"Move. Fast." He turned and raced toward the front of the bar, dragging her behind him.

"What is it?" But he either didn't hear or didn't care to respond.

They rushed up the stairs. Giorgio must have sensed them coming because the door swung open at the last moment.

"Where'd Horster go?" Taeg asked him.

"That way."

Taeg took off in the direction Giorgio pointed, and Maya had no choice but to race after him. "What the hell, Taeg?"

"Come on," was all he said. He ran a couple of blocks before pausing and turning a slow circle. Maya finally caught up with him.

"What's going on?" she asked in between pants.

He turned to face a narrow alleyway. "This way."

"Great," she mumbled when he disappeared inside. Nothing good ever happened in dark alleys. She would know.

Squeezing in behind him, she followed as he wound his way down the dank, smelly path. They came to a fork in the alley and Taeg paused, then turned right. They made it about ten more steps before four large men stepped out of an open doorway nestled in the dark. They were Others and they were scary as hell, with pierced brows and large tats covering portions of their bodies. And those were their least scary features.

"Shit." Taeg ground to a halt in front of her.

Well said. These guys were terrifying. She didn't consider herself a wimp by any means, but all her instincts of self-preservation screamed at her to get out of here. *Now.*

"What do we have here?" said one of the thugs, giving a pointed look at Taeg, then beyond him to Maya. "Looks like someone brought us a tasty snack."

Taeg held up his hands and stepped back a few paces, bumping into Maya. "I don't want any trouble, guys. I'm looking for a dude who came through here. Goes by Horster."

Another one laughed. "He doesn't look like much. We could take him with our eyes closed."

"Maybe we should go," she whispered into Taeg's back.

"I could take 'em," Taeg retorted. "Run back to Eros. Stay with Giorgio. I'll meet you there."

"But I can—"

"Nothing I like more than a fight," the first thug said to Taeg. Then he gave her a toothy grin. "Well, maybe one thing, right, baby?"

"Sorry, chuckles, but I don't swing that way," Taeg replied easily. Funny, he didn't sound scared. But he must be, right? These guys were terrifying.

"I wasn't talking about you, pretty boy. But you can watch, if you're still conscious."

Oh, hell no. Maya slipped her hand under her top and snatched the hidden dagger. She pressed the hilt into Taeg's side. "Here."

"Thanks," he said, palming it. "Now *go*."

She hesitated.

"*Go.*"

Maya turned and started down the alley, taking a hard left and racing toward the street.

"Oh look," she heard one of the thugs say, "he brought us a toothpick."

"Great," said another. "We'll need it to pick his bones out of our teeth when we're done with him."

She heard the unmistakable sound of fists hitting flesh. Someone let out a grunt. She stopped. Four to one. Those weren't good odds, especially when each of those men was almost twice Taeg's size. Could she leave him here to fight on his own? *What makes you think your odds will be better if you stay?* She wasn't stupid. Even trained, she was no match for their strength.

But she did have speed and agility on her side.

Oh shit, she was about to do something dumb.

She turned toward the sounds of battle and reached in her boots for her daggers. Holding their heavy weight, she raced back and rounded the corner, then came to a standstill to take in the scene. One of the four goons was already on the ground, either dead or unconscious, and Taeg fought the remaining three with an odd sense of calm about him.

"Go, Taeg," she whispered approvingly. She didn't know why she was surprised. He'd already proven he had strength and cunning.

She saw a flash of silver as Taeg sliced one of the men with her dagger. The man grunted when it slid through his shoulder, but it didn't stop him. He landed a solid punch to Taeg's cheek that momentarily dazed him, grinned, and cupped one fist in the other, lifting his arms overhead in preparation to bash his fists down on Taeg's skull.

That would snap his neck. It could kill him.

"Hey, you ugly fuck!"

Well, that managed to catch everyone's attention. They all froze, staring at her with equal looks of shock.

Perfect.

She ran toward them, and at the last moment did a little run up one of the walls before kicking off it, using that as momentum to arch into a dive. She knocked into the thug Taeg had sliced. He fell back and she went down with him, jamming both daggers into his neck. He gurgled as blood flowed out of the wounds, but threw her off before she could finish the job. She recovered one of her daggers. Doing a front roll, she jumped to her feet again.

"Damn it, Maya." Taeg started in on the other two attackers. But the one she'd tried to behead only had eyes for her. He got to his feet and faced her, yanking the remaining dagger out of his throat. Before her eyes, his wounds started to heal.

"Freaking demons." Their über-healing ability was so *not* fair.

He grinned and spat some blood before running at her with her dagger. She forced herself to hold her ground, waiting until he was a little closer before diving between his widespread legs. Hopping up and spinning around, she jammed the dagger into his back before he could turn to face her.

Despite the demon's tough skin, her aim was true. He froze, paralyzed.

Bracing her other hand on his back, she twisted the blade and yanked it out, then grabbed his hair and rammed the edge of the dagger into his neck. He gave one low gurgle as the dagger sliced clean through, separating his head from his body.

Thank God—and sharpeners—for quality blades.

Maya whirled in time to see Taeg slice the head off another one. The last one lay on the ground, already decapitated.

"Whoa. Good job, Taeg."

He gave her a dirty look while he used the demon's shirt to wipe the knife clean, though his own clothes were so bloody he might as well have used them. "I told you to run."

She bristled at his menacing tone. Of course he couldn't be grateful that she killed one of the men. He didn't want her to come to his rescue. "I don't follow your orders. Besides, I might have saved your life, for all you know."

"You damn near killed me, coming in here like some screaming banshee."

The first man Taeg had taken down uttered a low moan. Taeg rose and walked over to him, neatly and efficiently severing his head.

"Did you really think I couldn't handle four demons on my own?" he asked, nostrils flaring.

Well, she *had*. Now, after seeing him in action, she had a feeling she'd been dead wrong about that.

He wiped the blade again. "Are you hurt?"

"I…" She looked down at herself. Other than a few scrapes and cuts, she was fine. "No. How about you?"

Taeg strode over to her, lifting her chin to examine her face, then ran his fingers over her arms and stomach. She held her breath, trying to ignore the shivers that crept down her spine. Though he clearly wasn't feeling her up for the fun of it, her body still responded like he was.

When he'd satisfied himself that she was okay, he replied, "I'm fine."

Maya touched his lower lip, which had been split, but already appeared to be mending.

"Pretty impressive, demon," she said lightly. "You're not even breathing hard."

His lips twisted into a wry smile. He looked down at himself. "My shirt's ruined, though." Grabbing her hand in his own, he turned and headed toward the open doorway the thugs had first filed out of. "Come on."

"Where are we going?"

"We're still looking for Horster."

She glanced back at the fallen demons. "Are we leaving them there?"

"I'll call a cleanup crew once we're done with Horster," he replied.

Cleanup crew?

She had a feeling she didn't want to know.

The doorway led into a large, empty space that looked like it might have once been an office. Everything had been emptied from it, but loose wires and stray pieces of hard plastic littered the concrete floor. Taeg moved through the room into a narrow hallway. They passed a set of doors with faded lettering denoting men's and women's restrooms, and he treaded over to a partially closed door at the end of the corridor. Swinging it open, he stepped inside.

Horster sat on the floor, his back to a wall with his jacket beside him.

A man knelt down next to him, squeezing a needle into his arm. "Did you handle them, Riggs?" He looked up and cut off with a squeak.

Maya made out the glint of Taeg's teeth when he gave the man a feral grin. "Yeah, we *handled* them, all right."

The man stood up, shaking as he lifted his hands above his head. With two crooked buckteeth and his thin face, he resembled a rat. He wasn't much taller than her five-feet-two inches. "I…it wasn't my fault. I only did what Horster paid me to do. I'm just his supplier, man. That's all, I swear."

Taeg stared at him for a long moment before letting out a sigh. "Get the fuck out of here. Go."

The man flinched as he raced past them, as if he expected Taeg to change his mind at any moment.

Maya watched him go before turning back to Taeg. "The guy's a drug dealer. Why didn't you kill him?"

He gave a nonchalant shrug. "He's just a middleman. Kill him and three more will crop up in his place."

Well, that sucked. Because if Horster was any indication, that drug was seriously messed up. He lay on the ground, twitching and convulsing.

Taeg strolled over to Horster and knelt in front of him, pulling his head back so he could glare into his eyes. Not that Horster could look back, since his eyes rolled in the back of his head. "Horster. Fuck, man. Come out of it for a sec, will ya?"

He shook Horster until the man sobered up enough to realize someone was there. When he finally noticed Taeg, his eyes widened. "Ta—Taeg. Good to see you—"

"Cut the shit," Taeg bit out. "Where's the rest of it?"

"I..." Horster shivered uncontrollably, sweat covering his skin now. "I don't know what you mean."

"Save it, man. I know you only gave me part of what I paid for. Where's the rest?"

Horster reached his trembling hand into his jacket, fumbling around before he removed another folded-up piece of paper. He handed it to Taeg. "I—I must have forgotten it."

"Yeah, I'm sure," Taeg replied wryly as he unfolded the paper. "No doubt you would have conveniently remembered in exchange for more money, right?"

Ah, that's what this was about. Horster had been trying to screw Tacg over.

"How did you know?" Maya asked him. "I mean, you can't read Welsh."

Taeg glanced up at her with a grin. "I have my ways."

When she frowned at him, he elaborated. "The bottom of the page had a big arrow pointing right. Seemed pretty clear the information continued on another page."

Taeg rose and folded the paper, sticking it in his back pocket while he glared down at Horster. "Don't ever try to fuck me over again, or it'll be the last thing you do, got it?"

"I...yes," Horster rasped out, wincing as if he was in pain.

His eyes traveled down to Taeg's feet, and he inched his hand forward along the ground.

Next to him was another syringe, full of a milky white substance, not more than six inches from Taeg's heel. Taeg must have noticed it, too, because seconds before Horster closed his fingers around it, Taeg reached out and ground it beneath his heel.

"No!" Horster tried to lunge forward but messed up as he was, he only succeeded in falling onto his side.

Taeg shook his head and gave Horster a look of disgust. "Clean yourself up, man. This is pathetic."

He turned to Maya, and despite where they were, despite everything they'd just gone through, her heart still made a funny leap in her chest. "Let's get out of here."

঒৹৹ঌ

As it turned out, the walk back to Taeg's apartment didn't go by nearly as quickly as the walk to Eros had. Something to do with them being covered in blood. On top of that, Maya had road rash on one cheek to go along with the bruise on her forehead. Passersby did double takes and gave them a wide berth, but in true New York fashion, no one seemed to consider calling the police on them.

"You seem to be holding up rather well for someone who just killed a demon," Taeg observed quietly.

Maya stopped and turned to face Taeg. Confession time. She just couldn't hold it back anymore. "I've killed demons before. At least, I thought they were demons at the time. Now I'm not so sure."

He stiffened and searched her face for a long moment

before nodding. "I suspected as much."

All the air left her body in one big rush. "You're not pissed? I mean, for all I know they were complete innocents."

His face softened and he lifted a hand to cup her cheek. "You were only doing what you felt you had to do at the time, Maya. I can't fault you for that."

She hadn't expected that response.

He lowered his hand and wound it around hers, holding her tight as they continued down the street.

When they reached the steps to the building, Taeg fished his keys out of his pocket. Maya watched him unlock the door, drinking in the strength of his profile, the almost angelic glow that pulsed off him.

It seemed that now she'd started making confessions, she couldn't stop. "You know, for years I've studied every version of the Bible I could get my hands on, hoping I would someday find a way to banish demons for good."

He let out a low laugh. "Good thing for me that wouldn't work." Throwing her an understanding smile, he tugged on her hand. "Come on."

The events of the previous couple of hours had played themselves over and over in Maya's head, until she was left with two startling facts. One, Taeg had a lot of contacts and seemed to be pretty good at getting information. Two, he was a damned good fighter.

Holy crap, why hadn't she thought of this before? She knew exactly what to do. She also knew that in order to get him to agree, she'd have to tell Taeg the truth. *Madre de Dios.* She was finally going to talk about that horrible night.

They made it all the way up the stairs, to the outside of Taeg's apartment, before Maya got up the nerve to speak again. "I'll help you find the sword. For Brynn."

He paused, the key to the front door poised at the lock. When he turned toward her, Maya saw the glint of hope in his eyes, hiding behind a careful, expressionless mask. He spoke so quietly his words were nothing more than a whisper. "You will?"

"Yes, but on one condition." She took a deep, fortifying breath, and looked him square in the eye. "I want you to help me find and destroy the demons who killed my family."

CHAPTER ELEVEN

Maya held her breath while Taeg stared at her. She did her best to stand still, though inside she was falling apart. She'd never spoken of this before. Not even to her therapists, and there had been many over the years, hired by her adoptive mother to try to lure her into confiding in them.

Finally, without saying a word, he turned to unlock the door and opened it to let her inside. Maya slunk through, concentrating on putting one foot in front of the other. She felt so…fragile. And she hated it.

Behind her, Taeg locked the door. As if he sensed her inner turmoil, he placed his hands on her shoulders and guided her toward the couch. Taking a seat beside her, he hooked a finger under her chin and forced her to meet his eyes. "Okay. I want to know everything. Spill."

That simple command seemed to flood the dam she'd built inside her heart. Her lips opened, words she'd never spoken before tumbling out. "I was ten years old the first time I saw a demon. At least, I think he was. He had red horns. Two mouths instead of one."

"Maliki demon," Taeg confirmed.

"We lived on the outskirts of Puebla, in Mexico. Me, my father and mother, and my sister. She was eight. I was at the plaza with my father that day. He was talking to some friends while I jumped rope. That's when I saw him."

She remembered like it was yesterday. The monster walking down the street. How paralyzed with terror she'd been. He'd been more horrifying than the worst bogeyman she could have imagined. She couldn't stop staring.

"What happened?" Taeg prompted her.

"He saw me looking at him and grinned at me. Those two mouths…" She shuddered.

"Stay with me, Maya." Taeg closed his hand around hers, lending her strength.

"I ran to my father and told him I'd seen a monster. I pointed at him, and he noticed it. I didn't know my father wouldn't be able to see the same thing I saw. He was embarrassed. My father apologized to him and led me away. But I knew. I *knew*. When I looked back, the demon's eyes were on me."

Even now, when she thought back to that day, she still felt his power over her. The evil promises it spoke of. Maya tightened her fingers around Taeg's hand. "He came that night. Looking for me. And he brought a friend."

Taeg's eyes swam with unspoken emotion. "Oh, Maya."

Taking a breath, she continued. "I heard the scrape of something down the hall. It woke me up. My sister was still asleep in bed next to me, so I hopped off and tiptoed out of the room. I made it to the living room when I saw the shadows. I crawled behind a big plant and hid there while they passed by me. Even though it was dark, I could see what they were. Two demons. I…I didn't know what to do. I was so scared."

"Of course you were." Taeg squeezed her hand. "You were only a little girl."

"That's when I heard the screams. My mother. My father. After that, the sound of footsteps. In that moment, I knew. It was my sister, running down the hall toward their room. I…I wanted to scream at her to stop. To run the other way. But I couldn't. I was paralyzed. Eventually, her screams died, too."

"Maya," Taeg whispered, "you don't have to—"

She couldn't hold back now. The words had to be said. "That's when he came looking for me."

Donde estas, niñita? Te encontraré. Vine por ti.

"'I came for you,' he said. I scrunched myself into a ball and prayed. Prayed he wouldn't find me. The whole time I could hear his friend, hear the sound of him…" She closed her eyes, wishing she could forever forget the sounds of tearing flesh, of *slurping*, as the demons had feasted on her family.

"Don't say it, Maya. Don't even think about it."

But how could she not?

"When the demon came into the kitchen, I finally dared to move. I raced toward the door. It was cracked open from when they broke in. So I ran outside. Ran and ran some more. Maybe for half the night. I was still running when she found me."

Taeg's hand trailed up her arm. He gripped her shoulder tight. "Who?"

"Dr. Rossum. Helen. She was an archaeologist working on a nearby dig site. She knew my father, and recognized me. I… couldn't speak when she asked what happened. She suspected the worst, and had the local police called to my house. They found…the remains."

She took a deep swallow as she remembered those next few days. Coming to terms with the horror of what she'd seen. Knowing no one would believe her. "They never found the demons, of course. In the end they chalked it up to the work of a deranged madman. Helen, she took me in. Adopted me and brought me here, to her home in New York City. She saved my life."

"Oh, Maya." Taeg slipped his arms around her and pulled her into his chest.

She wanted to relax against him. To lean on him. She wanted that so desperately. But she couldn't. She didn't deserve it.

"Did you ever tell her the truth?" he asked.

"No, but she knew something was up. She took me to a friend of hers here in the city. He taught me everything he knew about fighting. Real fighting, the kind where only one person is going to come out of it."

"He did good, sweetheart. You're one hell of a fighter." Taeg stroked her hair in a gesture of comfort. Her mother used to do that, too.

No.

Maya yanked herself out of his arms. "Don't you get it? I killed them all. The demons came because of *me*. And I didn't do a goddamned thing to stop them. I didn't even warn my family."

She stared him straight in the eye, daring him to refute her.

"No, Maya," he said, reaching for her. "It's not your fault. You were just a child."

She slapped his hands away and jumped to her feet. The agony of the truth boiled up inside her stomach, eating her alive. "I'm a murderer, Taeg. I murdered innocent people. Demons. *Others*. Even my own fucking family."

"No, that's not true!"

She couldn't take it anymore. It was too much. All this time she'd kidded herself into thinking she was fighting evil, when the truth had stared her in the face the whole time. *She* was the evil one. She always had been. "My sister was only eight years old. I could have saved her."

Going on pure instinct, Maya turned and headed toward the door. She had to get out of here.

Taeg grabbed her just as her hand closed around the lock. He whirled her around, and her fist shot out automatically, catching him in the face. "Let me go."

"No."

"Let me. Please. *Please.*" She didn't know what she was begging for, but Taeg responded by grabbing her in a bear hug and picking her off her feet. In three long strides, he was at the couch. He sat down with her in his lap, pinning her when she fought to get up. She struggled to get free, but he wouldn't let her go.

"It wasn't your fault, Maya. It wasn't your fault."

She shook her head. He was wrong.

His eyes blazed with intensity. "Sweetheart, just forgive yourself. Please."

Just like that, all the fight went out of her, leaving her with nothing but a bundle of raw nerves and a body filled to bursting with emotions. Burying her head in his neck, Maya finally, *finally*, let them out. Cries of raw agony burst from her throat. She allowed the tears to come, allowed herself to *feel* for once, until she was at last blissfully empty.

❧

Long after Maya had cried herself hoarse in his arms, she lifted her eyes and gave Taeg a shaky smile. "I guess that was a long time coming."

"Why didn't you ever confide in your adoptive mother?" he asked her. "Don't you think she would have believed you?"

She pursed her lips as she considered his words. "You know, I think she probably would have. I guess I wanted to pretend it never happened."

He looked at her evenly, a surge of emotion fueling his words. "It truly wasn't your fault. Most adults in your position would have frozen at the sight of two demons, much less a ten-year-old child."

She shrugged like she believed him, but in the end she said, "Maybe."

That was a start, at least.

Taeg clasped her arms and gently tugged her upward. He wiped the remains of her tears from her face. "Are you okay?"

"Yes." She appeared to realize she was still sitting on his lap. Her cheeks turned a light shade of pink. She scooted off him and sat beside him on the couch.

His body belatedly reacted to her former closeness, and he stifled a curse. At least it hadn't done that while she'd been crying on his lap. That would have been highly inappropriate. He leaned forward to disguise the sudden shift in his jeans. "Are you sure you're all right?"

With a nod she said, "Yes. I guess I held it in for too long."

The look on her face was heartbreaking and arousing at the same time. She was a strong one, his little fighter. "I swear, Maya, I'll help you find the bastards who did this. And together we'll kill 'em good."

He didn't know what had possessed him to say that, to make a promise he probably couldn't keep, but he couldn't have held the words back to save his own life.

"Thank you, Taeg." She gave him a brilliant smile before glancing down at her bloody clothes. "I... Mind if I use the shower first?"

"Be my guest."

"I'll be quick." She stood and rushed toward the bathroom.

Taeg watched the door shut, then examined his own bloodstained outfit. Since he was reasonably sure he didn't have to worry about her running away anymore, he decided to flash over to Keegan's to borrow his shower.

He returned in less than ten minutes, and she was still in the bathroom. With a sigh, he slumped onto the couch. Much as he tried not to think about Maya showering in his bathroom, it was impossible. Like trying not to breathe.

The door unlocked and Maya walked out, clad in a short, silky robe he'd brought from her apartment. Her long, wet hair clung to her, creating enticing wet spots all over her robe. How the hell was he going to handle being close to her? Just the sight of her drove him to distraction.

She saw him and stopped, narrowing her eyes. "How did you manage to shower?"

"Flashed over to my brother's."

"Oh." She arched a brow. "It must be nice to be able to do

that."

He grinned. "Yup."

Maya hesitantly leaned against the doorjamb. "I'm sorry about my little breakdown. The pity party's over and done with. Promise."

Taeg stifled his sigh. "You know, Maya, it's not a crime to feel."

A ghost of a smile crossed her face but she didn't respond.

"Are you positive you're okay?" he asked her.

She nodded. "I will be once the demons are dead."

He didn't respond. What could he say? That the likelihood of her locating two maliki demons who she didn't know by name were slim at best? And that was assuming they were even here on Earth.

"Can I ask you something?" she asked, her voice clouded with uncertainty.

He froze. Something gave him the feeling he wasn't going to like her question. "What is it?"

"Back at your brother's apartment, when you were talking about Leviathos, you said he used to be your friend. What happened?"

Aw, crap. He didn't want to tell this story. But now that she'd confided in him, how could he not do the same? "Leviathos and I practically grew up together back in Infernum. He was my best friend as far back as I can remember."

"Go on," she urged, pushing off the doorjamb and coming to sit next to him on the couch.

"I…betrayed him."

"How?"

He rested his elbows on his knees. "We were teenagers,

and he fell in love. Her name was Ana, and she was an ishtari demon. Beautiful. She loved him, too. They bound themselves to each other—that's the equivalent of engagement in our world."

"And?" she pressed.

And he'd been an idiot.

"One night after hanging with him, I came home to find her in my room. Naked." He turned away, the old, familiar sense of guilt tightening his throat. "I was young and dumb. A total shit. I should have sent her away, but…"

"You slept with her," Maya whispered.

"Yup." He let out a humorless chuckle. "Some friend I was, huh?"

She shrugged. "We all make mistakes."

"Yeah well, Leviathos didn't see it that way. He came over to return something I'd forgotten, and he found us in bed together."

"Oh, Taeg."

"He flipped. Had every right to. From that moment on, he hated me more than anything. No matter how many times I apologized, he swore revenge."

She made a soft noise, but she spoke without a hint of judgment. "I can understand him being angry, but from what I've heard, it sounds like he's gone overboard. Even if he did love her, that doesn't merit trying to destroy an entire world."

Taeg shook his head, daring to meet her eyes. "He doesn't see things the way you and I do, Maya. He's always had an envious nature and this…it seemed to unhinge him. It changed him completely."

"Whatever the past, it doesn't excuse his actions, Taeg. And *you're* not responsible for them."

Right. If only he believed that.

"You're not," she repeated firmly. "No matter your faults, you're a good man. Don't ever doubt that."

Had she actually said that to him? He examined her face, so open and giving. So unlike the prickly Maya he'd first met. His chest constricted. The Maya he was seeing right now, she might be his undoing. "You know, coming from you, those words mean a whole hell of a lot."

She smiled at him and licked her lips, her eyes going unfocused. She inched a fraction closer.

Oh, man. This was crazy. Just a short time ago she'd wanted to kill him. Now she sat here, looking very much like she wanted him to kiss her. And damn, he wanted to. So badly.

Breathing in deeply, he straightened his back before he could give in to the insanity.

Maya's eyes glinted and she momentarily ducked her head. But when she looked back at him all she said was, "Are you going to bring me back to my apartment, now that I've agreed to help you?"

Yeah, that would be the smart thing to do. But for some reason, he was reluctant. Maybe because in many ways she seemed so vulnerable. Or maybe because she was so important to his mission. He couldn't even tell anymore.

"I'm heading upstate to visit my friend who speaks Welsh tomorrow," he finally said. "I thought you might like to come with me. Since you don't have to work for a few more days, it only makes sense for you to stick around until then."

"I do have school, you know." When he didn't reply, she groaned. "Fine."

Inwardly, he sighed with relief. In a few days she could go

back to her place and he'd come to her when he needed her. But for now, he wanted her here. Whether that made sense or not.

"You can take the bedroom," he told her.

"You're not going to try and tie me up again, are you?"

Taeg opened his mouth to make a smartass retort, but in the end he only said, "No. Good night, Maya."

She nodded and stood, heading into the room before closing the door.

He stared at it for a few moments, as if he might be able to use X-ray vision to see inside. *You can be a real dick sometimes.* Maya had poured her heart out to him tonight. Had confessed things she'd never told anyone. Her whole family had been stolen from her—her parents and her younger sister—and she'd only been ten years old herself, for devil's sake.

She'd shown him a softness he bet she rarely let through. And now here he was, ready to take her down the rabbit's hole again. Repaying her kindness by throwing her headlong into danger. Because he needed her. Right now she was his only hope of destroying the book, and Brynn would never be safe until that happened. He couldn't betray Keegan. Not again.

As alluring as Maya was, as much as he ached to be her knight in shining armor, he couldn't. His other mission was too important. Family came first. If he managed to destroy the book, then he would focus on getting revenge for Maya. Until that happened, he needed to keep his distance emotionally. He might not be able to give her problems the focus they deserved, but at least he could keep himself from seducing her. All he could promise right now was hot, dirty, casual sex, and something in his gut told him she wasn't a casual kind of girl.

Yet, after a mere three sleepless hours, Taeg cursed himself for vowing to stay away. Because damn it all, she was right next door, and he couldn't close his eyes without imagining them together. And he knew he couldn't go to sleep without unintentionally dreamscaping with her. He was too weak where she was concerned.

Funny thing was, the biggest turn-on wasn't Maya's smoking body, but her fierce and fearless attitude. She'd taken on a group of demons today, for devil's sake. The woman had metaphorical balls of steel, and that was sexy as hell.

She needs to rest. And she sure didn't need his sorry ass dreamscaping with her while she was trying to do it. He told himself that over and over. But eventually the inevitable happened. He fell asleep.

Once again he stood at the house from last night's dream, breathing in the palpable terror in the air. The demons were here.

Damn. She couldn't keep reliving this. It would drive her insane.

He walked down the dark hallway and into the living room, heading toward the potted plant Maya huddled behind. Kneeling in front of her, he placed his hand under her chin and forced her to look up. "Maya, stop."

Her image morphed, no longer that of a frightened girl hiding in her house but the full-grown, luscious Maya he knew. Very slowly, the panic in her eyes receded, replaced by relief and, if he wasn't mistaken, pleasure. She wore one of the outfits he'd packed for her, a slinky black nightgown that ended at mid-thigh. Her lips curved into a welcoming smile.

"Shit." When he rose to his feet and turned away from her, he noticed they were back in his bedroom. He stalked across the room, coming to a stop in front of the window. The image of her as a woman was so at odds with the terrified little girl he'd seen that he didn't know how to react. How had she survived the agony of that horrifying night without losing her mind?

But then, with a whisper of fabric, she stood right behind him.

"What's the matter, demon?" Her seductive voice sent a shiver of longing down his spine. As if she sensed it, her fingers trailed down the same spot. "Don't you want me?"

Taeg turned to face her. "You know that's not it."

Maya lifted a brow at the clear proof of his desire. "Obviously not."

Her hand reached out to cup him, fingers closing around his girth, and he let out an involuntary hiss. She looked up at him with a mixture of allure and vulnerability that made his blood boil. "Taeg. Make me forget."

Oh devil, he wanted to. But hadn't he just resolved to leave her alone?

He caught her hand and drew it away with a muffled groan. "We shouldn't."

"It's *my* dream."

Yeah, and she really thought that, didn't she?

He examined her face. Eyes half-glazed with desire. Lips moist and parted. Her heavy breath forced his attention down to where the hardened pearls of her breasts poked against the fabric of her nightgown. He had a feeling few people, if any, had seen her clad so provocatively. That she even had an outfit like this pointed to a smoldering sexuality deep within her, one she no doubt preferred to keep hidden under a layer of bristle. What an enigma she was.

"Damn, Maya, you're breathtaking," he admitted.

She smiled, then caught her lower lip between her teeth. "Please, just for a little while, make me forget."

It was her plea that did him in. Here, in their shared dream, there were no responsibilities. No consequences. Here, maybe—just maybe—he could act on the way he felt. He drew his arms around her, closing the distance between them. She lifted to her toes when he lowered his head, and her parted lips brushed against his in a butterfly kiss that shook him to his very toes. When the tips of her full breasts brushed his chest, he couldn't help but groan. Her tongue reached out to glide along the seam of his lips. He cupped the lush fullness of her ass and lifted her so he could press his arousal against the juncture of her thighs.

"Taeg," she sighed against his lips.

Taking her mouth in a deep, erotic kiss that only hinted at all the things he wanted to do to her, he stumbled a couple of steps forward. As could only happen in a dream, those few paces were all it took to get them to the bed across the room. He laid her back onto it and covered her body with his own.

"Don't leave me," she whispered.

As if he could.

Resting his full weight on her, he forced himself to continue kissing her slowly, when all he wanted to do was lose himself inside her in a mad rush. He broke the kiss and sat back onto his legs so he could look down at her. With her face flushed and body heaving under her slinky nightgown, she had an earthy sort of beauty even a goddess would envy. "You're exquisite, Maya."

Her eyes fluttered open. "Taeg—"

"Shush. Let me look at you."

For a moment he feared she would protest, but in the end she licked her lips and watched him from behind half-shuttered eyes. When he'd looked his fill, he tugged the thin straps of her nightgown down her shoulders, baring her full breasts to his view. "Beyond exquisite."

He stroked them, running his thumbs across the taut buds. He couldn't resist leaning down and tugging one nipple into his mouth. She moaned as he ran his tongue around the bud, then lightly scraped his teeth across it.

She thrust her fingers into his hair and tugged him down hard. "More."

He broke away with a hoarse laugh.

"Don't get greedy now." Sitting back again, he ran his fingers along her pubic bone, now barely covered by her gown. With one quick jerk, he tugged the fabric up around her waist, baring her delectable body. A low groan escaped him at the sight of her slick, honeyed flesh. He ran his forefinger along the seam of her parted folds, borrowing her moisture, then slid his finger inside her. "Wet for me?"

"Don't tease me," she replied. Her inner walls closed around him, and suddenly he wondered who was doing the teasing. Damn, how he ached to be there. Not just that. He wanted this to be real, not a dream.

"Do you remember how I told you I could turn into air form?" he asked her.

She opened her eyes to shoot him a look glazed with desire. "Yes."

"Would you like to see it? *Feel* it?"

Maya didn't respond, but if the narrowing of her eyes and

ratcheting of her breath was any indicator, the answer was yes.

With a grin, he dissipated into air. His molecules dissolved into air particles that burst across the room. There was no pain, only a sense of lightness and the easing of pressure from his physical form. He was now colorless and undetectable, and the feeling was beyond exhilarating.

His clothes fell onto Maya. She gasped and lifted to her elbows, looking around the room.

He concentrated on squeezing the air particles into a tight ball, then aimed it at Maya, forcing a burst of air across her body. His clothes billowed off her, floating to the ground. She moaned at the sensation and fell back onto the bed.

While he didn't have the same level of sensation in air form, he could still feel. It would be akin to a whisper of breath along his body, if he technically had one right now. But to Maya, he would feel like a breeze. One that could run along her flesh at will. And right now his mission was to make her body go into pleasure overload.

In the dim recesses of her mind, Maya recognized she was dreaming. But it was one she hoped would never end. Taeg had dematerialized right before her eyes. He'd simply gone *poof*, his clothes falling down to cover her. After that, a delicious wind had fluttered them away.

As if a million fragments of air individually stroked her, a breeze blew across her nipples, tugging and twisting them, while light strokes of wind brushed her legs, arms, and stomach. She panted and moaned, instinctively squeezing her thighs together. Already on the verge of a climax.

Although she knew this was a dream, she couldn't help but wonder—could he do this in real life? The intensity of the air increased as it brushed her entire body, making her flesh quiver and her knees tremble. She moaned and arched her back at the onslaught of sensation. It was enough to send her over the edge. She cried out as she convulsed, splintering into a million little pieces…

And awoke.

"Holy hell." She focused on her surroundings. She still lay in Taeg's bed, with the covers tight around her waist.

That's right. It wasn't real.

Laughing quietly, she sat up and smoothed the hair plastered to her sweaty forehead. That had been the wildest dream she'd ever had. Had she actually cried out in real life? She hoped not. But then, something told her Taeg would have come running if she had.

Thank goodness. If he had come in to check on her, how would she have explained that? She had a feeling he would have taken one look at her flushed face and guessed she was dirty dreaming about him. He might have even tried suggesting they bring the dream to life.

Scary thing was, if he had, she wasn't sure how she would have answered him.

With a low groan, Maya lay back down in the bed. How was she going to get any sleep now?

෩෧

Taeg came awake with a start. Dream-coitus-interruptus once again. "Oh fuck."

If he had known Maya would wake up as soon as he'd made her come, he would've taken much, *much* longer. That had been amazing. To feel the whisper of her hardened nipples against his air form. Hear her naughty little moans of ecstasy. Fucking orgasmic. Only thing was he couldn't come while in air form. Which left him with a huge problem now.

He kicked the thin sheet off and yanked his boxers down, closing his hand around his erection. He was so hard it hurt. Three pumps was all it took. He came with a tortured groan, thinking of Maya the whole while.

Yeah, so much for keeping his distance.

Taeg let out a deep sigh as he rose and headed to the bathroom to clean up. They were going to have a real problem if he couldn't sleep without dreamscaping with her. As delicious as it was, it wasn't exactly restful sleep. Already he felt the effects of sleep deprivation from the last two nights.

How was he going to keep his hands off her when he could all too easily remember how gorgeous she looked when she came? He'd never wanted anyone as badly as he wanted Maya. And that spelled trouble, pure and simple.

Chapter Twelve

"You seem to think I'm some sort of miracle worker. I've already given you all the information I have."

Leviathos stifled a curse at Garin's words. He examined the information the shifter had placed in front of him. "You're sure this is the woman?"

Garin nodded from his seat across the table. He picked up a handful of salted peanuts from the small, dirty-looking bowl set in between them and tossed them into his mouth.

Leviathos stifled a shudder. It had been Garin's idea to meet at this seedy hotel lobby. He normally wouldn't be caught dead in a place like this. The devil only knew how many unwashed hands had touched those peanuts.

"I tracked her scent back to her apartment and broke in," Garin said. "There were photographs there that matched the description you gave me, and hers was the only scent I picked up on. She definitely hadn't been there for over a day. I looked up the records and she's the owner of the apartment."

"Maya Flores," Leviathos mumbled. Well, this didn't make

much sense. Nestled among the pile of documents was a birth record, one that lacked the distinctive watermark of an Otherworld forgery.

"She's a human," he said to Garin. "What could Taeg possibly want with her?"

"Beats me." Garin shrugged and grabbed another handful of nuts.

Leviathos shuffled through the thin file of information Garin had hastily compiled. "What of this adoptive mother— Helen Rossum?"

"She died a couple of years ago and left the apartment and all her belongings to the girl."

Leviathos backtracked to the adoption papers Garin had found. "It says here she wasn't adopted until she was eleven. What happened before then?"

"Don't know. I got a contact back in Mexico. He can do some digging around, see if he finds anything on her."

"Do that." Leviathos was onto something here. He could almost taste it.

"You know, you might be getting worked up over nothing." Garin lifted his beer to his lips and took a long swallow. "From what I saw of this girl in her photos, she's one major piece of ass. Maybe he's just getting his freak on. Wouldn't be the first, or even the millionth, demon to do the dirty with the local human population."

"No." Taeg wouldn't be associating with a human unless she had something to offer him. A one-night stand, sure. Immoral whore that he was, he no doubt had plenty of those. But this was quite obviously not that. He might not be Taeg's best friend anymore, but that much he still knew. He'd be willing to bet on it.

"Suit yourself." Garin shrugged carelessly. "It's your dime. I can research her as much as you like. In fact, I wouldn't mind getting acquainted with the broad up close and personal."

Leviathos set the file down and looked the shifter dead in the eyes. "You're not to touch her, got that?"

Garin bristled. "What do you care?"

"If she's of some use to Taeg, she might be useful to me." And maybe with her he could break Taeg once and for all.

"Ah." Garin gave him an understanding nod and a wink. "You want to tap that, too, huh? Don't blame you."

"Stop thinking with your dick for one second, will you?"

"Right. Sure. Tell yourself whatever helps you sleep at night."

Leviathos ignored him He didn't care in the slightest what Garin thought. And if the woman turned out to be useless, Garin could have her for all he cared. But if she was capable of something special, well, perhaps he could find a way to exploit that.

"Focus on finding out more of her background." Leviathos pulled a large wad of bills out of his pocket and slid them across the table. "That's what I'm paying you for."

"You're the boss," Garin said. His eyes gleamed with greed as he picked up the stack of bills.

Leviathos stood and left without further conversation. He couldn't wait to get out of this dank hotel. It made his flesh crawl.

Garin would do as he was told. The promise of more money made him a loyal, if somewhat incompetent, lackey. But Leviathos wasn't about to depend completely on him. No, now that he knew the woman's name, he would try to dreamscape with her. Perhaps he could learn more about her that way.

He could only hope that Taeg hadn't confided in her about a demon's ability to communicate telepathically with humans. If luck was on his side, he'd know what Taeg was up to by the end of the week. Once he knew what Taeg was playing at, he could finally get the revenge he desperately craved.

∽∾

After a night of restless sleep, Maya crawled out of bed sometime in the late morning. When she opened the door, Taeg was still asleep on the couch. From the way his sheet twisted around his lower body, she had a feeling he might have slept as restlessly as she had. By the time she showered, dressed, and exited the bathroom, he was already awake.

"Good morning," she said when he sat up on the couch and ran his hands through his sleep-rumpled hair. The sight evoked images of him lazing around in bed, and her flesh grew warm in response. He was too hot for his own good. Or hers.

"Harrumph," he replied as he rose and headed toward her. Against her better judgment, her heart rate sped up. But he didn't approach her like she'd thought he would. He simply edged past her and into the bathroom. She told herself she wasn't disappointed.

No, she was relieved.

Yeah. Right.

She headed into the kitchen and rummaged around in his fridge, then started making breakfast. Amazingly enough, she felt better this morning. Confiding in Taeg last night had made her feel lighter. Freer. And maybe he was right. Was it fair to blame herself for mistakes she'd made when she was only ten?

After fixing a couple of plates and setting them on the small table tucked into one corner of the kitchen, she made some coffee. She heard the opening of a door a second before Taeg's voice sounded behind her.

"Something smells good."

"I made breakfast." Taking a sip of her coffee, she turned to face Taeg. And, when she saw his shirt, promptly choked on the hot liquid.

"What's wrong?" he asked.

Written in bold red letters across his T-shirt were the words *Awesome in Bed.*

Below that, in tiny print, she noticed for the first time the words *I Can Sleep for Hours.*

"Uh…nothing." Maya took a hasty seat at the table, certain her cheeks matched the color of the words on his shirt. What could she say, that the first three words on his shirt had called forth imagery she couldn't stop from running through her mind?

Taeg only smirked as he walked over to the coffeepot and poured himself a cup. "We'll leave for my friend's place around six o'clock this evening. It's a bit of a drive, so I figured we'd spend the night there and come back tomorrow morning."

"How far is it?" Maya asked in between bites of her eggs.

"About two hours." He took a seat across from her and leaned back, grinning while he placed his arms behind his head. "Should give us plenty of time to chat."

She tried not to cringe at that thought. Two hours of

being no more than inches from him in a cramped sports car sounded like a journey to one of the nine levels of hell. And that wasn't even taking into account his lack of driving skills. The man was too arousing for his own good. How would she handle being so close to him?

"So"—her voice cracked, and she cleared her throat before continuing—"your friend will be able to decipher the papers Horster gave you?"

"Yes." Taeg nodded and picked up his fork. "The real question is whether that will lead us to the sword."

"What do you think?"

He shrugged. "Most people believe Excalibur is a myth because the sword has never been found. Or if they do think it exists, they don't believe they could blow through Merlin's magic in order to recover it. My guess is yeah, it'll be at one of those places, ready and waiting for someone like you to find it."

Taeg sounded so sure of his words that she couldn't help but stare at him. "And what happens if we find it?"

"*When* we find it, I'll destroy the book. And once I find Leviathos, I'll destroy him, too."

He cocked a brow as if daring her to argue with that. Like she was one to judge. How many demons had she killed, and for far less serious offenses?

When she said nothing, he leaned over his plate and shoveled two forkfuls of eggs into his mouth. She caught herself staring at the way his lower lip moved when he chewed on his food, and acknowledged the inevitable. She was attracted to him. And after everything she'd learned about demons in the past few days, it wasn't as horrible a thought as it had once been.

Not every demon was evil.

There. She'd said it. She'd laid it all out.

In the end, though, it didn't change anything between her and Taeg. If she was going to help him find the sword and he was going to help her track down her family's killers, then that meant they'd be working together for some period of time. Neither of them could afford the distraction and uncertainty of taking things beyond the professional level.

No matter how hot she found him.

And don't you owe it to your parents' memory not to get involved with a demon?

The thought materialized out of nowhere, surprising her with its intensity. That wasn't what was stopping her. Was it? Maya banished the worry from her head. There was no use in examining it further. It didn't change anything.

She stared at Taeg for a little while longer before letting out a shaky laugh. "What an unlikely pair of allies we make—a demon and a demon-hater."

Taeg gave her a cocky grin. "Sweetheart, you just never met the right demon."

Shortly before dusk, Taeg snuck a look at Maya from his seat behind the wheel of Dagan's car. In the hour and a half they'd been traveling upstate, the landscape of steel and glass had morphed into quiet roads and maple trees, but she'd been eerily silent the entire time. The woman ran hot and cold like nobody's business. It was almost as alluring as it was frustrating.

Yeah, he had issues.

"Penny for your thoughts."

"They're worth more than that," she replied.

Wasn't that the fucking truth? Right now he thought he'd give the entire contents of his bank account to know what was going on inside that puzzling head of hers.

She finally spoke. "When are we going to start searching for the demons who murdered my family?"

Taeg fought the urge to wince. "I called a contact of mine earlier today and asked him to run a search for maliki demons in Mexico. I figure we can start there, then branch out if we need to."

Amazing how easy the lie passed through his lips. He hadn't done squat about her problem yet. Brynn and Keegan came first.

"Okay. How many of these malikis do you think there are?"

"All over the world?" He let out a disbelieving laugh. "Thousands, probably."

She sucked in a breath. "Why? Why can't they stay in their own world, where they belong?"

Okay, that hurt, but he tried not to take offense. "Maya, Infernum is a nasty place to live. It's dark, it's hot, and there are no modern conveniences. Like electricity. Nobody wants to stay there."

"They can just *leave* because their own world sucks?"

"Demons are allowed to leave their dimension for a variety of reasons. Usually it's a temporary allowance, but a lot of them don't go back."

"I don't understand. Don't humans know about this? Why doesn't anyone try to stop them?"

"You're right. You *don't* understand." He held back an

impatient sigh. "There's travel between all dimensions, and every world has a leader who sits on the Elden Council. Your Earth leader is aware of what's going on."

Maya gave him a sharp look. "By Earth leader do you mean the president?"

"He's only the leader of the United States," Taeg said. "But to answer your question, I don't know who Earth's Council member is. The only ones who do are those who sit on the Council."

She shook her head. "I don't get your politics. How could anyone willingly let in creatures who mindlessly kill and torture? Why allow travel between dimensions at all?"

"I for one am glad they do," he replied lightly. "Otherwise I'd be rotting in Infernum."

"It's your world, isn't it? Some would say that's where you belong."

Her sharp words lingered between them like a bad smell, and this time Taeg couldn't help but be offended. For some reason he'd thought she'd begun to see him as more than just a *demon*.

After a few moments of pointed silence, she heaved a soft sigh. "I'm sorry, I didn't mean that. It's just frustrating."

"I get that. I do. But things aren't as simple as you'd like them be."

"You're right," she admitted stiffly. "They aren't."

Just like that, his anger melted away. This couldn't be easy for her, changing her entire worldview in a few short days. In a way he was amazed she'd come as far as she had.

"We're here." He turned into the long, curving road that led up to the estate.

She perked up, taking in their surroundings. "Where

exactly are we?"

"Right outside of Poughkeepsie."

The car jiggled and bounced as the narrow road turned into a cobblestone path. After some time it curved, and the house came into view.

"Whoa," Maya breathed. "You didn't tell me your friend lives in a mansion."

He gave her a grin as he parked in the semicircular driveway. "You didn't ask."

She drank in the sight of the two-story, Classical-style home with its limestone façade. Even he had to admit it was quite impressive, though not as impressive as the outline of Maya's lush figure against the inky darkness.

Turning back to him, she said, "Is everyone you know rich?"

"Elain has had hundreds of years to gather her wealth." She'd been turned by a vampire in her native Wales back in 1642, and she'd proven quite adept at business dealings over the centuries.

"Her?" she asked, her voice sharp.

He couldn't help but be pleased by that. "Yup."

She was silent for a moment. "She's not human?"

"Most definitely not. So please"—Taeg nodded toward her boots, where he was sure her daggers were concealed— "try to refrain from using those."

Maya appeared to consider his words. "Okay."

She moved to open the door, and he got the urge to flash outside and open it for her. So he did.

Startled, Maya jumped, then pressed her lips together, sliding out of her seat. "I'm not sure if I'll ever get used to that."

Some mischievous part of his brain urged Taeg to step toward her. Okay, maybe it was his cock doing the thinking. Whatever. He obeyed without questioning it too much.

She let out a gasp when the front of her body sensually rubbed against his own. She shifted to the side so her back leaned against the side of the car. "You're crowding me."

Taeg followed her, placing his hands on either side of her. He bent forward, taking perverse pleasure in the way her breathing accelerated and her pupils dilated. The scent of honeysuckle and spice assaulted his senses, making him hunger for something he shouldn't.

"Let me do the talking in there," he whispered into her ear. "And for devil's sake, listen to me if I tell you to do something. Elain is decent enough, but she's far from human and can be quite fickle."

"What"—Maya gulped, and when she spoke again there was a tremble in her voice—"what does that mean?"

Her breath fanned out against his neck and his cock tightened in response. He purposely pressed tighter against her, knowing she could feel it. Some sick part of him wanted to remind her that while she held contempt for demons, she was also attracted to one. Not very sporting of him, but he found he didn't quite give a damn.

"What I mean, little slayer, is that you don't want to unintentionally anger her. Or worse, catch her interest. Be as dull and uninteresting as possible. In other words, *don't be you.* Got it?"

"Ye—yes," she gasped.

Her eyes were even more unfocused than before. With her cheeks flushed and her lips moist and parted, she looked one hundred and ten percent fuckable. His previous admonitions to stay away from her were for the moment forgotten. All he could think about was kissing her for *real* this time, and not just in a dream.

He tilted his head toward hers and moved forward. His lips were mere inches away when she placed her hands on his chest and pushed.

"Taeg, we shouldn't," she whispered, her voice as unsteady as he felt. "We're supposed to be working together and…and we're too different."

The implications behind her words were obvious. She was human and he was demon, therefore, not good enough for her.

Damn it, what was he doing?

He backed off, putting some distance between them. He was supposed to be focused on finding the sword, not on kissing his pretty little slayer senseless.

Keep focus, douchebag.

Besides, she was right. They were too different.

He turned and headed for the front door. "Come on."

Yeah, actually he was glad Maya stopped him. The last thing that needed to happen was for them to become attached to one another. For so many reasons.

If only his cock could be happy like his brain. Unfortunately, in its semi-aroused state, there was no way that was going to happen.

Swallowing hard, Maya stumbled after Taeg. While he sauntered forward like he didn't have a care in the world, her legs had gone weak with lust. She feared they might not hold her. Hadn't he been affected by their almost-kiss at all?

Okay, well, she knew he'd been *affected*. She'd felt the proof of that high on her hip. But that wasn't what she meant. He'd almost kissed her, then acted like it didn't mean a thing. What a confounding man.

Demon, Maya. Not a man. Have you forgotten those red eyes?

"Oh shut up," she muttered irritably. Her brain couldn't seem to leave that one alone.

"What?" Taeg asked.

"Uh, nothing."

He practically flew up the eight or so steps it took to get to the front entrance, then rapped on the heavy oak. Less than ten seconds later, the door gave an imperial groan as it swung open. On the other side stood a butler. An honest-to-goodness *butler*, for Christ's sake. He appeared to be in his mid-to-late sixties, with a shock of white hair across his head and rheumy blue eyes.

"Good evening, sir, miss," he said in a regal British accent. He stepped back to allow them inside. "The madam is expecting you."

"Thanks, Jeeves," Taeg replied.

The front door opened to a long hallway decorated with checkerboard marble flooring. Wood-paneled walls were painted a creamy white.

"The parlor is this way," the butler said. He led them to a door down the hall.

"Yeah, I do remember from last time I was here," Taeg said.

The butler sniffed, opening the door and stepping to the side.

Maya entered the room and peered around in openmouthed shock. Given the Classical décor of the façade and the hallway, she hadn't expected this. At all. The cozy parlor was dimly lit and decorated in shades of red and black that were far more suitable to the Moulin Rouge than to a late nineteenth-century mansion. Black brocade drapes covered the far wall, running from the ceiling to the floor. On another wall, twisted strips of fuchsia silk lined a large, gilded mirror. Two cushioned chairs and a settee were covered in rich burgundy velvet. The whole room screamed luxury and decadence.

"The madam will be with you in a moment," the butler droned.

Maya turned around to see Taeg nod at the butler. "Thanks, pal."

With another loud sniff, the butler stepped out of the room and closed the door behind him.

"That guy's a regular barrel of laughs, isn't he?" Taeg quipped.

She opened her mouth to answer, but a curtain of velvet fabric on the wall behind Taeg caught her eye. The ends were partially draped behind iron hooks, billowing the fabric open just enough that she could see the glint of metal underneath. Were those *iron manacles* on the walls?

"Um…who exactly is this friend of yours?"

The door swung open and a woman stepped inside. Although the term "woman" seemed far too tame to describe her. She was more like the vision of Aphrodite one might find in a painting at the Metropolitan. With long, curly hair the color of flame, shocking blue eyes, and alabaster skin so unnaturally smooth and pale that it could have been carved from ivory, it was clear she was no human. An electric blue dress fell to mid-thigh, highlighting her slender curves and long, lean legs. Although she appeared younger than Maya, she was effortlessly chic in a way that made Maya, in her jeans and purple blouse, feel like the dorky college girl she was.

The woman's blatant appraisal of Maya turned to stark lust when she turned to Taeg. "Taeg, darling. It's wonderful to see you again."

Maya sucked in an involuntary breath when the tone of the woman's voice made her gut clench with an emotion she couldn't deny. Jealousy. She forced herself to stay calm. For all she knew, this woman and Taeg thought of each other as brother and sister.

"Good to see you, too, Elain," Taeg said. "You're looking beautiful as always."

Elain gave him a low, seductive laugh and crossed over to him, threw her arms around his neck, and pulled his head down to hers.

So much for her theory. Brothers and sisters definitely did not greet each other like that.

Maya forced herself to remain stiff and silent, though she couldn't stop her hands from curling into fists. Just because she didn't want to get involved with Taeg didn't mean she liked seeing him with another woman.

When Elain tilted her head to the side, revealing a glint of tongue snaking into Taeg's mouth, she'd had enough. Her bones ached with the force of holding herself back. "You have *got* to be kidding me."

Elain broke away from Taeg and they both looked at her.

His eyes were narrowed, clearly warning her to keep her mouth shut. *Be boring*, as he'd advised her.

Elain examined Maya once again, then turned back to Taeg. "What interesting little morsel have you brought for me, darling?"

Chapter Thirteen

Maya twitched in her spot, avoiding Taeg's imploring glare. She could practically hear him cursing her in his mind. Why couldn't she have kept her mouth shut? So much for remaining uninteresting. But when he replied to Elain, his voice was calm.

"Elain, I'd like you to meet Maya. She's a graduate student studying archaeology at NYU, and she's been helping me with my research."

"A human?" Elain surveyed her for so long that Maya had to fight the urge to squirm. Finally she turned back to Taeg. "But darling, she can't even speak Welsh, can she? Even if she can, she couldn't be nearly as fluent as I am."

Of course she'd have to point that out.

"I have *other* uses."

When both Elain and Taeg turned to her, she realized she'd put too much of an emphasis on the word "other." Damn, she hadn't meant to do that. Maya turned and made a show of examining the brocade on the wall so they wouldn't see her embarrassment.

"You plan on spending the night, don't you?" Elain asked Taeg. Was it just Maya, or was there loaded innuendo behind those words?

"Yes." His response was just as quiet. "As long as you don't have any other visitors here."

"I sent Manuelo to the city for the night. I assumed I'd have no need for a Feeder this evening."

Feeder? What on earth was that? And why did Maya have a feeling she was missing a lot of what was going on? But the last thing she wanted to do was reveal her ignorance in front of Elain. She'd ask Taeg when they were alone.

Taeg murmured something Maya couldn't hear. She turned around to see Elain standing mere inches from him. Her palms leisurely slid up and down his chest while he whispered something into her ear. As if she could sense Maya's eyes on her, Elain turned to her, and she gave her a grin that held a hint of challenge in it.

Maya gritted her teeth when her gut clenched again. *Don't give her the satisfaction of showing a reaction. Besides, he's not yours to fight over.*

Elain finally broke away from Taeg and faced Maya straight-on, tilting her head to the side. "But where are my manners? I almost forgot about you humans and your... base needs. I've had Jenkins prepare a meal for us."

"That's not necessary, Elain," Taeg said.

"Don't be ridiculous. I won't be accused of being a poor host." She waved a hand in the air. "Besides, we have all evening to decipher your papers."

Elain sashayed forward, bypassing Maya and heading toward the door. Only when she'd flung it open did she say,

"Well, what are you waiting for?"

Maya stayed rooted in place, focused on Taeg. He approached, that warning glint still in his eyes. She knew she should stay quiet, but she couldn't help herself. "You and your *friend* seem to be pretty chummy."

He grabbed her elbow and forcibly whirled her toward the door. "Remember what I said earlier," he said low in her ear as he led her out of the parlor. "Be boring like you've never been boring before. She's more dangerous than you might think. In fact, the less you speak the better."

Well, wasn't this great? She was expected to sit through an entire dinner with an irresistible demon who drove her crazy and the gorgeous *Other* who clearly had the hots for him. And to top it all off, not only did he want her to keep quiet, but she wasn't even allowed to use her daggers on the bitch?

How was she going to make it through an entire evening of this?

ౠ

Maybe bringing Maya along hadn't been the best of ideas. When Taeg had thought up the plan, keeping her close had been his biggest concern. He'd momentarily forgotten that Elain was his sometimes-lover who no doubt expected them to pick up where they'd left off. Now he not only had to deal with Elain playing footsie under the table, but also with Maya glaring daggers from her spot directly across from him.

Elain had forgone the opulence of the formal dining room, with its massive oak table that seated sixteen. They sat in a far more intimate dining alcove located off the kitchen. If he asked, she'd probably say it was because there were only three of them at this small square table. But he had a feeling she'd done it so he'd be within easy reach of her. Even now her hand closed around his knee, traveling a path up his thigh. Trying to stake her claim.

Taeg cleared his throat and shifted so that her hand fell away.

Her eyes narrowed and her lips tightened in obvious displeasure, but she turned to Maya without making any comment. "I do hope the food is palatable. Given that I haven't eaten in over three hundred years, I wouldn't know."

In between lobbing him vicious scowls, Maya had glumly picked at her food, but she snapped to attention at Elain's words. "Over three hundred years? Wow." She initiated a pointed perusal of Elain's body. "You look good."

Though she didn't say it, the words "for your age" were clearly implied.

Taeg almost choked at the obvious dig, and from the way she stiffened, Elain hadn't missed it, either. He uttered a silent prayer of thanks when she didn't rise to the bait. She trailed a hand down his arm and gave him a steamy glance.

"Yes, forever preserved at nineteen. Lucky for me, sagging will never be an issue." After a moment of marked silence, she added, "Too bad you missed that boat, my dear."

He mentally threw his hands up in the air. What had he been thinking, bringing these two together? If they could end the evening without one of them trying to kill the other, it would be a miracle. Lucky for him, instead of snapping out a response, Maya let the matter drop. She didn't even ask any questions about what Elain was, as he'd half-expected her to.

Maya directed a glance at his plate, which he hadn't touched. "Not hungry?"

"Not really." He shrugged and tilted his chair back slightly. "I could go another month without eating a bite."

"A month?" Maya dropped her fork with a loud *clang* and leaned forward in her chair. "Are you serious?"

He'd forgotten how little she knew about demons. For all the time she'd spent researching how to kill them, she'd never bothered to actually learn a thing or two about them. "Dead serious. It's a genetic thing."

She stared at him like he was some sort of science project she ached to dissect. And yeah, even that turned him on. Twisted.

He almost forgot about Elain sitting at his side. She must have noticed it, too, because when she spoke, her voice was cold as ice. "You two don't seem to know each other very well."

"That's not a requirement, is it?" Maya replied flatly. She sat back in her chair and picked up her fork once again. "We're working together on this one project. Nothing more."

Ouch. Although he couldn't say he was surprised, her cold rebuff stung. It was a clear, and knowing Maya, a quite deliberate disclaimer of any ownership claims on him. Elain didn't miss it, either, because she perked up in her chair.

Maya didn't say another word for the rest of the dinner. Elain, on the other hand, wouldn't shut up. She talked about everything from life in the eighteenth century to once dating a famous mobster. The woman talked so damned much, he wondered how he'd ever found her attractive to begin with.

"Do you remember the night we met at Opiate?" Elain let loose with a throaty laugh. "Why, I thought we'd never make it out of the club—"

"You know, it's getting late." Taeg rose to his feet. There

was no way in hell he wanted Maya to hear that story.

Maya appeared relieved and stood up as well. "I agree."

"Oh, I forget about you humans and your odd sleep schedules." Elain slid back in her seat. "You slumber away the best parts of the day."

After leading them down the hall and up a flight of stairs, Elain stopped in front of a door. It opened to a spacious room that was fairly sedate with its mauve and chocolate tones. "You can sleep in here, Maya."

"Thanks." Maya peeked in the room, then glanced at Taeg. He gave her a reassuring nod, about to tell her to go inside, when Elain spoke again.

"You know, we never did settle the matter of payment for my services."

Taeg's heart dropped when she tapped a forefinger across her lips as if considering what she should ask for. Oh damn, this wasn't going to be good.

"Is she part of my payment?" Elain finally asked, tilting her head as she looked over at Maya.

Taeg could practically feel Maya recoil at those words. "She's off limits. As I said, she's only here to help me."

"Very well." From the way Elain's lips curved, he could tell she wasn't at all bothered by that. "So, the usual then?"

The insinuation behind those words was deliberate, and by the sour-lemon look on Maya's face, she'd picked up on it. He opened his mouth to make it clear Elain wasn't talking about sex. But then he recalled Maya's words at dinner. Her rejection of him earlier by the car. She'd made it clear a million ways from Sunday she didn't want anything to do with him like that. Worse, he'd told himself time and time again that it was for the best. He and Maya were wrong for each other in so many ways.

If she thought he was going to sleep with Elain, why disabuse her of the notion? And if it made her jealous, well, that wasn't his fault, was it?

"Yeah," he said, turning to face Elain. "The usual."

Taeg did his best to ignore his guilt at the momentary hurt that flashed across Maya's face. She had rejected *him*, after all. To top it all off, he couldn't get attached to her. Attachment meant emotions, and emotions made people do stupid things.

Family came first. He had to remember that.

"Good night, Maya." Taeg turned, letting Elain lead him down the hall. She slithered one of her arms under his.

"I'll put you in the room next to mine," she said, though the naughty tone of her voice made it clear to anyone who listened that she didn't think he'd be spending any time there.

"Sounds great."

Elain was attractive. Sexy. Not a demon-hater. And she was into some real kinky shit. Chains on the walls. Whips. He should be excited that she wanted him to spend the night with her. Why then did he feel like he was being led to his own execution?

❧

"That bitch."

Maya paced the expanse of her borrowed room. Sitting across from Taeg and Elain at dinner had been hell. Pure torture, having to watch her run her hands all over him. If she wasn't mistaken, Elain had gotten grabby under the table, too. The woman was like an octopus.

Although Taeg hadn't looked like he enjoyed all her

attention, he also hadn't told her to back off. Far from it. Seemed quite clear he was more than willing to go with Elain and play her game.

"Couldn't they at least have waited until they were alone? So disrespectful."

That was why she was upset. It surely had nothing to do with the fact that Taeg was probably hooking up with Elain at this very instant. Oh, who was she kidding? Despite what he was, she wanted him. And even though it was no doubt for the best, the thought of him hooking up with someone else was driving her *in-s-a-a-ne*.

If only she could have done something tonight. Sitting there like a mute had gone against her nature. She wasn't someone who just let things happen to her. Not anymore. But tonight, because Taeg had asked her to, that was what she'd done. And now she was miserable because of it.

"Damn you, Taeg. This is all your fault."

He was an arrogant, low-down prick who probably hit on anything with two legs. If he thought she was going to waste two more seconds thinking about him, he had another thing coming. The best thing she could do would be to go to sleep and forget all about him.

She shuffled toward the bed before pausing.

No, wait.

Better yet, she should find him and tell him his mind games weren't going to work on her. If she'd managed to survive a demon attack that killed her entire family, not to mention single-handedly taking out more demons than she could count on one hand, she wasn't about to fall for some demon Casanova's tricks.

No, they were in this for what they could provide each

other. She'd help him find the sword, he'd help her find her family's murderers. That was it, nothing more. The sooner he realized that, the better. In fact, she would tell him in no uncertain terms. That way it would be out in the open, and they'd be free to focus on the important stuff.

Mind made up, she stomped over to the door and pushed it open. She rounded two corners and passed countless closed doors before she started questioning the wisdom of her strategy. If she managed to find Taeg, which given the size of this place wasn't guaranteed, what if he was with Elain? She didn't want to see that.

Maybe she should go back to her room. She could always have this talk with him in the morning, when she was better rested and wasn't fuming mad.

Maya turned one more corner and wavered there uncertainly before leaning back against the wall. She thumped her head against it. This was ridiculous. She was being totally crazy. She started to turn back when she heard a soft sound.

What was that?

Turning back around, she noticed for the first time an open door at the end of the hallway. The only open door she'd seen this entire time. Her feet crept forward, stepping one in front of the other until she stood no more than a dozen feet away from the doorway.

This was craziness. She should go back to her room. But then she heard the noise again, louder this time. It sounded like… a moan.

A moan?

Oh, hell no.

Caution fled like the wind. She was too far gone not to look now.

❧

Taeg let Elain lead him to the other end of the house, but when she tried to push him into her bedroom, he stood his ground. "I thought I was getting my own bedroom."

"What difference does it make?" When he didn't back down, she waved a dismissive hand in the air. "Fine. Suit yourself."

Turning, she strolled to a nearby door and swung it open, stepping aside with a flourish. "Your room."

He stepped inside a room decorated much like Maya's, except in muted scarlet and gray. Nothing like Elain's luxurious quarters, he knew from experience. Still, it would do.

Elain sauntered into the room after him, sliding a finger along the wall while she ambled aimlessly throughout the space. "Your human is an interesting creature."

"She's not my human." Taeg strode over to the bed and took a seat. Making sure the two women hadn't tried to kill each other had taken more out of him than he'd expected. "I told you, she's only helping me."

"If you say so." Her tone made it clear she didn't believe him. She turned and crossed to where he sat, taking a seat next to him. "Don't tell me you haven't noticed her curves."

Great. Now he had a jealous vampire to contend with. That was never a good thing, especially if he expected Maya to sleep under the same roof as her. Taeg forced nonchalance and a hint of seduction into his voice. "She's well-built, for a human. But then I like my women a little less fragile, don't I?"

Elain grinned at him, appeased. She trailed a hand up his

chest. Tilting his head to the side, she leaned into him. "Now, for my payment."

Taeg forced himself to relax when her teeth scraped his throat. The initial bite was always unnerving. To this day he wasn't quite sure how he'd trusted her enough to do it that first time. He must have been really drunk.

Her teeth sank into his flesh with a small burst of pain. Then she took one long draw, and it was gone. He groaned when his body went boneless from an overload of pleasure. As he'd discovered with that first bite, being bitten by a vampire was almost as pleasurable as having an actual orgasm. If only he could enjoy it. But that wasn't going to happen tonight.

He collapsed back onto his elbows, only vaguely aware of Elain following him down while she continued to suck his blood in rhythmic swallows. One of her hands snaked under his shirt, hitching it up. She rubbed her hand along his chest. The silky glide of it on his flesh, along with the feel of the blood leaving his body, coalesced into one mass of sensation that made his cock go hard. Elain moaned as if she could sense his erection. Hell, she probably could. The woman was like a bloodhound.

But when her hand traveled down to close over the outline of his erection through his jeans, he forced himself to face the truth. His body might respond to Elain's bite, but he couldn't have sex with her. Not when someone else was on his mind.

Long, dark hair. A lush, compact body. Eyes that blazed with passion and anger. That was who he wanted. Maya, his little demon-slayer. He could practically see her in his mind—his sexy, angry avenger—hands propped on her hips, poised to reach for a dagger.

No. She'd be in attack mode, preparing to rip him a new asshole.

"What the fuck?"

Yeah, she'd probably say something like that.

Wait a second…

Someone had actually said that.

Taeg jerked his head to the side, disengaging Elain's fangs. After a second, the blood haze cleared enough for him to realize what he saw.

Oh, shit.

He hadn't been imagining Maya. She actually stood at the doorway. And yeah, if the heaving chest and bright red cheeks were any indication, she was pissed with a capital "P."

Taeg followed her angry gaze down his body, to where Elain's hand still cupped his now rapidly deflating erection. He wrenched out of her grasp, ignoring her protests when he jumped from the bed. "Maya, I can explain."

"Explain?" Maya huffed. "Explain what, that you're a man-whore?"

That shocked him into freezing in place right in front of her. He tried to swallow the snort that bubbled in his throat. "A…what?"

Probably not the best time for him to find humor in the situation, because she snapped her leg up in a front-kick that caught him right in the crotch.

"*Oomph.*" He bent over into a defensive posture as pain spread throughout his entire torso, bringing stars to his vision and a trail of vicious curses to his lips.

Elain's amused laugh trilled from where she sat sprawled across the bed. Taeg ignored her and braved a look up, just in time to see his little slayer flee the room.

"Have you no shame?" Maya ground out as she retreated.

Shame? After that kick, it would be a miracle if he ever had *children*.

CHAPTER FOURTEEN

Why did this house have to be so damned big?

After what seemed like a small eternity, Maya finally rounded the third corridor and made it into her bedroom. She slammed her door shut and paced the room. Of all the things she had expected to see, that certainly hadn't been one of them. An image of Elain flashed through her mind. Pale flesh looking cool as marble. Bloodred lips. Her admission that she hadn't eaten in over three hundred years.

She'd been sucking on his blood. Actually *drinking* it!

A vampire. Elain was a vampire.

Taeg had already told her such creatures existed, but still, seeing one in action was more than a little unnerving. How could he let her suck his blood like that? Wasn't he afraid she'd take too much? Was it possible to take too much blood from a demon? Why would he let her to do that to him?

Oh, come on. Wasn't it obvious he found the whole process arousing? He'd had a hard-on, for God's sake.

Embarrassment warred with anger, turning her into a

seething mass of emotions. Why had she insisted on tracking Taeg down? Once she'd found them together, why hadn't she quietly backed out of the room rather than blurt out the first thing that came to mind? And why oh why did this all matter so much?

She had no claims on Taeg. She'd made that quite clear to the both of them. So then why did she want to tear Elain limb from limb, and very, very slowly? And she wasn't even going to get into what she wanted to do to Taeg.

As if on cue, the door swung open, slamming against the wall. She jumped and turned to face the doorway.

"*You.*" Anger churned in her gut at the sight of him, making her ache for a fight.

Taeg stepped inside the room, his red eyes narrowing in on her. "Who else were you expecting, the fucking queen of England?"

The sharp tone of his voice, along with his pronounced limp, made it clear he was upset about her well-aimed kick. She instinctively shrank back before she remembered: she didn't retreat—she fought back.

He was angry with her, was he? Well two could play at that game. "You may be a demon, but you weren't raised in a barn. In the future, knock before you enter my room."

Taeg stalked toward her. "I came here to apologize, but about halfway here I realized I have nothing to apologize for. What was it you said earlier tonight? Oh yeah. 'We're working together. *Nothing more.*' You've told me over and over again how you could never be attracted to a demon."

How dare he bring this back on her? *He'd* hit on *her.* More than once. And then he expected her to sit back without protest while he made out with another woman? Well sorry, but that wasn't her style.

"Because they're repulsive," she shouted. "You don't proposition someone and then make out with someone else on your next breath!"

"And you don't kick a man in the balls," he retorted acidly.

She felt an unexpected burst of guilt and shame at those words. She had hit him pretty hard, and she didn't need to have balls to know how much that would hurt. Still… "I don't see any men around here. Just a sorry half-drained demon."

"That's it." Teeth gritted, he reached for her.

She leapt to the side to avoid his fumbling grab. Extending her arm, she swung it toward him, striking him across the back. It sent him flying across the room, where he hit the wall.

He surprised her by chuckling. Cracking his neck, he turned to face her. "You can't stand it, can you?"

She kept her hands up, body in attack mode. "What?"

Taeg grinned. "The way you feel about me."

Her mouth dropped open and she straightened. "You are so full of yourself."

"Wanna kick my ass? Give it a shot." He came at her, arms raised in a boxer's stance. She latched onto one of his arms and brought her knee up, aiming for his solar plexus. Not even she was mean enough to go for the groin again. Taeg's muffled grunt told her she hit the spot. She didn't have time to enjoy the victory, though. He grabbed her leg before she could lower it and yanked upward, sending her sprawling to the ground.

"*Ungh.*"

He was on top of her before she could process the wooden floor slamming into her back. His masculine scent assaulted her senses, making her feel drunk off his essence. Making her want him. Why did she have to respond so strongly to him? She didn't want to feel this way.

"Have I ever told you what a difficult woman you are to talk to?" he grumbled as he stared down at her. But there was a glint in his eye.

He thought this whole thing was funny, did he? She'd show him funny.

Shoving up on his chest, she managed to get enough space between them to jam her knee into his gut and push up. He flew backward with an ease that made it clear he was just fucking with her. Letting her get some hits in.

She maneuvered to her feet. "What's your game?"

"Ha." Taeg leapt to his feet and hopped from side to side. "I only wanted you to feel like you're getting somewhere."

"Are you *patronizing* me?" She swung at him with a series of kicks and jabs that he mostly countered, though one or two connected with his flesh.

"Just blowing off steam," he replied in between shots. "Thought we could both use a little of that."

Blowing off steam. He was right. And that was annoying.

"Why did you let her drink from you?" Her own words surprised her, mostly because of how hurt she sounded. She had no reason to be hurt. None whatsoever.

"What other form of payment does a vampire value?" He grunted when he took a knee to the side. "Look around you. She doesn't need any more money. Would you rather I let her drain you like she asked?"

Wait. Earlier Elain had mentioned something about Maya being her payment, hadn't she? And he had refused. He'd offered himself instead. That earlier conversation took on a whole new meaning, and once again guilt stirred in her gut. Well, it wasn't like Taeg had confided in her or anything.

"You could have told me, you know."

"Yeah, somehow I didn't think telling you Elain was a vampire would make you feel any better about spending the night here. Was I wrong?"

Her anger melted away and she froze in place. "You're right."

Taeg grinned, and a split-second later pushed her backward. Her back banged lightly against the wall closest to the bed, and he pinned her in place with his arms. "I often am."

Lord, he was close. The warmth from his body permeated her bones. His soft glow practically illuminated her flesh. Maya shut her eyes, as if that could erase the image of him standing right in front of her, or the arousing scent oozing from his pores. Why did she have to want him so badly? She hated herself for asking the next question when she didn't want to know the answer. But she couldn't stop the words from spilling out of her mouth.

"Does Elain's price include sleeping with her?"

He was quiet for so long she opened her eyes to look up at him. And sucked in a breath. He stared at her like she was the most delicious meal he'd ever seen. Like he wanted to consume her. And God help her, it made her want to be consumed. Her heart gave one loud *thump* before resuming its beat at triple normal speed.

"Would it bother you if it does?" he finally responded.

"I…"

Chickenshit, his eyes seemed to be saying. "So, what? Is it that you'd like to join the both of us?"

It took several full seconds for the meaning of his words to sink in. Once they did, she let out an indignant gasp and slapped her hands against his chest. "You vile, disgusting... demon."

"That's what I am, sweetheart. Don't you forget it." He pushed away from the wall and turned toward the door.

His easy dismissal of her stung more than she could have imagined. What, he thought he could come in here with his lame-ass non-apology, provoke a fight, and then walk away? Screw that.

"Where do you think you're going?" Maya grabbed his arm and swung him around. "This isn't finished."

ॐ◦ॐ

Not finished?

Taeg stared at Maya without responding. He knew this wasn't finished. It hadn't even started. He was trying to leave before it did. Seeking her out had been a mistake. He'd known that while he was doing it. But he hadn't been able to help it. He'd been driven by the need to explain himself, even though he knew it was for the best if she thought him a self-obsessed tool. And now, watching the way her chest heaved and her eyes narrowed in anger, it was all he could do to not fall on her like a slavering beast.

"Damn it," he growled, closing his eyes. "Why couldn't I have just stayed with Elain?"

"What?"

The timbre of her voice told him he'd said the wrong thing. What else was new?

"You said it yourself earlier. Taking things any further

when we're supposed to be working together would be a mistake. Especially since you'll never think of me as anything other than a demon," he finished bitterly.

Maya's glare softened. "Taeg, less than three days ago I thought demons were evil souls from Hell. I...I know now you're not evil. But fifteen years of programming is hard to overcome just like that."

"I get it. I do." This attraction they felt for each other was something they couldn't follow through on. Not when they both had their own agendas. It wasn't meant to be. Even if his body burned for her touch. "Let's forget all about this. Partners, right?"

He didn't wait for her response before turning back toward the door.

"Taeg. Wait." Maya spun him around again.

"What?"

This time she did the one thing he would never have expected. She yanked his head down, slanting his lips to hers. His mouth parted in surprise and her tongue slipped inside, rubbing along his with an intensity that made him groan.

Suddenly they weren't playing anymore. Their tongues collided, tangling over and over in a sweet dance that banished all but one thought from his head. This was so much damned better than a dream. Her sweet essence enveloped him, urging him closer to her. Her taste, the feel of her pliant body beneath his. It was the most exquisite form of torture he could have ever imagined.

"I want you so much," she admitted hoarsely.

Her words coursed through him like wildfire, setting his body ablaze. Never in a million years would he have thought she'd admit it. And the power of those words, coming from her, was an aphrodisiac of the finest kind.

"You know I feel the same, little slayer."

"Yes, I can feel that." She gasped on her next breath, arching up toward him in a catlike stretch. The movement pushed her breasts against his chest, tearing a groan from his throat. Right now, nothing mattered but the feel of her body against his. The sensual slide of her tongue as it stroked a hot trail along his neck, sending shudders over his whole body.

Damn, but he wanted her. With a sense of desperation that overrode everything else. The sword, the book, none of that shit mattered right now. Nothing mattered but his overwhelming desire to demonstrate to Maya how much she drove him wild.

"Your body is amazing," he confessed, snaking his hands under her blouse and sliding it upward. At some point she'd removed the dagger and scabbard she kept hidden under there, so all he touched was silky, warm flesh. Unbelievable how much drive and strength could come from such a small, feminine body.

His fingers caressed the rigid peaks of her breasts over the lacy black fabric of her bra. So feminine, so arousing. "Perfect."

Her fingers closed over a few locks of his hair. She moaned and gave his hair a sharp tug, bringing him in for another kiss.

This was heaven.

For the first time maybe ever, his need to give pleasure overwhelmed his desire to get off. His cock ached where it lay against her thigh, begging to plunge deep inside her. But he ignored that, focusing on Maya. On her body and her satisfaction.

A soft laugh trilled from the doorway, startling them out

of their embrace.

Taeg turned to see Elain leaning against the open doorway, a knowing smirk on her face. "And here I thought you two would be fighting."

"Elain, I…" He shifted uncomfortably, not sure what he should say or do. Maya stiffened at his side, but said nothing.

"Sorry, you two. Playtime is over. Now it's time for business." She nodded to Taeg. "I'll meet you in the library in five minutes. Alone. Bring the papers you want me to decipher."

He watched her leave before turning to Maya. She wore a shuttered expression, making him wonder what the hell was going through her mind. "I need to—"

"Go." She nodded without meeting his eyes. "I know it's important."

It was. He needed to remember that. "About what just happened—"

"I'm tired," she interrupted. "Let's talk tomorrow, okay?"

Taeg left the room feeling more confused and uncertain than ever.

‾‾‾‾‾‾

"You're a fool."

Taeg blinked at Elain, who sat in the armchair directly across from him in her small but opulent library. Both chairs were covered in lush burgundy velvet that contrasted with the striking gold and purple hues of the room.

"Tell me how you really feel," he half-joked.

"You're falling for a human." She kicked off her shoes and curled her legs under her. The movement pushed her dress up her thighs, making it impossible to miss she that wasn't wearing any underwear.

Taeg cleared his throat and looked away. "I don't know what you're talking about."

"Right." She answered with a low, throaty chuckle. "If that's the case, why are we in the library right now instead of in my bedroom?"

Shit. How was he supposed to answer that question?

Elain scoffed. "You know, I never would have pegged you for the type to become involved with a human. They tend to be weak and fragile. I would know, having once been one myself."

"Not all humans are alike." Why was he defending humans? He should be denying this.

"What's so special about this one? I know it must be more than the package, lovely as it may be."

She seemed genuinely curious, but he didn't have an answer for her. At least, not one that didn't make him seem like a total tool. Clearing his throat once again, he dug the papers out of his pocket. "Here."

"Like I said." Elain's eyes danced with laughter. "Fool."

"Thanks."

She snatched the papers out of his hand. "You're lucky you stumbled upon me. How many other people do you know who can read Welsh?"

"Not a one." Taeg waited impatiently for her to finish both pages before he spoke again. "What is it? Possible locations for the sword?"

"Not exactly," she hedged, as she carefully folded the papers and handed them back to him.

"What, then?"

"It tells the story of three sisters who know where Merlin buried the sword. According to that, the Vivi sisters were rumored lovers of Merlin, and he entrusted them with the sword's location, believing they'd never reveal it to someone who wasn't worthy. These papers contain directions to where the sisters can be found."

"Okay." Taeg sat forward and propped his elbows on his legs. "But Merlin lived a long-ass time ago. What are the odds these chicks are even still around?"

"Pretty good, I'd say." Her lips twisted into a little smile as she nodded toward the papers in his hand. "The directions start with 'once past the faerie veil.'"

He knew what that meant, being half-fae and all. They were from his mother's world. "Faelan."

"Yes. The Vivi sisters are dark faeries."

"Dark fae?" Fucking great. His gut told him these sisters were trouble, pure and simple. Dark fae were powerful and unpredictable. They also lived a long freaking time, and their abilities grew stronger with age.

"They will be dangerous," Elain said.

"Yup, that's just my luck." He rubbed a hand across his weary eyes. This felt like it had been the longest night of his life.

"Don't forget that finding the sisters is only the first step. After that you have to prove your worthiness."

"Piece of cake, right?" If only he actually believed that.

"We'll see," she said. "I do believe you're able, but the question is whether you will be willing."

"What's that supposed to mean?"

Elain laughed as if she knew something he didn't, but she sobered with her next words. "If you do learn of the sword's location, how do you plan to get past the invisibility spell? Not even the Vivi sisters can help you with that."

That was where Maya came in. No way he was telling Elain that, though. "Let me worry about that part."

She nodded her head in agreement. "I'll transcribe the directions for you."

"Thank you, Elain."

When Taeg moved to rise, Elain stopped him with her next words. "Do you wish to continue where we left off earlier?"

It didn't take a genius to figure out she wasn't talking about feeding from him.

"I promise you won't be disappointed," she added huskily, dropping her feet to the floor and bending toward him so her breasts practically spilled out of her top.

With a sense of detachment, he noted how arousing she was. How easy it would be to say yes right now. But his heart wasn't in it. "I'll take a rain check."

"I thought you might say that." She abandoned her alluring pose and curled back in her seat, a mixture of exasperation and amusement written all over her face. "I suggest you conquer your current bout of prudishness before you meet the Vivi sisters."

Her tone didn't bode well.

"What's that supposed to mean?" he asked, sharper than he'd intended.

"Those papers suggest some different ways in which they might seek to determine your worth." She laughed again. "Let's just say they are rumored to be quite inventive."

Her words dropped like a lead weight in his stomach. "And that would mean what?"

"They are apparently quite insatiable in the bedroom. Why

do you think Merlin was so enamored of them? You've heard the stories of his weakness for women."

Frustration coursed through him. An avalanche of thoughts invaded his mind, one of them finally making its way to the forefront.

If Maya were to find out about this, she would seriously kick his ass.

Chapter Fifteen

Clomp… Clomp.

"*Donde estas, niñita? Te encontraré.*"

"No." Maya shook her head in denial.

The demon bypassed her hiding spot and traveled down the hall. In the recesses of her mind she knew this was a dream. Remnants of the past, reliving themselves in her head. But she couldn't shake it. Once again she was that little child, caught in a nightmare she couldn't awaken from.

When the screaming started, she curled herself into a ball. She couldn't stop it, no matter how much she tried. Paralysis gripped her every time she had this dream. Why couldn't she do *something*?

Footsteps sounded again. A figure stepped out of the hallway and into the room. Even from her spot in the shadows, she saw it wasn't either of the two demons who'd murdered her family.

Two booted feet appeared in front of her, practically aligned with the tips of her bare toes.

"Taeg?" she whispered.

For a moment the nightmare faded away as she allowed herself to hope. He was here to help her.

But then the figure inched closer, into the moonlight. It wasn't Taeg, but a complete stranger. One with flashing green eyes that betrayed him as non-human.

Her stomach knotted when the man regarded her curiously, then shifted his attention to the screaming down the hall.

"This haunts you," he said.

"Who…who are you?"

The stranger's eyes settled back on her. "What happened here?"

"I…I don't understand."

The screaming stopped abruptly, leaving only the sounds of feasting, of flesh being torn from bone. The man tilted his head, as if drinking in the sound. He stepped back and swiveled to walk down the hallway.

Maya tensed, half-rising from her position on the floor. Curiosity filled her, but she wasn't about to follow him. Not when she knew full well what she'd find.

After a few moments the footsteps padded along the floor again, signaling the stranger's return. He stared at her, his eyes still expressionless. "This was your family? Murdered by maliki demons?"

This had never happened in her dream before, at least as far as she could remember. What figment of her imagination was this? "Yes."

"The demon's faces, they waver between humanlike and their true form. Why is that?"

"I don't understand," she said. "Who *are* you?"

His brows furrowed, his expression turning speculative, then awestruck. "You could see through their glamour, couldn't you?"

"Why are you here?" she whispered.

He remained silent, studying her intently before speaking again. "Were these demons ever found?"

A burst of anger pulsed through her body, lending a hard edge to her tone. "No."

An expression of understanding crossed his face. "Ah, so this is what you seek? Vengeance?"

"Vengeance?" she echoed. "I—yes…vengeance."

The scene faded into nothingness. She blinked, and when she reopened her eyes she was lying in a strange bed. "What the…"

The events of the past few hours came back to her in one blinding recollection. Seeing Elain drinking Taeg's blood. Fighting with him. Kissing him. "Oh God."

Sitting up, she rubbed the sleep from her eyes. When had things become so complicated? Until a few days ago, her mission in life had been clear—find a way to banish all demons to Hell, and destroy the ones who'd killed her family. Now she had to worry about things like whether or not demons were evil, not to mention deal with the confounding man who'd made her question everything to begin with.

She'd *kissed* Taeg. Allowed him to touch her. And she'd enjoyed every minute of it. How far would it have gone if Elain hadn't interrupted them? Would she have slept with him?

He didn't understand. How could he? After her parents' death, with the exception of her adoptive mother, she'd never let anyone get close to her. Loving meant risking loss, and she couldn't deal with any more of that in her life. Other than that one lousy experiment with her lab partner when she was an undergraduate student, she'd never been with a man. And Taeg had been with a lot of women.

What if she slept with him and he thought it was horrible? How could she bear that?

She couldn't think about this right now. Exhaustion wound through her, making her eyes heavy. She lay back down, shutting them.

Please, not another nightmare. I can't keep dreaming about this. That would drive her insane. And now she was adding strangers to the cast of characters in her dreams? Proof that she needed to get herself back on track.

'Vengeance,' the stranger had said. He had probably been her subconscious reminding her of what was important. Not Taeg, as tempting as he might be.

Her family. She had to bring them peace.

శాంర్డ్

The human was far more interesting than he'd initially given her credit for. Troubled, but interesting. She could *see* through glamours. Leave it to Taeg to discover a gem such as she. Excitement lent a quiver to Leviathos's hands. Before he could forget their faces, he dug out a pad and sketched rough drawings of the maliki demons he'd seen in the woman's dream. He pulled his phone out of his pocket and dialed Garin.

"Hello?" the wolf-shifter answered.

"I've got some sketches for you. Two maliki demons who murdered the woman's family when she was a girl. Talk to your contacts, see if we can figure out who these demons are."

"What does this have to do with anything?"

"I don't pay you to question, I pay you to *do*."

There was a brief pause on the other end of the line before Garin spoke again. "Whatever. It's your dime."

"I'll text you the pictures."

Leviathos hung up and glanced at the sketches once again. If he could find the whereabouts of these demons, he might be able to use that to coax more information out of the woman. What use did Taeg have in mind for her? One thing was clear: there had to be a good reason Taeg wanted a human who was immune to glamours. And he'd bet it had something to do with the book. The memory of something he'd once heard tickled his mind—a powerful glamoured object. Hmm…he'd have to think about that.

The slip of paper he'd gotten from Horster lay in a crumpled square on his desk. He picked it up and smoothed it out to examine the geographic coordinates written on it. Belpheg had been right. He'd heard rumors of a hidden portal several hours from the city, one reportedly created in secret by a disgruntled employee of the Council. The coordinates Horster had managed to uncover led them right to it. They were the same on every dimension, so if Belpheg got ahold of them, he could use the portal to travel here to Earth. For obvious reasons, Leviathos didn't want that.

Leviathos rose and walked to his kitchen, where he turned on the gaze stove. Now that he knew the location, he didn't need this slip of paper anymore. He set it to the stove, and it quickly burned to ashes.

The portal was his ticket to the book, kept under lock and key by the Council. He was close. So near to the power it contained. But before he made his move, he had to know what Taeg was up to.

If this Maya was helping him, he would steal her right out from under Taeg's nose, the way his former friend had done with his first and only love, Ana.

After all, he knew what Maya wanted most.

Like him, she sought vengeance.

And he might just be in a position to give it to her.

He turned and headed back to his living room. Before he could cross the room, the air crackled with static electricity, making him jump. Belpheg's figure suddenly appeared, and Leviathos's heart began to race. He'd just barely managed to rid himself of the evidence. Luck was on his side after all.

Belpheg's gaunt frame straightened as his eyes searched the room. He turned and saw Leviathos. "There you are."

"I'd appreciate it if you announced yourself *before* dropping in." Leviathos lowered his hand from his chest, willing his heart rate to even out.

Belpheg cocked one brow. "That's not possible."

Perhaps not, but thanks to a local black market witch, Leviathos now had in his possession a spell that would block Belpheg from projecting his image near him. He was saving that one, though, for when it would truly come in handy.

"What do you want?" Leviathos barked.

"Have you met with Horster yet?"

Leviathos's heartbeat sped up again. He took a breath, thankful Belpheg couldn't hear the rapid *swish* of his heart inside his chest. "No, but we spoke on the phone. He's still searching for the location of this supposed portal. He isn't sure if it truly exists."

"Damnation." Belpheg's lips tightened. "Perhaps you

should impress upon him the importance of this mission."

Acting as if Belpheg's words rankled him, Leviathos wrinkled his brow. "I have. Don't you think he knows how important it is? Once I have some information, I'll contact you the way you showed me."

Belpheg had shown him how to meditate so that his spirit could project onto an astral plane that Belpheg had created. Creepy, but it could come in handy at some point, Leviathos supposed.

Belpheg's gaze searched him for one long moment, and Leviathos did his best to infuse sincerity into his expression. Finally Belpheg nodded. "Good. We'll be in touch."

He disappeared, leaving Leviathos to relax. The sooner he got the book, the better. Belpheg was starting to annoy the hell out of him.

ॐ

Morning couldn't come soon enough for Maya. She was tired of all the nightmares. Tired of wondering if Taeg had spent the night in his own bedroom, and if so whether he'd been alone. Tired of this house and its snide immortal owner. So when the knock sounded on her bedroom door shortly before noon, she was more than ready to get the hell out of there.

"Come in."

Taeg poked his head in the door, those red eyes of his looking bleary like he hadn't slept, either. And maybe he hadn't.

That jerk.

He arched a brow as if he could hear her thoughts. But when he spoke all he said was "Ready to go?"

"Hell yeah." Was she ever.

She followed him to the front hall. Thankfully, there was no sign of Elain. Probably still sleeping, if that legend about vampires was true.

Her butler waited for them at the front door, however. When he saw them walking down the hall he opened the door to allow them out. "Good day, sir, miss."

"Yeah, you too, Jeeves," Taeg replied. "Stay fun, pal."

The butler merely sniffed and closed the door shut in his face.

"Always up for a good time, that guy."

Maya didn't bother responding. She walked to the car and waited for him to unlock it. Not even the slogan on his T-shirt—*I'm Not Lazy… I Just Don't Give a Damn*—was enough to make her crack a smile right now.

She slid into the seat and sat silently as he drove off the property. Palpable tension filled the air. Taeg must have felt it, too, because he only drove a few minutes before breaking the silence.

"Nothing happened," he said.

"What?"

"With Elain." His fingers tapped the steering wheel. "I didn't sleep with her or anything."

"It's none of my business." But true as that might be, she couldn't help the waves of relief that rolled through her. For the first time since they'd gotten in the car, she turned to face him. "What was the payment she demanded last night?"

"Blood."

Elain had been satisfied with nothing more than his blood. That Maya actually found that to be a relief was a testament to what the past few days had been like.

"Elain mentioned something last night," she said to Taeg. "She said she didn't need a Feeder. What's that?"

"Feeders are humans who act as blood donors for vampires."

"Willingly?" Who the hell would do that?

"The act of being fed on by a vampire is arousing. Almost orgasmic. Can you see how some people might be lining up to volunteer for that?"

The memory of Elain's hand cupping Taeg's erection crept into her mind. She couldn't imagine ever agreeing to be fed from, orgasmic or no. But maybe that was just her.

"Elain said she was once human. Does that mean vampires are created?"

"Sometimes I forget how little you know about the other races." Taeg laughed. "Okay, here's basic vampire biology for you. Vampires are both made and born. Those who are born are actually beings from another dimension called Enevora."

"Vampires came to Earth from another dimension and made more vampires?"

"Yes. It's been happening for as long as travel has been allowed between dimensions. Vampires have the ability to make new vampires by altering the DNA structure through blood exchange."

"Like a virus," she said.

"Exactly. Elain was created by a made vampire, so she's second-generation at the very least."

This was crazy. Maya thought the worst thing she had to worry about were demons. Now she had vampires to fear, too?

"Wait." She straightened and looked back at Taeg. "Can vampires only infect humans?"

"No. They can infect any living creature."

"You're half-fae and half-demon. If you were infected by a vampire…"

"I'd become a fae-demon-vampire," he finished. "I'd have the traits I was born with, as well as those inherited from my vampire creator. The necessity to drink blood to survive, aversion to the sunlight, the ability to create more vampires."

"Holy crap."

"Exactly. It's a crazy multiverse, Maya. Crazier than you know."

Why would Earth's leaders allow vampires, if they had the ability to infect everyone around them? They could irrevocably alter life on every single planet. That didn't make sense. It was also way too much to ponder right now, so she moved on to the next subject.

"What did Elain have to say about the sword?"

Taeg hesitated. "The papers Horster sold me contain directions to three fae sisters who might know the sword's location."

"Really?" Not as good as the location of the sword itself, but close enough. "When are we going to go see them?"

He scratched his chin, scruffy from a day's growth.

"What is it?" she asked him.

"*We* won't be visiting them. Just me. They don't live here on Earth. They live in Faelan, the dimension the fae originate from."

She gaped at him. "How are you going to get there?"

"I'll petition the Council for allowance. But not until tomorrow. There's a gig I'm working for my regular job that I've put off for far too long. I plan on taking care of it tonight."

"Regular job? You have a regular job?"

Taeg chuckled and cast a wry glance at her. "What did you think I do all day, sit around and wait for hot, angry chicks to kidnap?"

"I…" She looked away, rubbing her arms. "I guess I never thought about it. What is it that you do?"

"I'm a Detainor for the Elden Council. My brothers, too."

"A Detainor?"

"Inter-dimensional bounty hunter." His smile was all teeth, giving him a predatory look. "I track down bad guys and bring them back to the Council for judgment."

"Like a demon cop?"

"Something like that." He snickered as if he found the note of amazement in her voice amusing.

"What exactly classifies as 'bad' to the Council?"

"A lot of the same things as on your world. Rape, murder, mass destruction. For the most part, these things are technically prohibited. I hunt down the demons suspected of breaking the Council's laws."

"What do you mean, for the most part?"

"Some races can't help but do these things. Incubi and succubi feed off others' life forces. Vampires occasionally take too much blood and kill their victims." He shrugged. "The Council makes allowances for things like that."

Ok-a-a-ay…just when she'd begun to think this Council might be good, he had to go and ruin it for her.

"I see I've finally rendered you speechless," Taeg said.

"You could say that." If she lived a million years, she wouldn't understand his world. So many moral shades of gray. "What is it that you have to do tonight?"

His swirling red eyes fixated on her. "I have a meeting with a contact who's got some information on a demon I'm hunting. Leader of a small local drug ring that sells *score*. Small-time shit, but big enough that it's hit the Council's radar."

"Where are you meeting him? That bar we went to the night other night—Eros?"

"No." Taeg let out a laugh. "That place is too tame for Benny, my contact."

"Too *tame*?" If this Benny character thought Eros was tame, she didn't think she wanted to know what he considered fun.

"There's an Otherworlder club up in Harlem that he likes to go to. It's called Opiate."

Opiate. That name sounded familiar. Finally, she remembered where she'd heard it. "Elain said that's where you two met."

He fidgeted in his seat. "Yeah."

Great. How many other bimbos did he have waiting for him at that club? Would they be anxious to take Elain's place? Maybe he picked them up in droves and chose whichever one suited him best at that particular time. Like a harem.

"I'm going with you," she said.

Okay, where did that come from?

Taeg's husky laugh filled the interior of the car, sending an involuntary shiver through her. "I don't think so, little slayer. That place is too dangerous for you."

"More dangerous than Eros?"

"Yes."

"But I can handle myself," she reminded him. "Or have you forgotten?"

"I've no doubt about that, but you've never seen a place

like this. It makes Eros look like Sunday school. Creatures of all shapes and sizes, ready and eager to let their freak flags fly."

A tiny ball of apprehension knotted up Maya's stomach. From his description of the place, it wasn't anywhere she'd normally volunteer to go. But she wasn't about to back down now. If this kind of stuff existed in the city, she should at least be aware of it. "I don't care about that."

"You should." Taeg sighed. "Listen, Maya, it's not just that. Opiate caters to the dregs of Otherworlder society. Misfits and outcasts. To say that the place is risqué would be a major understatement. I don't think you could handle it."

She bristled at his words. After everything she'd seen, everything she'd survived, she wasn't about to back down just because she might have to face some freaky *Others*. Even if the thought of being in a club packed full of them made her skin itch like she had a major case of hives.

"I can handle it," she insisted. "Besides, didn't we decide we're partners?"

"Not in this. This has nothing to do with my mission, or yours."

"It's a club full of *Others*. Seems to me like that's exactly where I should be looking if I want to find my family's murderers."

Taeg snorted. "You think you have a chance in hell of finding them in a local Otherworld club? What are the odds of that?"

Good point, but she wasn't giving up. The reasons were more complicated than she cared to examine, but nevertheless, she didn't want him going alone. "I'm going with you, and that's that."

Taeg shook his head. "Suit yourself. But if you want to tag

along, you're going to have to do everything I say, and I mean it."

Argh, he could be so annoying. "Fine."

"Fine." His fingers drummed on the steering wheel and he gave her a brief glance. "Are we gonna talk about what happened between us last night, Maya?"

What could she say? She couldn't tell him the truth: that she was scared to take things any further between them. "I need some time to think about everything. Okay?"

His hand tightened on the wheel, but his voice sounded normal when he replied, "No problem."

They drove the remainder of the way in silence.

Maya waited until they were back in the city to ask, "Do you think you'll be able to get the sword's location from the fae sisters?"

"Oh, I'll get it," he said darkly. "One way or another."

CHAPTER SIXTEEN

"You're taking her to Opiate with you?" Ronin was clearly amused.

"She insisted," Taeg replied. "And she can be pretty damn insistent."

Ronin laughed, long and loud. "I never would have believed it. My big brother Taeg, pussy-whipped."

"Screw you."

Next to him, Keegan let out a snort. "Yeah, Ronin, give it a rest. He'd have to actually get some in order to be whipped, wouldn't he?"

"Screw you, too," Taeg snapped at Keegan. He never should have confessed he hadn't slept with Maya, but when Keegan had asked him point-blank, he hadn't been able to deny it.

Taeg downed the remainder of his whiskey before stepping from Keegan's terrace back into his apartment. He'd brought Maya here so he could fill his brothers in on what he'd learned.

Once Brynn had heard he was taking Maya to Opiate,

she'd insisted on taking her out to buy some club-appropriate clothes. Keegan had tried to get her to stay home, but she'd brushed off his objections. Bram and Reiver had looked less than pleased as they'd followed the women out of the apartment.

They'd come back about an hour ago, and from the teasing grin Brynn had given him, he had a feeling the outfit was going to be killer. Not that it mattered. He'd want Maya even if she was covered in day-old goat's blood.

Keegan and Ronin stepped into the living room behind him.

"Have you thought about this?" Keegan asked. "She damn near freaked out when it was just our group. How do you think she'll react in a club full of non-humans?"

"Especially the kind of non-humans who go to places like Opiate," Ronin added. "Devious and shifty, the whole lot of them."

"We all make the occasional trip to Opiate," Taeg reminded them.

"Point made," Keegan said.

Taeg thought about it for a minute. "You know, I'll think she'll handle it fine. Maya's tough. She's seen shit you wouldn't believe and come out stronger for it."

"Sounds like you admire her." Keegan knocked back his glass of whiskey, then yanked Taeg's empty glass out of his hand and headed to the bar set up on a side table. He generously refilled both glasses and handed one to Taeg.

Taeg watched him. Why did he look so smug? "You sound like you want me to like her."

"Why not? She's tough. She's beautiful." Keegan shrugged. "She might be perfect for you."

"You're crazy," Taeg said. But inside he couldn't help but think Keegan had a point. Maybe, once this was all over they could find out. Aw hell, what was the point in even contemplating this? If he wasn't careful, he'd get attached to his little slayer without having spent one night in her arms. And that would be fucking insane.

"Don't mind him." Ronin smirked. "Now that he's hitched, he wants everyone to feel his pain."

"Best thing that ever happened to me." There was no mistaking the stark honesty in Keegan's voice.

"Come on, give it up," Taeg teased him. "The old ball-and-chain isn't around to hear you."

But inside, he knew Keegan was right. Brynn was the best thing that had ever happened to him. That was why Taeg had to make sure she'd be safe, no matter what.

There was a moment of steady silence before Ronin spoke. "Have either of you gotten any news about Leviathos?"

Taeg sighed. "Not a freaking thing. He keeps off the radar a damn sight better than our father ever did."

"Let's not forget, in many ways he's smarter than our father was," Keegan said. "And less conceited, which gives him an advantage over Mammon."

"Maybe he has no plans to get his hands on the book," Ronin ventured.

Although Leviathos hadn't been heard from since he'd escaped when they captured Mammon, it was the first time any of them had ever suggested he might not want the same thing Mammon did.

"Don't be ridiculous," Taeg snapped. If there was one thing he knew about Leviathos, it was that his envious nature would lead him on a path straight to the book. He wanted to rule worlds, like their father had. And more than anything, he wanted his revenge.

"Ronin has a point," Keegan said. "After all, we haven't heard a thing from him, and he's bound to know where we are. All this trouble for the sword may be for nothing."

Okay, coming from Keegan, that was just stupid. His hand involuntarily tightened around the glass and it gave a *crunch* as it cracked. "So what, should we leave Brynn unprotected? What about the baby? *Your* baby? Don't you even care?"

Keegan's back went rigid and he set his glass down on the side table. "You better watch what you say, little brother. That's *my* fucking family you're talking about."

"Then act like it, bro," Taeg shot back. "You're living in a dream world. I'm sure it's great and all, getting to play house with someone who loves you, but you need to get your head out of your ass. Until the book is destroyed, we're all in danger."

"That's it," Keegan growled.

He lunged across the room so fast Taeg barely saw his fist before it connected with his jaw. He staggered, the glass in his hand falling to the floor and shattering on the hard wood.

Damn, that hurt. Keegan always did have ham hocks for hands.

Taeg turned toward his big brother, the coppery taste of blood filling his throat. He and Keegan used to fight all the freaking time, but Keegan had mellowed out big-time since marrying Brynn.

It was a shame. He'd missed this.

The glint in Keegan's eye said he was game for a brawl, so Taeg grinned at him. "Let's do it."

Ronin let out a long-suffering sigh from his spot across the room. "Here we go again." But at least he didn't try to use his calming ability on them this time.

Glass crushed under Taeg's feet when he lunged at Keegan. His fist landed with a glancing blow to his brother's cheek. Keegan laughed and swung at him with an uppercut that made him take a bite out of his tongue.

"Son of a bitch." He swallowed the blood pooling in his mouth and closed his arms around Keegan, capturing him in a body lock. They staggered across the room, each trying to get the upper hand.

"Oh my God." Maya's muffled gasp stopped them both cold.

Taeg let go of Keegan and turned to see Maya and Brynn standing in the entrance to the living room. Maya stared at the both of them in shock. And yeah, he'd have to be blind to miss what she was wearing.

Well, fuck me three ways from Sunday.

Her outfit was hotter than he could have ever imagined. A poured-on, sleeveless blue dress that pushed her cleavage way up and dropped down to mid-thigh, and her signature knee-high black boots. Her hair had been straightened and hung nearly to her waist, showcasing the sexy hourglass shape of her body. He didn't notice he was drooling until Keegan gave him a light punch in the gut.

"You look…hot," Taeg managed to choke out.

Maya frowned. "What's wrong with you two?"

"Uh…just letting off some steam," he mumbled, wiping the small stream of blood trickling from his mouth.

"Never mind them." Brynn gave the both of them a dirty look. "This is pretty normal around here."

Maya turned to Brynn. "They fight like this all the time?"

"Not nearly as much as they used to, which means about once a week," Brynn said.

Maya looked at him, surprise written all over her face. "I thought you only got off on fighting with me."

There was a moment of marked silence before everyone else broke into laughter. Maya's cheeks turned bright red, as if she'd just realized she said those words aloud. Devil's balls, she was so freaking cute.

As the laughter died out, Brynn directed a pointed glance at Keegan, then at the broken glass littering the floor. "You're going to clean that up. Now."

"Sorry," Keegan mumbled.

Brynn shifted her attention to Taeg, freezing him with a glacial glare until he, too, grumbled an apology. Raising a brow, she said, "You've got blood on your shirt."

He looked down. "Shit." When Maya looked horrified, he said, "Don't worry. I'll be fully healed by the time we make it downstairs."

"Come on, you can borrow one of my shirts." Keegan clapped him on the shoulder and headed toward the hallway.

Brynn faced Maya. "See? All is forgiven. Fighting is like breathing to these boneheads."

Taeg swallowed his automatic snide comment. He wasn't about to mess with a pregnant lady. "Be right back."

He followed Keegan out of the room.

"Men," he heard Maya mutter.

"Yep," Brynn agreed. "Demon or human, they're all the same."

He barely processed the insult. No, he was too busy thinking about his little slayer and how luscious she looked in that dress. It highlighted every curve of her body, and she had plenty of them. Damn, but she was just about perfect.

Perfect for you.

Keegan's earlier words echoed in his head, kicking around in there until they were all he could think about. How the hell was he going to keep his hands off Maya tonight?

You're not.

He looked at his crotch and muttered, "Shut up, dick. I'm in charge here."

"What did you say?" Keegan called out, looking back at him.

"Uh…nothing."

Yeah, and just to prove he was wrong, one more thought of Maya and the damned traitor rose to life, right there in the hallway of his brother's apartment.

It was going to be a helluva long night.

ॐ∘ॐ

Maya sat in the passenger seat of Dagan's car while Taeg drove them to Opiate. A school of butterflies had taken flight in her stomach. She pressed down hard in an effort to calm her nerves, reminding herself she was the one who'd wanted to go with Taeg. She still did, but the prospect of facing yet another place filled with *Others* made her nervous as hell. Especially after what Brynn had told her about the club.

"Make sure you stick close to Taeg. Opiate can get a little bit scary."

"Scary how?"

"It's hard to explain." Brynn had hedged, busying herself with helping Maya straighten her hair. "It's not that I think anyone will try to hurt you. It's just…well, make sure you stay alert."

The whole exchange had left her feeling on edge. She turned to study Taeg, who looked hotter than normal tonight, if that was possible. Black slacks took the place of his usual jeans, and he'd borrowed a gray lightweight sweater from Keegan. His hair was casually tousled, as if he'd just hopped out of bed and run his fingers through it. Or maybe someone else had, after spending a long, sleepless night in bed with him.

Just the sight of him made her wet. It was so unfair that he could make her feel this way without even trying.

When he swiveled his head to throw her a questioning look, his red eyes reflected against the light of the streetlamps. "What's up?"

She wasn't about to confess her real thoughts. "What can I expect at this club?"

"It's like Eros, but a little more hardcore. You'll see all kinds of Otherworlders there—gargoyles, vampires, werewolves. Mostly shady types."

"What about humans? Will there be any there?"

"The only humans you're likely to see will be there with Otherworlders. Humans who are attracted to the supernatural. Or Feeders." His eyes blazed. "Stick by my side the entire time. Follow my lead. Do what I tell you."

She let out a snort. "You'd love that, wouldn't you?"

"Maya," he said with a note of warning in his voice, "you promised."

That's right, she had. Damn it. "Fine."

He grinned. "That's a good girl."

"Fuck you."

"Love to," the smartass replied.

Okay, she wasn't getting anywhere with this verbal exchange. She turned to stare outside the window, memorizing the streets as they passed them by.

After a few minutes he reached out and grasped her hand. "It'll be fine, Maya. Promise."

His warm, husky voice melted her worries away.

"All right," she said softly, stifling a shudder when his thumb started a lazy caress along the back of her hand. The man was like a furnace. The kind that could make any woman want to burn.

They finally pulled up to a relatively quiet street in Harlem. It was pretty dead this time of night. A tall, heavily muscled man in a black suit stood on the sidewalk next to where Taeg had stopped. He opened the passenger-side door.

She gave Taeg a puzzled glance, but he was already stepping out of the car. He tossed the keys to the man. With a shrug, she climbed out of the passenger side.

The man inclined his head in a gesture of respect, all the while giving her an appreciative once-over. "Ma'am."

"This way." Taeg casually looped an arm over her shoulder. His touch sparked an involuntary shiver throughout her whole body.

"Cold?" he asked her.

"No."

She instantly regretted her automatic response when he smiled, as if he'd guessed the real reason for her shiver. He didn't comment on it, though, but simply examined her with a blatantly sexual perusal. "I like your dress."

That was no surprise. The thing was so tight it left nothing to the imagination. She'd argued when Brynn had picked it out, but Brynn had reassured her that even with this outfit on, she'd look like a nun compared to most of the other women at the club.

"Thanks. It's made of jersey, so the fabric will stretch if I need to fight." It was the only reason she'd finally relented and agree to wear it. Well, that and because she could wear her regular boots, with the daggers tugged inside their compartments.

"How many fights do you think you're getting into tonight?"

"Never hurts to be prepared."

Taeg appeared to consider her words, then nodded. "You're right."

He led her in between two buildings housing storefronts that were closed and gated for the night. They entered what looked like a normal city alleyway—dark, smelling of piss, and littered with stray bits of garbage that had flown in off the street. Creepy, as alleys tended to be.

"Are you serious? The club is down *here*?"

"Wait and see." Several yards in, past a set of dumpsters, a green metal door cut into the wall. Taeg led her to it and rapped sharply with his knuckle.

The door swung open to reveal another man, almost a clone to the valet in terms of size and manner of dress. He must have recognized Taeg, because he inclined his head and moved aside to allow them entrance.

"What's up, Vinnie?" Taeg said to him, not bothering to wait for a reply as they walked by.

Directly ahead of them was a small reception area. A short, oily demon sat behind the tall, enclosed desk.

"Taeg, pleasure to have you with us, as always," he said in

a high-pitched voice.

Taeg nodded his head in acknowledgment. "Noch."

Noch turned to look her up and down. His eyes lingered on her cleavage. "What an enchanting guest you have."

Eww. She'd have to scrub for an hour tonight to rid herself of the dirty feeling of his lecherous gaze on her.

Taeg didn't respond to Noch. He steered her toward a set of red-carpeted stairs that led to the second floor. The walls of the narrow staircase were painted a deep red, and the banister was covered in a black-and-white zebra pattern.

They reached the top of the stairs and she gasped at what she saw. "This place is insane."

He shrugged without bothering to reply, and she shifted her focus back to the interior of the club.

Rounded booths were scattered throughout the room, the black round tabletops accented by the zebra pattern covering the seats. On one side of the room, a large bar lined the wall, the backdrop a mixture of dark red wall and metal scrolling. The look might come across as gaudy in some locations, but here, it lent an aura of mystique to the place.

But as interesting as the decor was, that wasn't what had caught her eye. It was the people. The club was jam-packed with them, mostly *Others*. One of the booths housed a small group of what she suspected were vampires, deep in heated conversation, their flawless porcelain skin almost glimmering in the dim light. More creatures were scattered throughout the space, some with horns protruding from tough grayish hide, or large talons curling out of monstrous hands.

A man with a goatlike lower body edged closer to her while leering, as if he was purposely trying to brush his privates against her.

Nasty.

Maya stifled a shudder and scooted in toward Taeg. "Where exactly are you meeting this contact of yours?"

Taeg scanned the crowd. "Benny could be anywhere in the club. Might not even be here yet. He's not the most predictable when it comes to meetings."

"Great." Her stomach felt like a lead weight. This place gave her the freaking creeps. She didn't know how long she'd be able to stand here without trying to kill something. Namely that freaky goat-man. Her fingers itched to close around one of her daggers.

As if he sensed her extreme discomfort, Taeg pulled her closer to his body. "Relax. You're safe with me."

Safe. Funny, he didn't feel *safe* at all. He felt dangerous. Exciting.

She did some scanning of her own, but didn't see anyone resembling those two demons from so long ago, whose faces were forever burned into her memory.

"Taeg," a melodic voice called out from somewhere ahead. Maya looked up to see a gorgeous blonde slinking toward them. She wore a tiny strip of black cloth that could barely be called a dress and a wide smile on her perfect face. Her long, flowing locks gave a seductive sway as she walked.

Maya tensed when the woman stopped in front of them, sparing her no more than a quick, dismissive glance before she turned her attention to Taeg.

"I missed you, darling," she hummed in that heavenly voice.

A face that could be carved from marble. A to-die-for voice. Just like Dagan.

Siren.

Maya glared at Taeg. "Why am I not surprised?"

He gave her a wide-eyed, innocent look before turning to the woman. "Hello, Nadia, this is my date, Maya."

Nadia ignored that, sliding her hands up his chest. "Why haven't you called?" she asked with a pout.

The nerve of the woman, to put her hands on him when she knew he was with someone else. Even if she wasn't technically a "date" date, Nadia didn't know that.

Maya bristled, about to snap at her when Taeg grabbed Nadia's wrist and removed her hands from his body. His reply was ice-cold. "I told you I'm with somebody."

Nadia's face scrunched in anger. "But—"

"Good night," Taeg said firmly before taking hold of Maya's waist and leading them in the other direction.

She had to admit, that felt good. Resisting the urge to shoot Nadia a triumphant glance, Maya said, "I'm surprised you turned her away."

"Come on, Maya. I'm not so bad."

Those soft-spoken words made her feel ashamed of her cattiness. Just his intent, no doubt.

Taeg stopped in front of the large bar, which was far less crowded than she would have thought considering the sheer number of people in the place. The bartender was a tall man with golden skin, piercing blue eyes, and long, brown hair that failed to hide the pointy tops of his ears. An *elf*?

When the bartender made his way to them, Taeg said, "Hey, Crull, can we get two house lagers?"

He wanted to drink? *Now?*

"What are you doing?" she hissed.

"Don't want to look like I'm working." Taeg shrugged. "Might make some people nervous."

Huh. She hadn't thought of that. "Does everyone here know what you do for a living?"

"Not everyone. But enough that the word could easily spread if people start to get anxious." He motioned toward two empty barstools, then sat down on one.

She thought about that as she took a seat. "Doesn't that make your job dangerous?"

He let out a husky laugh. "Most Otherworlders want to avoid the Council. They mean serious business, and fucking with one of their employees would piss them off."

The bartender plopped the beers down in front of them.

"Thanks, man," Taeg said to him. "How's it going?"

"Slow." The bartender flashed him an easy smile. "Business or pleasure tonight?"

"A bit of both."

Crull looked her up and down, then gave Taeg a knowing wink before sauntering off.

She flushed at his obvious reference. Lifting her glass to her mouth, she took a sip. The cool liquid slid down her throat, leaving behind the taste of honey and spice. "Wow, this is delicious."

"You should know it's way more potent than regular beer."

She stared at the seemingly innocuous amber liquid in her glass. "But it tastes so good."

"That's what gets you into trouble. If I were you, I'd drink no more than half that glass."

Hard to do, when it tasted like nectar of the gods. She took another deep sip, licking her lips to get every last drop, not considering how that might look until she saw his indrawn breath and the narrowing of his eyes.

"Careful," he whispered into her ear. "Too many moves like that and you may start a brawl."

His gruff words, combined with the heat of his breath on her neck, sent a tremor of lust coursing through her body. Lord, he knew what to say to make her go weak. Maya saved herself the trouble of having to respond by lifting the glass for another deep sip.

Taeg noted it, arching a brow. "Brownies do make the best beer."

"Brownies?" The mere word caused an unpleasant twist in her guts. She plunked her glass down onto the countertop.

He laughed. "So predictable, sweetheart."

Busted.

After a minute she was glad she'd set the liquid down, because a wave of heat crept down her throat to the pit of her stomach, warming her from the inside out. "Wow, this stuff *is* potent."

"Warned you." He pulled his cell phone out of his pocket and glanced at the screen, then glanced around the room once again. "Where is he?"

"What about over there?" She pointed to an area farther back, separated from the main part of the club by a gauzy curtain that was so sheer it was almost see-through.

Taeg stiffened, looking uncomfortable. "He's probably not back there."

"Don't you think we should check?" When he hesitated she rose up from her barstool and grasped his hand. "Come on."

"Maya, I don't think—"

"You want to find this guy, don't you?" She rolled her eyes and made her way through the crowd of people, carefully avoiding goat-man while she dragged Taeg behind her. The tiniest wave of dizziness speared her vision. Lord, was she buzzed already, from a few sips of that stuff? It didn't bother her right now, though. She felt looser than usual, and that wasn't so bad. She could use a little loosening.

They neared the far end of the club and she drew back the curtain, then came to an abrupt standstill. "Oh," she said in a small voice.

So this was why Taeg had been hesitant about coming to the back. This area of the club seemed to be reserved for couples in various stages of undress. Unless she missed her guess, and she didn't care to look closely enough to confirm it, a fair number of them were getting it on right here.

When she made no further move forward, he muttered, "Might as well look for him while we're back here." Taking the lead, he dragged her behind him.

Everywhere she looked provided a new reason to blush. In one corner a vampire stood with his arms around a woman whose blouse was unbuttoned and half off her body. He bit into her, right above one breast, cupping the other, her bra pushed aside. On another spot along the wall, a second goat-man was doing things she didn't dare contemplate to a human woman who faced away from him. *Yuck.*

Maya swallowed hard and looked away. "What exactly do you do when you come here?"

Taeg at least had the grace to look embarrassed. He grimaced, focusing on the opposite end of the room. "I sit at the bar. This place has good beer."

"Uh-huh." She didn't quite believe him. He seemed all too familiar with this part of the club, quickly steering her through the crowd while scanning the patrons' faces. She kept her focus anchored on him, careful to avoid witnessing more peep shows.

"He's not in here," Taeg finally stated.

She breathed a sigh of relief when he turned and led them back toward the main part of the club. Funny how much more manageable it seemed now that she'd seen what was in the back.

The loud, pumping bass from the music cut out and a slower song started up. All around her couples pulled each other into embraces and swayed to the rhythm. Some didn't stop there. She saw plenty of wandering hands.

Truthfully, this part of the club wasn't that much better.

A little devil on her shoulder prompted her to turn to Taeg. "Let's dance."

He stopped in midstride with an expression of disbelief. "Are you serious?"

Okay, maybe she never would have suggested it if she wasn't slightly buzzed, but right now she didn't care. "Why not? Your contact isn't here yet. Might as well do something until he arrives."

The look in his eyes made it clear he was about to refuse. "Maya—"

"Come on," she insisted, lifting her hands to his chest. "It's just a dance. It won't kill you."

"It might." But in the end he sighed and wrapped his arms around her waist, giving a sensual sway of his hips.

She loved a man who could dance. And Taeg could dance. The natural rhythm he exhibited made her wonder what else he did exceptionally well. Closing her eyes, she gave herself over to the feel of his body against hers. The hard ridge of his chest beneath her palms. He was so hot. Like a campfire, heating her entire body until even her skimpy dress seemed like too much fabric.

What would it be like to have his naked flesh pressed against hers? To have him cover her with his warmth while he drove into her again and again? She could practically imagine the feel of his heated and hardened arousal against her. Just the thought of it was mouthwatering.

Lord, where was this coming from? She shouldn't be enjoying his body against hers so much, or fantasizing about him in bed. Inside her.

"Stop it." His voice was tight. Strangled.

Her eyes flew open. "What do you mean?"

He stared down at her, his eyes blazing with lust and some other emotion she couldn't identify. "Unless you want me to take you right here, stop rolling your hips into me. I'm not a fucking saint."

Her mouth dropped open. She hadn't been, had she?

Oh hell. She might have been rubbing up against him like a cat in heat without even noticing it. The demon turned her on that much. She dreamed about him most every night, for chrissake.

She licked her lips, opened her mouth to apologize. What came out instead was an obvious dare. "You wouldn't."

Taeg's expression hardened, lust pouring off him in palpable waves. "You love to challenge me, don't you, little slayer?"

He was right. She did, especially when it was obvious how much he enjoyed it.

Her thighs clenched and answering moisture gathered. He closed his eyes and took a deep inhale before opening them on a grin. Could he *smell* how turned on she was right now?

Taeg sobered. "You know, I've never wanted anyone half as badly as I want you. Even if most of the time you're trying to kick my ass. I've tried to deny what I feel for you, but I can't."

Wait, this wasn't what she'd expected. Declarations of lust, maybe. But this sounded far more serious.

"I know you want me, too," he continued hoarsely, "despite the fact you keep trying to deny it."

"I…" When she realized she couldn't disagree, she trailed off. Much as it frightened her, she did want him.

"Maya, I've told myself over and over again it's not a good idea to complicate things between us, but I'm starting to wonder what the hell we're fighting this attraction for."

He wasn't the only one. She'd never been nearly as attracted to anyone else before. And despite what he was, she had the feeling they might be astonishingly well-suited. After all, what mere human would ever understand about her past?

Taeg had not only listened to her sordid confessions, but he'd helped her to see that she couldn't continue blaming herself for her actions as a child. He accepted her for who she was, bad attitude, stashed weapons, and all. What was more, he actually *liked* those things about her.

Holy crap, he might just be perfect for her.

That realization steeled her spine. What else could she be waiting for?

Oh jeez. Was she actually going to do this? Make love to a demon?

Not a demon, Maya. Taeg.

"Taeg." She took a fortifying breath. "I—"

"Shit." He stiffened, focused on something behind her.

"What?" She stopped abruptly and tried to turn, but Taeg wouldn't let her.

"I think I saw…*shit.*"

"*What*? What is it?"

"The fugitive I've been searching for. The one Benny was supposed to give me information on tonight. The fucker is actually *here.*"

CHAPTER SEVENTEEN

Maya tried to turn around again, but Taeg held her still. He forced himself to continue swaying back and forth with her while keeping his eyes on the demon. "Keep dancing. I don't want to call attention to myself."

What the hell to do? He wanted to get the creep. The guy was a scumbag drug dealer, and this job was worth a lot of money. But he was with Maya.

"Aren't you going to bust him?"

"Apprehending him could be dangerous, and I don't want to leave you here alone."

She stepped out of his arms. "I'm pretty sure I can keep up. Now go get his ass."

He should have known she'd react that way. She was so predictable when it came to capturing demons.

At that moment, the fugitive looked up and his eyes widened in recognition. He turned and ran for the door.

"Son of a bitch." Taeg tightened his hold on Maya and raced after the demon, shoving people left and right to clear the path.

"What's happening?" she shouted over the din of the crowd.

"He spotted me. He's running."

If only Maya wasn't here. He could flash right in front of the guy. But he didn't dare do that now. No way was he leaving her behind in this crowd to fend for herself, not even for five minutes.

They reached the carpeted staircase and started down them when Vinnie called out to him from behind. "Taeg, if you're looking for the guy who raced out of here, he went upstairs. Toward the roof."

"Thanks." He immediately switched directions and headed up, freeing Maya's hand only when they'd reached the roof.

There. The demon sped toward the edge of the building, clearly planning to leap the five-foot distance separating this roof from the next.

"Stay here," Taeg ordered. He shifted his focus and in the span of one instant flashed directly in front of the creep.

"Shit," the demon yelled.

Taeg braced his weight as the demon barreled into him at full speed. He went down hard but quickly rolled over, gaining the top position. He swung his fist at the demon, catching him square on the cheek.

The demon's head snapped to the side. He spat out blood with a harsh, grating laugh. "You'll pay for that."

He held up one of his hands and, with an audible *pop*, his retractable claws broke the flesh on his knuckles. The ivory-colored bone claws on vestag demons had always reminded him of the comic-book hero Wolverine. Not only were they sharp as hell, but they were a little frightening. He'd die before admitting it, though.

"Ooh, I'm so scare—"

The claws sliced into him before he could finish his taunt. They ripped through his shirt, tearing long gouges in his side.

"Son of a bitch." Rolling off the demon, he sprang up and glanced down to where searing pain tore through his stomach. Thankfully the wounds weren't that deep. "This is my brother's shirt, asshole. He's gonna be so pissed."

He backpedaled when the demon jumped to his feet, releasing the claws in his other hand. Damn it. Reaching behind him, he freed the dagger he kept strapped in a hidden sheath at his back. "Hey, Betty, wanna play?"

The rhythmic click of booted heels running along the rooftop preceded Maya's arrival. But even the vestag demon's mouth dropped open in shock when she hopped into place next to Taeg, a dagger in each hand.

"What the devil are you doing?"

"Helping you," she said without taking her eyes off the demon.

Helping him? Was she insane?

"I do this for a living, you know. I think I can handle one measly vestag demon on my own," Taeg said.

"Yeah, he doesn't need any help from a little girl." The demon sneered at her. Then, as if just realizing what Taeg had said, he glowered. "Hey!"

The demon lunged at him, slicing his claws in a long arc. Taeg jumped back, then jabbed the dagger up and into his guts. With a muffled *oomph*, the demon stopped cold, but then he groaned in pain, his whole body twitching as something rammed into him from behind. The demon lifted his head to shoot Taeg a bewildered glance.

What the fuck?

He released his grip on the knife and walked around the demon, letting out a barking laugh when he saw Maya with her dagger jammed into the demon's back.

"Good thing demons are hard to kill. Otherwise I'd be out a quarter of a mil right now."

"What?" she gasped, her eyes going wide. "That's how much you get paid to bring him in?"

"Yeah, but only if he's still alive."

She stepped away, a look of shock on her face, but when the demon tried to stagger forward she twisted her dagger and pushed down hard, dropping him to the ground.

Taeg observed all this while trying to figure out if he should laugh or be pissed off. "You know, you'd make a damn good addition to our team."

Her eyes widened and a pleased smile crept to her face. "Really?"

He took a good look at the demon. With two knives buried in him, he wasn't going anywhere anytime soon. Normally he'd escort him to the Council, but that wasn't going to happen with Maya around.

Taeg dug his cell phone out of his pocket and dialed Ronin. "Yo, bro, I'm on the rooftop of Opiate. I've got the mark bagged and tagged, ready to go."

"No shit," Ronin replied with a hint of interest. "I thought you were meeting with Benny tonight?"

"Benny didn't show, but the mark did. Go figure."

Ronin whistled. "That's some good luck."

"Tell me about it."

Maya circled the demon, staring down at him like he

was some freak attraction in a sideshow circus. "Now I need someone to escort him to the Council. Can you do it?"

"I'll be there in twenty."

CHAPTER EIGHTEEN

If she lived to be a hundred years old, Maya didn't think she'd ever top the sight of Ronin flying onto the roof of the club, his wings flapping masterfully as he landed. Large, white, and full, they looked exactly how she imagined an angel's wings would. One quick shrug of his shoulders and they were gone, as if they'd never been there at all.

"Way to be inconspicuous," Taeg said.

"I kept to the shadows. Besides, you know how most people are. If anyone saw anything, they'd probably think it was just stress."

Taeg grunted. "Or too much alcohol."

Ronin stepped over to where the unconscious demon lay on the ground. His shirt sported two ragged rips where the wings had apparently torn through. He gave the demon a quick glance and then looked back and forth between her and Taeg. A grin tugged the corners of his mouth up. "Gave you some trouble, did he?"

"I could handle him fine," Taeg snapped.

Okay, apparently he was irked that she'd helped him. But what had he thought she'd do—stand by and scream like a girl while he fought the demon to the death? That wasn't her. He should know that by now.

"I'll take care of the demon," Ronin said.

"Thanks, bro." Taeg knelt and rolled the demon onto his side, and yanked the dagger out of his stomach. The demon twitched and let out a soft yell before going silent. He wiped the bloody knife on the demon's clothes, then re-sheathed it. Then he repeated the action with her dagger. Standing, he handed the now-clean weapon to her. "Come on. Let's get out of here."

He strode toward her and grabbed her hand.

"But your stomach—"

"It's fine. Already healed up."

She had time to do no more than lift the corner of his shirt to confirm the bleeding had stopped before he tugged her forward with an impatient frown on his face.

"I want to get out of here before patrons start heading up to check things out," he said. "I have a feeling attendance will die down rapidly if demons start figuring out they aren't safe from the Council's reach here."

Considering they'd raced through the entire packed club to apprehend the fugitive, Maya thought it might be a little late for that particular worry, but she didn't argue as she followed him.

They passed Vinnie on the way down the stairs. He examined Taeg. "Get him?"

"Yeah," Taeg said, clapping him on the shoulder. "Thanks to you."

Vinnie cocked a brow. "You're lucky I was doing the

rounds when he tried to escape. Next time try to keep it out of the club, though. We don't want to sketch our patrons out."

"I hear you, man. And I appreciate it."

With those words, Taeg continued forward, keeping a tight grip on her hand. They made it outside and into the car before he spoke again. "So that was your first bust. What did you think?"

She grinned at him. "It was fun."

His lips twitched. "I thought you'd say that. If it weren't so dangerous, I'd hire you on as my assistant.

Maya gave him a dirty look and he laughed. "That's right, I forgot. You'd probably want *me* to be the assistant, wouldn't you?"

Joker. She shook her head, staring out the window.

"Seriously, slayer," he continued in a soft tone. "You did good back there. Even if you do have a hard time obeying directions."

"Thanks." She didn't bother to hide the smile that crept to her face. Praise felt nice. Especially by him.

Taeg's right hand reached out to take hers. "Listen, it's been a long day, and tomorrow I need to make that trip to Faelan. Let's go back to the apartment and get some rest. I'll be nice and let you have the bed again."

The thought of sleeping in his bed made her pulse race. Because tonight she didn't want to be in it alone.

Oh Jesus.

Now that all traces of alcohol had cleared her system, she was more nervous than she'd ever been in her life. It was one thing to dream about doing naughty things with a demon, but to actually do them? And he was so experienced, while she… wasn't.

Maya closed her eyes and rested her head on the seat. She concentrated on taking deep, even breaths. It would be okay. No big deal. People did these kinds of things all the time. Some with demons, though most of them probably didn't realize it.

"You okay?" he asked her.

"Yes," she whispered. *Just nervous. And excited.*

When the car came to a rolling stop in front of Taeg's apartment building, he got out and walked around the car. After opening her door, he held his hand out to her. Maya took it and rose to her feet. Her legs gave a mortifying wobble. She was so nervous. How was she going to make it through this night?

"You sure you're okay, sweetheart?"

She gave him a weak nod, trying not to let her embarrassment show. "So you caught the guy you were looking for, huh?"

"Yeah. Lucky break." He led her to the front of the building, unlocking the door and holding it open for her.

With each rhythmic clunk of her boots on the steps, her heart pumped faster and louder. By the time he unlocked the front door and moved aside for her to pass, she was a bundle of raw nerves, ready to explode at the slightest provocation.

"Maya." Taeg closed and locked the door before turning back to her with a frown on his face. "I can tell something's wrong."

"No, it's just—"

"Listen, about what happened back at the club. About what I said." He shifted in place, nervously running a hand along the back of his neck. "You don't have to—"

"Oh, shush." Holding back a laugh, she moved forward to place her fingers over his lips. Here she was, freaking out about sleeping with him, and he thought she wanted to reject him again. Well, there was only one way to let him know how she felt. She gave him a slight push and his back hit the door.

"What are you doing?" he asked, his eyes widening.

Running her hands up his chest, she only had one millisecond to enjoy the look of shock on his face before she rose to her tiptoes and covered his mouth with hers. At first his lips were tender and slack under hers, as if he still hadn't caught on. But then he exploded with movement. A low groan rumbled in his chest and he closed his arms around her, pulling her in so tight she could hardly breathe. But hey, who needed to breathe?

He cupped her backside, lifting her up to mold his erection between her thighs. He was so hard, and she felt so empty. She squirmed against him, trying to calm the ache between her thighs, but it wouldn't go away. There was only one thing that would alleviate the hunger she felt now.

Taeg broke away, breathing hard. "Do you have any idea how much I want you?" he whispered hoarsely into her ear. "How much I've wanted you from the moment I first saw you?"

"Yes," she whispered back. "Because I want you just as much."

He groaned and carried her toward the bedroom. His red eyes, the eyes that would have once filled her with hate, glittered with passion. "Let's not wait any longer."

৵৵

Maya looked up at him with an expression he never thought to see from her. Desire. Longing. She *wanted* him. Right now nothing else mattered.

He set her on her feet and grasped the hem of her dress, sliding it upward.

She placed her hand on his. "Wait."

He frowned. "Wait?"

She bit her lip, looking nervous. "The lamp is on. Aren't you going to shut it off?"

That was what worried her? Thank the devil. For one second he feared she'd decided to stop, and that would've killed him. He gave her a little grin. "Why on earth would I do that, slayer? I want to see *every* inch of you."

She fidgeted and brushed her hair off her shoulders. "What about…protection?"

"Protection?" He should have known she'd worry about that. "We can use it, but just so you know, demons don't carry any diseases and demon-human pregnancies are extremely rare."

"Yeah, but they do happen. Just look at your brother."

He shook his head. "Brynn's part demon, even if it is a tiny part. Otherwise, the odds are pretty damn slim."

"But still possible?"

"Statistically speaking, you're more likely to win the lottery ten different times than get pregnant from me."

"Really?" When he nodded, she looked down before shyly lifting her eyes. "In that case, let's leave it. I want to feel you skin-to-skin."

He practically choked at her words. They evoked sensual images of the two of them that had him nearly crawling out of his flesh with desire. Not only that, but they were evidence of how much her opinion of him had changed over the past few days.

She *trusted* him.

"I want that, too, sweetheart."

When she urged his hand upward, he lifted her dress to reveal tiny black panties. One more tug and her breasts came free.

His cock hardened with a painful intensity. "You are so fucking *beautiful.*"

She stepped back and hesitated for the briefest of moments before she hooked her thumbs under her panties and slid them down.

For a moment he forgot how to breathe. She was even more beautiful than in his dreams, if that was possible. That bare, heavenly spot between her thighs called to him, making his cock pulse in anticipation.

Down, boy.

He pressed his lips to hers, teasing her with a flick of his tongue against the seam of her mouth. She sucked it inside. Letting out a loud groan, he wrapped his arms around her and maneuvered them to the edge of the bed.

He finally broke the kiss. "You have a body made for pleasure, little slayer. One that should be worshiped."

She only moaned, pulling him in.

He trailed kisses down her throat. Along the upper curve of her shoulder. Devil, he couldn't take it anymore. Her breasts arched upward, enticing him to have a taste. So he bent and took one into his mouth while he kneaded the other.

"Oh," she cried. "That's so…"

Mmm…sugar and spice. And a million other tastes that made him ache to come right then and there.

"Have you dreamt about me doing this?" his inner devil

prompted him to ask. When she didn't answer he sucked harder, tugging on her nipple before switching to the other breast and lavishing the same attention on it.

His hand crept down to her legs, still pressed together. If he had his way, she'd have them spread in the most wanton of ways before the night was through. Her body was made to tease. He slid two fingers between the crease of her thighs, groaning at the moisture he felt there.

"Taeg," she gasped.

Hell, even her voice was sexy.

"I have to know what you taste like." Sliding off the bed, he dropped to his knees in front of her. Damned if she didn't look apprehensive.

"What are you doing?"

"Just relax, sweetheart."

Her chest heaved. She was so enticing, the hardened tips of her nipples begged for his touch. His mouth. Soon enough. Right now he had other things on his mind. He placed his hands on her knees and pushed her legs open, baring her to his view.

"Taeg!"

"Slayer, just looking at you makes my mouth water." She was slick with moisture, the tiny pearl of her clit begging for his attention. So he gave it, with one long lick.

"*Whoa.*" She tensed and jumped beneath him.

"Relax," he said with a laugh. If he didn't know better, he'd say she'd never had anyone go down on her before. But that had to be freaking impossible. He gave her another stroke before running his tongue around her clit.

Her legs shook and she dug her hands in his hair, tugging on it painfully. Devil, but she was wound up tight. Letting go of her knees long enough to unwind her hands from his hair, he gently pushed her back onto her elbows.

She gave him a look that was half-perplexed, half-aroused.

"Lean back." He turned his attention back to her body, spreading her knees farther before closing his mouth around her and sucking in on her clit. She let out a cry, arching her lower body off the bed.

Damn, but she had the sweetest taste. He could feast on her for hours without tiring.

"Sweeter than candy," he breathed. Then he proceeded to show her just how sweet she tasted, licking and sucking until her legs shook uncontrollably and she screamed.

His cock gave a hard thump in his pants, as if to say, *What about me?* He ignored the pain.

She let out a loud gasp and tugged his head up from between her legs. "That was...incredible," she panted, and the look on her face said she meant every word.

"Sweetheart, that was only the beginning."

෨෧

She was in heaven. She was in hell. This was torture of the most amazing kind.

How could I have gone my whole life without experiencing this before?

If she'd had any doubt about Taeg's sexual prowess before, she didn't now. The man was a sex god. Even after he'd given her the most amazing orgasm ever, he still worked her with his mouth and tongue. His fingers rubbed along her seam, making her ache for more. She was beyond the point of embarrassment.

"Please." She arched her hips upward.

"What do you want?" he asked with an impish grin.

"I…"

"Do you want my fingers inside you?"

"Yes!" That was what she wanted.

His smile was devilish. He lowered his voice to a hoarse whisper. "What about my tongue?"

Her eyes widened. "What?"

"Do you want my tongue inside you?" The look on his face made it clear there was no shame in wanting that. Desiring that. Oh no, it was obvious that *he* wanted it. And that was the biggest turn-on of all.

"Yes." Her head fell back onto the bed.

His laugh was soft and silky, eliciting an answering hum from between her thighs. "I want that, too, slayer. More than you know. Let me show you." His mouth closed around her clit, sucking hard. At the same time two fingers slid inside, pumping in and out of her with a rhythm that set her blood to boiling.

Oh…holy hell.

She lifted back onto her elbows, her thighs tightening around his head when he replaced his hand with his tongue, sliding in and out with long, deep strokes that drove her insane. Then his fingers joined the action and she was gone. Clutching his hair in her hands, she ground herself into him, shrieking when her release overtook her.

Stars exploded in her vision, blinding her with bursts of color. She must have lost touch with reality for a moment because when she came to he was lying next to her, still fully clothed, but panting as if he'd just run a marathon. He rolled to face her and slid his fingers up and down her hip, gracing her with a slow, satisfied grin.

"You are breathtaking, slayer. Don't you ever forget that." Bending, he pressed a firm kiss to her lips. He tasted of salt and her feminine essence, and it was astonishingly arousing.

"That was…amazing," she confessed when he pulled away.

"Agreed." He grimaced and the reason for that became immediately clear. He was still hard as a rock beneath his pants. How could she have forgotten, even for a second? He'd spent all of his time on her, without showing any concern for his own pleasure.

A *demon* had given her two mind-shattering orgasms, without taking anything for himself in return. How wrong she'd been. How ignorant. Well, the least she could do was pay him back in kind. Her heart thudded as she reached for his shirt and tugged it up. He helped her lift it over his head. But when she reached for the button of his slacks, he placed his hand over hers.

"Maya, are you sure?"

More than ever. She wanted him. Needed him. "No way in hell we're stopping now."

When she guided him onto his back, the sound he made was halfway between a laugh and a growl. He watched through half-lidded eyes while she tugged his zipper down, then slid his slacks off his body, pausing only to take off his shoes and socks. His boxers were tented to impossibly large heights, eliciting a panicky moment of self-doubt. What was she supposed to do with *that*? But when she pulled them down, freeing him, all of her niggling doubts faded away and instinct took over. This was a dance as old as time.

He was so breathtaking. So hard.

"So big," she gasped.

A ghost of a smile crossed his face. It turned into a groan when she brushed her fingers across the tip. His cock pulsed beneath her, and suddenly it was imperative that she taste him. Closing her fist around him, she made an experimental swipe of her tongue along the tip.

"Sweet devil." He canted his hips. "You're going to kill me."

"Sorry," she said, though she grinned. She wasn't sorry in the least. Payback was a bitch, wasn't it? She traced her tongue from the base to the tip, and from the sound of his groan, he liked that, too.

Hmm...maybe there was no wrong way to do this. Closing her mouth around him, she slid up and down, sparking a rhythm that seemed to drive him crazy. She couldn't resist teasing him. "You like this?"

"You know I do." He chuckled. "So it's going to be torture, huh, slayer?"

"Just returning some of what you gave me."

His lips twisted into a wry grin. "Catch on quick, do you?"

She repeated her movement, licking and sucking his thick shaft until at last he grabbed her head and started pumping his hips. The answering pulse between her legs made her breath catch. Even though she'd already come twice, something had been missing. *This.*

She needed him. Inside her. Pulling back, she looked at him from between hazy eyes. "I want you. Make love to me, Taeg. *Now.*"

He hesitated. "Are you certain this isn't something you're going to regret tomorrow?"

The man was the most infuriating mixture of gentleman and rake. Right now, at least, she wanted the man who didn't give a damn about the consequences. Well, she had an idea how she might convince him. Crawling forward, she straddled his body.

With a muffled curse, he flipped her onto her back quicker than she could blink. Placing his hands on either side of her face, he stared into her eyes as if he might catch a glimpse of her soul. The look on his face was deadly serious, and for one moment she thought she saw a glimmer of uncertainty.

"You realize this changes everything, don't you?" he asked.

"It already has." And it was true. Everything was different now.

With a nod of acknowledgement, he positioned himself between her thighs. His cock nudged her entrance and she felt a split second of panic. The one time she'd done this, it hadn't been so much fun. But then he thrust forward and the panic disappeared. He felt so *good*, stretching her as he filled her. She wrapped her legs around his waist, pressing her nails into his back to urge him forward.

Sweat beaded on his forehead. He stopped, closing his eyes on a strangled curse.

"What's wrong?" Her voice didn't sound like her. No, it sounded like a wanton creature, eager to take whatever she wanted.

"You're so tight." He opened his eyes to lob her with a suspicious glance. "You have done this before, right?"

"Of course." She wasn't doing it wrong, was she?

Relief crossed his face.

"Well, once."

"*Once?*" He looked down at her in disbelief.

"I didn't like it very much."

"Aw, fuck me." He groaned, dropping his forehead to hers.

"What's wrong?" Didn't he want her now that he knew she had almost no experience?

"Nothing's wrong." He pressed a kiss to her lips. "That's just a lot of pressure."

"Oh, that's all?" Excitement flowed through her veins. "Well, don't worry about it. You've already beat my first time, hands down."

He laughed and on her next breath, pushed into her with a stroke that slid him all the way home. She let out a soft cry at the unfamiliar sensation of fullness. Lord, he was… One thrust of his hips and she lost all ability to think. She became one mass of sensation, rising up to meet every plunge, flexing her hips to take him in deeper.

"Okay?" he asked on a gasp.

"More," she moaned, digging her nails into his hips to drive him faster. He slid almost all the way out, then back in, quickly building up to a fierce, powerful rhythm. "Please."

"What? Tell me what you want," he demanded.

What did she want? She couldn't even think. Finally her lips formed the word she was searching for. "Harder."

"Fuck yeah," he growled. He pulled away long enough to turn her onto her hands and knees, then drove into her from behind, fully seating himself in one quick stroke. She arched her back, crying out at the unexpected invasion. He didn't give her time to adjust, just pounded in and out with a speed that had her gasping for breath. "More?"

He'd be the death of her. "Yes!"

With a low rumble, he dropped a hand underneath her,

lightly slapping his fingers over her clit before rubbing them against it. That was enough to send her over the edge. She came with an ear-splitting shriek, only dimly aware of his low, answering groans. She fell, face forward, onto the bed and he followed, pumping his release into her with a loud, hoarse cry.

Later, when she could finally think again, there was only thing on her mind: *What the hell?*

She'd expected good sex. No, great sex.

But this?

This had surpassed her expectations. In fact, it had been something else entirely.

CHAPTER NINETEEN

For the third night in a row, Taeg couldn't sleep. But this time it wasn't because he was thinking of sex. Scratch that. He *was* thinking of sex. Just not of having it.

Maya lay asleep at his side. Well, passed out was more like it. Other than his hoarse "Still alive?" and her mumbled "Yeah" they hadn't exchanged two words before she'd conked out.

What had happened earlier?

He'd had sex before. Tons of it, in fact. But what he'd had with Maya wasn't sex. It was a life-altering experience. An explosion. A fucking miracle. Every single little thing he didn't need right now. He was in real trouble. His plans for keeping his emotional distance from her were pretty much screwed.

Truth was, he'd come to care for Maya. Really care for her.

One more thing to add to his plate.

He rubbed his hands across his eyes. Right now he needed more responsibility the way he needed a hole in the head. But it was too late. He'd already gone and gotten himself tied to her. He couldn't undo that now.

If only he could be like Dagan. Carefree. Willing and eager to boink any attractive woman who looked his way. Oh wait, he *had* been like that once. Hadn't he?

No matter which way he looked at it, he owed Maya the truth. Not only that, but he owed her his allegiance, the way she'd given him hers. Who was he to say his family's problems were greater than her own? Once he got back from Faelan tomorrow, he'd call his contacts and see what he could find out about the maliki demons. They could split their time between that and tracking down Leviathos.

Maya stirred and awoke, jolting up in bed. She appeared disoriented at first, then apparently remembered what had happened between them, because she pressed her lips into a shy smile. The corners of her eyes tugged upward. After a moment's hesitation, she lay down next to him, sliding the sheet up over her breasts.

A sense of uneasiness drifted in the air between them, leaving him confused and uncertain. He should confess. Apologize and tell her he'd fix things. But everything was so new between them. He didn't want to drive her away just when they'd reached this new level of closeness.

Keeping his mouth shut seemed to be the better option right now. Hell, if he could get some guys to start tracking her family's killers tomorrow, maybe he wouldn't have to tell her he'd initially reneged on his bargain.

"How was it growing up with an evil demon for a father?" Maya asked, surprising the hell out of him.

"Why would you ask me that?"

"I've been thinking about it a lot." She shifted onto her side to face him. "I had wonderful parents. I can't imagine having a bad one."

He stayed silent for a while, trying to find the right words. "It was awful. We were possessions to him, not people. More like shiny baubles. Keegan and Ronin with their wings, me with my ability to flash, and Dagan breathing underwater. When we didn't do what he wanted, he would beat us."

"Did that happen a lot?" She traced a finger along his chest, though he was pretty sure it was unconscious on her part.

"All the time. Ronin had it worst." Every time he thought about that, he wanted to hunt his father down in prison and beat his brains in. "He was nine or ten when our father took him, whereas the rest of us were still infants. Keegan stepped in for Ronin whenever he could."

"How did the four of you turn out so normal?"

"Don't know. Our mothers' blood, maybe? Or maybe it was having each other."

She smiled, one of those genuine smiles that was so rare coming from her. "You really love them."

"With all my heart," he responded simply. "And what I love, I protect."

The air between them grew thick. Her eyes met his, and for a moment he couldn't look away. They were stuck in a nonverbal exchange that he didn't even understand. Whatever it was, it left him weak and shaken and desperately in need of a drink. Then again, there were better ways to relax.

He looked at Maya. "Did I ever tell you I can morph into air form?"

Her cheeks turned pink and she turned away. "Yes."

"Remind me to show you what I can do with that."

"Okay," she said breathlessly.

"First things first, though." He rolled onto his side facing her and ran a finger in between the curves of her breasts. "Remember those ties I used to restrain you to the bed?"

"Yes." Her voice was cautious, and a little bit suspicious. With good reason.

He glanced at her meaningfully.

"Taeg," she responded.

"Come on, little slayer, live dangerously for once." He slid one hand under the sheet, cupping her breast, and she arched her back.

"I don't know," she said, but her tone made it clear her resolve was weakening.

"Tell you what." He gave her a soft, slow grin. "I'll let you do me first."

CHAPTER TWENTY

Sunlight filtered in through the heavy curtains, sending slivers of light dancing across the room. Maya knew it was daytime, but *when* in the day was a total mystery. She shifted slowly, trying not to wake Taeg, who lay asleep beside her.

Oh boy, was she sore today. Her whole body felt limp and used, in a delicious, wanton sort of way. Yes, she was relaxed, but this wasn't the best state to be in if she had to fight demons. Good thing she didn't plan on killing Taeg anytime soon.

Grinning, she arched her back into a slow stretch. Fabric tugged at her wrist. She found one of the ties still attached to it. Lord, he was so unabashedly sinful. Much of last night was a blur, but she remembered all the ways he'd insisted on taking her. And she'd gone along with his every suggestion. Who knew she was such a sexual creature?

Stark realization slapped her in the face. She was falling for him.

Oh shit. This wasn't a simple case of lust. She wouldn't

have let it go this far if that had been all. No, she'd let him into her body because he'd managed to worm his way into her heart. In a handful of days she'd gone from thinking all demons were evil creatures from Hell to falling for one.

What would her mother say?

Somehow—*somehow*—she thought her mother would be happy for her. For letting someone else in. For trusting again. She might even have liked Taeg, with his easygoing attitude and zest for life. What a freeing thought.

Now the question was, if she was falling in love with him, what was she going to do about it? That was the million-dollar question, wasn't it? If there was a possibility that he returned her feelings, did that mean that they could be together? They were so different.

She'd most certainly be giving up the chance at children if she chose to be with him. Her hand inadvertently crept to her stomach. Honestly, she never thought she'd have children. The world was too crazy and she was too focused on finding her family's murderers. Add to that her inability to confide in other people, and it was pretty much guaranteed she'd end up old and alone with thirteen cats.

We could always adopt.

Listen to her. One night in the man's arms and she was already planning out their future. *Slow it down, Maya.*

A low buzz cut through the silence.

"Taeg," she whispered. "Your phone."

When he didn't budge, she rolled to face him. He lay on his stomach, head resting on a crooked arm. She took one long moment to simply admire him. Even in sleep the toned muscles on his back showed off his power and dominance. The very things he'd demonstrated to her in depth last night.

The sheet had ridden down while they slept, and it revealed the upper curve of his ass. Rounded and tight, the way a man's rear should be. Lord, but he was drool-worthy.

And right now, he's with me.

The buzz sounded again, low but insistent, jolting her out of her reverie. "Taeg." She nudged his shoulder. "Your phone is ringing."

"Mmm, okay," he mumbled, flipping onto his back. "But you have to be on top this time," he added in a soft slur without opening his eyes.

He thought she wanted to go another round? Sweet heavens. But when her attention shifted downward her mouth dropped open in disbelief. Asleep as he was, he was still ready for her. Heat flared between her thighs. For a moment she considered hopping on board and enjoying the ride. But then the damn phone started up again.

Crap. Joints creaked as she crawled out of bed, searching out his phone. She found it in the side pocket of his discarded pants. "Hello?"

There was a beat of silence before a man's voice replied. "Where's Taeg?"

"Um...sleeping." She fidgeted at the obvious indication that he lay right beside her.

"Can you wake him? It's Keegan."

"Sure." She strode to the bed and leaned over Taeg. It took several violent shakes to awaken him.

"Wha—?" He sat up, giving her a disgruntled look before he realized she was stark naked. Heated interest crossed his face and he reached for her.

"Not now." She handed him the phone. "It's for you."

The grouchy look came back to his face. "Hello? Yeah...

What time is it now?" He rose to his feet, unabashed in his nakedness. "Fine, I'll head over there."

Disconnecting the line, he perused her once again, taking his sweet time about it. When he spoke, his voice came out a sexy rumble. "I like what you're wearing."

"I'm not wearing anything."

"Exactly." His lips curved into a grin and he yanked her into his arms, burying his face in her neck. He was so warm. Smelled so good. And he was ready to go, yet again.

"What was that about?" she asked before she could lose her train of thought.

His hands trailed down to the curves of her rear, urging her closer. "Keegan spoke with the Council liaison earlier this morning, and figured he'd get approval for me to visit Faelan while he was at it."

His fingers trailed down the cleft of her backside and she shivered. "Does that mean you're leaving now?"

"I should," he whispered into her ear. He touched the tip of his tongue to the outer shell of her ear before he moved in for a long, hot kiss.

She lifted her hands to the back of his head and tugged him farther down, unable to help herself. Crazy how the man could make her want him desperately, no matter how many times they'd already made love.

When he slung one arm around her waist and pulled her up, sliding his other hand down her behind and between her legs, she broke away with a throaty moan. "I thought you had to go."

He winked at her, a naughty twinkle in his eyes. "Hell, it can wait a little longer."

Three hours later, after convincing a reluctant Maya to let him drop her off at his brother's apartment so she could spend the day with Brynn, Taeg found himself in Central Park. People spread out all over the great lawn and hill. The scent of flowers mixed with the aroma of hot pretzels and fried foods. Man, he loved this place.

A large boulder lay on the perimeter of the hill, surrounded by an invisible force field. It repelled all non-Otherworlders, preventing them from seeing anything within it. That was the only way an inter-dimensional portal could exist in a place as populated as this.

The force field made a slight sucking sound as it accepted him. Anyone happening to be looking at him would see him disappear, just like that. But knowing humans, they would probably chalk it up to the harsh glare of the sun or a strange trick of the eyes.

He stepped out of the portal to find himself on Faelan soil. The hot, humid air practically clung to his skin like a lover's sticky caress. Didn't matter what time of year it was in Faelan. The weather here was always the same.

Night had already fallen in this dimension, not that it made much of a difference where he stood right now. The Nimri region of Faelan, home to dark elves and faeries, was always foggy and stormy. Sort of like some B-movie portent of gloom and doom.

He dug out the directions Elain had written down for him and read them before opening up a fae path and stepping into it. Too bad he couldn't use his flashing ability to travel between dimensions.

It took only a millisecond before he stood in front of a gray, rocky cliff. The top extended into several jagged edges that resembled the teeth of a maliki demon. Perched on flat land between two of the crooks stood a small, two-story home made from the same rock as the cliff. It looked like one good thunderstorm would be all it took to knock the structure over.

As if on cue, a ragged thunderbolt tore through the sky, briefly illuminating the house.

"Spooky."

Why hadn't he materialized directly in front of it?

Brows creasing, Taeg tried to flash closer, but the fae path deposited him in the same exact spot.

"Son of a bitch." The home and surrounding cliffside had been bespelled against travel by fae path. Looked like he was going to have to do this the old-fashioned way. He allowed himself one small shudder before he found some purchase in the rock and started his ascent. One thing was for sure — these Vivi sisters were hard to get to. Maybe that was part of the worthiness test, because as far as he could tell a person would have to be either courageous as hell or completely nuts to attempt this.

Good thing he was one of the two.

At least the long ascent gave him time to reflect. And as was always the case lately, it was Maya he thought of. He'd gone and done it: he'd slept with her, even after he'd repeatedly told himself to stay away. Even knowing it would complicate things in a way he didn't need right now. Looking back on it, he'd been lost from the very beginning. She was just so...so *Maya*. Everything about her drove him insane.

Though practically Taeg knew he should be kicking

himself for what had happened last night—and this morning—he couldn't bring himself to regret it. Not when she made him so freaking happy.

After a harrowing climb that included hanging on by no more than two fingers a couple of times, he finally crawled onto the narrow ledge that served as the front step to the house. Rising to his feet, he lifted the knocker, but before he could use it the door opened with a soft *creak*.

He stepped inside and pushed the door shut behind him. One quick glance was all it took to confirm that the inside of the place was as creepy as the outside. The entrance opened up to a great room, with walls the same rough-hewn stone as the cliff and cobwebs covering the rickety wooden furniture. Directly ahead were wooden stairs leading to a second floor.

Looks like the housekeeper took a decade off.

After clearing his throat, he called, "Is anyone home?"

A soft squeal from upstairs preceded the slapping of feet running across the floorboards. After a minute, a figure appeared on the stairs.

"A visitor? We rarely have visitors," the woman exclaimed in a singsong voice. She practically floated down the steps, the white cotton of her short sundress swaying behind her. She looked around his age, though he knew appearances could be deceiving. Her long black hair flowed down her back, in perfect contrast to the bluish-gray cast of her flesh. Large midnight-blue eyes examined him thoroughly.

Dark fae. This must be one of the Vivi sisters.

He stifled the involuntary shudder that rose within him at the sight of her. Dark fae were scary as shit, with their ability to manipulate energy. They possessed unpredictable powers, and they weren't afraid to use them. Their kind couldn't be trusted. Figured Merlin would have gotten himself caught up with a trio of them.

"Portia, Emy, we have a visitor," the woman called out as she meandered toward him, looking like she might want to eat him. Hell, for all he knew, she might try to.

"A visitor? A visitor?" he heard from upstairs.

"Um." He uneasily backed up until he hit the door. "I'm here searching for—"

The woman launched herself at him, rubbing her body all over his like a cat. "Mmm, how lucky. Such a delicious visitor you are. We rarely get visitors."

"Whoa." Not quite what he'd expected. He shrank backward into the door, trying to peel her off him. "You don't get out much, do you?"

More thumping sounded out along the stairs.

"For shame, Dressa," said another voice. "Did you think to keep him for yourself?"

Taeg looked up to see two more women moving down the stairs. Their manner of dress and appearance were similar to the one plastered to his front.

"I told you we have a visitor," Dressa replied. "Isn't he yummy?"

"Yes, he is." Another woman stopped in front of him and rubbed her hands over his chest and thighs. "Delicious."

"Ladies. Please." He slapped their hands away. Funny, he'd thought they'd be less grabby and more flat-out frightening. Maybe they were so used to being alone that they were dying for any bit of company they could get.

"Ladies, I'm here because I'm searching for Excalibur," he managed to get out.

That got their attention. They stopped and backed up,

giving him matching looks of surprise. Something shifted in the air, until it grew stale—foreboding.

Uh-oh.

"The sword of Merlin?" said Dressa, her expression shuttering.

"I've been told he may have confided its location to you. Is that true?" he asked.

"Tell him, Dressa," urged one of the sisters. She smiled at him, but there was nothing reassuring about it. No, it was menacing. More like what he'd expected.

"The location of the sword?" Dressa looked at her sisters before turning back to him. "Yes, we know where it is. It can be revealed only to one who has proved his worthiness."

And you aren't worthy, her tone implied.

"Though you still wouldn't be able to see it," sang the woman who stood behind Dressa.

Taeg gave a meaningful glance backward, toward the front door. "The test of worthiness wasn't getting up here?"

"Of course not, silly creature," Dressa chirped.

"Too easy," agreed another sister.

Shit. So much for wishful thinking.

"Okay. What's the test of worthiness? How can I take it?" he asked carefully. These fae were dangerous. Cunning. And if he didn't miss his guess, more than a little unhinged.

The women looked him up and down, examining him thoroughly, as if taking his measure and finding him lacking.

"What is your purpose for seeking the sword?" Dressa asked.

"Me and my brothers want to use it to destroy a dangerous book. If it isn't destroyed, it could ultimately lead to inter-dimensional destruction."

"Truth," sang one sister.

Taeg looked over at her in surprise. She was a truth-sayer? How rare were they?

Dressa appeared to consider his words before nodding. "That is a noble cause. You may now prove your worth to us."

"Okay. Great. How?"

Her lips curved into a wicked smile that sent a shiver of apprehension through his entire body. Her finger trailed suggestively down his chest. "We've been alone for so long."

"We'll have fun," one of the other sisters crooned. "So much fun."

Elain was right. These women *were* freaky. Figured. As great a sorcerer as Merlin had been, he hadn't been known for thinking with his head. At least, not the big one.

How the hell was he going to get out of this situation without offending them?

He broke away from the women, clearing his throat as he stepped further into the great room. "Listen, I need to get back real soon, so if you can just straight-up tell me what I need to do…"

When he turned to face them, he froze in place. All three had slipped the thin straps of their dresses over their shoulders, and they now pooled at their feet. The women wore nothing other than the naughty grins on their faces.

"Oh, hell," he whispered, his chest tightening. "Uh, listen—"

As one, they sauntered toward him.

He blindly retreated. A month ago, he might have found this exciting. Who knows, maybe he would have actually dug the danger of being with dark fae sisters. But now, after

Maya… This was his worst nightmare.

His back hit something, halting his retreat.

"Look." His voice cracked, and he coughed before trying again. Maybe, if he was lucky, he could bullshit his way out of this one. "Not that you ladies aren't gorgeous. I mean, really, you are. But I'm sort of seeing someone and she would kick my ass if anything like this happened so, if you don't mind, maybe we can find another way to prove my worthiness."

The sisters stopped, confusion marring their beautiful faces.

"I'll do pretty much anything else. Hell, I'll even clean your house, and believe me, I think only someone who was truly worthy would volunteer for a task like that, 'cause *damn* this place is filthy."

Shit. He was rambling.

"You mean, you don't want us?" Dressa asked, looking stumped.

Another sister formed her lips into a pout. "But it's been so long since we had a male visitor."

"Yes, and are we not beautiful?" the third sister asked, stroking her hand down her chest and pinching the nipple of one full breast.

"Sure you are." Taeg looked away before his body could involuntarily respond. "Like I said, it's not that at all. It's just, you know, I'm kind of in a relationship."

He winced. Damn, he sounded like a tool. Why the devil hadn't he sent Dagan on this mission? This would've been right up his alley.

"Do you not desire the sword so greatly?" Dressa asked.

They all looked at him expectantly.

"I do, it's just…"

"We promise you won't regret it," the second sister cooed.

"We'll be gentle as lambs," the third agreed, giving him an impish grin. "Unless that's not what you want."

"No…no, I can't," he said.

"It is the only way to prove your worthiness," Dressa said in a tone that brooked no argument.

Shit.

Taeg let his head fall back against the wall, closing his eyes. His chest constricted tighter, threatening to cut off his air supply.

He never would have expected this, being forced to make *this* kind of decision. If he said *no*, he might be giving up his only opportunity to destroy the book and stop Leviathos once and for all. But if he said *yes*, he'd be betraying Maya…

Son of a bitch. The one thing he'd been trying to avoid. Hadn't he promised himself that he would put family first? That nothing else was more important than making sure Brynn was safe? Then he'd gone and fallen for Maya. She'd snuck her way into his heart, with her spunk and attitude and kick-assery. She'd made him forget his objective.

It sucked, and he wished he didn't have to do this, but he knew where his loyalties lay.

He had to do the right thing here.

Taeg lifted his head to look them straight-on. "I'm sorry, but I can't. It would hurt someone I care about deeply. I can't do that to her. If it means I give up my chances of getting the sword, then so be it."

"Truth," trilled the truth-sayer.

All of a sudden Dressa snarled, her face twisting into an ugly scowl as she raised a hand in his direction. A ball of energy flew from her fingertips, knocking him back against the wall, holding him in place like an invisible straightjacket. He couldn't move, couldn't even lift his fingers. In the span of an instant she stood directly in front of him, digging her fingers into his throat. Thunder clapped outside the window, reflecting her somber mood. Something dark and dangerous flashed in her eyes as she tightened her fingers, cutting off his air supply. "What if I told you the penalty for refusing was death? Would you be so quick to say no then? Do your loyalties run *that* deep?"

Oh shit. If she was trying to convince him to play her little sex game, this sure as hell wasn't going to do it. His balls shriveled in defense, as if trying to make their way back inside his body, and his muscles quivered from his fruitless effort to move. Well, he'd be damned if he would let himself be intimidated. Let them try and kill him if they wanted to. He had a few tricks up his sleeve, too. If he could just get her to stare into his eyes long enough, he would charm the hell out of her—that was, *if* the place wasn't also bespelled against that. Unfortunately her gaze was stuck somewhere below his eyes, right around his mouth. Maybe if he pissed her off even more…

"Listen, I know you don't get out much, but no means no, lady. *Ain't. Happening.*"

Her eyes widened and flew up to meet his eyes, but she turned away after a fraction of a second, facing one of her sisters.

"Truth," the sister sang.

A speculative expression crossed Dressa's face. "You would truly choose death over an evening of pleasures?"

Taeg's stomach roiled at the menace in her voice. "Is there a third option?"

One of the other sisters trilled with laughter.

"What is it, Portia?" Dressa asked her.

"His most precious gift," Portia responded between giggles. "Would he be willing to part with *that*?"

My most precious gift? What the fuck could that be?

"Clip his wings! Clip his wings!" Portia sang, breaking out into a maniacal cackle. "Broken birds can't fly."

"Wings?" What did they think he was? He didn't have any wings.

But Dressa's eyes narrowed and she gave him an appraising grin. "You're an air sylph, are you not? A *flasher.*"

His gut clenched, and he swallowed hard.

Dressa must have read the look of dread on his face, because she laughed. "Sacrifice your ability to flash, and I'll give you the coordinates."

"My…" He knew she could manipulate energy. And she was strong. Damn strong. Could she actually take his ability to flash from him? And if so, could he bear to part with it?

"Oh, hell," he whispered.

Her brows arched. "Sacrifice is the key to proving worth. Any warrior worth his salt will tell you that. So what will it be: loss of your abilities, or…" The fingers of her free hand suggestively closed over the crotch of his pants.

Taeg stifled a curse, trying to jerk away from her touch. But he still couldn't move, prisoner to the energy that pressed him to the wall.

Fuck. He couldn't begin to imagine living without the ability to flash. But the other thing…

That wasn't an option. Not with Maya in his life.

He closed his eyes and swallowed past the heavy lump in his throat. "I'll lose the flashing."

For a long moment, silence hung thick in the room. Then Dressa let out a low laugh, removing her hand from his throat. Suddenly he could move again.

"Congratulations, warrior," she said, edging back. "You have proved your worthiness."

Taeg opened his eyes, not sure he'd heard correctly. "*What?*"

"Only one pure of heart and noble of intention can wield the sword. Your loyalty in the face of both threat and temptation is admirable. You have shown yourself to be a worthy man, and therefore will be rewarded with the coordinates to its location."

"Though you still won't be able to see it," trilled the third sister.

The tight feeling in Taeg's chest eased, leaving him feeling a million times lighter. Like he could float on air. He'd gotten the sword's location without having to betray anyone he cared about. Without anyone getting hurt.

"*All fucking right.*" He cleared his throat, straightening. "So the threat to take away my ability, that was just a test, huh? I can still flash?"

"Oh no, warrior."

The other two sisters shrieked with laughter, and Dressa's lips curved into a cruel smile. "What I said to you was true. Every worthy hero must make a sacrifice. You have made yours, the loss of your most precious gift."

"But—"

"Now stand still." She lifted her hand, wiggling her fingers at him. "Oh, and this is going to hurt. *Quite a bit.*"

CHAPTER TWENTY-ONE

Taeg reached the portal back to New York City close to midnight. Without his ability to flash, it had taken him a whole lot longer to get back to the portal. He'd even gotten lost a few times.

Damn. Things didn't seem the same now. From now on, he'd have to rely on things like public transportation. And walking. Hell, this sucked. Big-time. But it had been worth it. He'd gotten the location of the sword. He could finally begin to make amends to Keegan and Brynn for all the times he'd failed them.

The trek back to Keegan's seemed to take an eternity, and he was more than a little anxious to see Maya again. When he stepped into the apartment, he found Reiver in the chair set up in the foyer.

Reiver greeted him, then nodded toward the living room. "She's in there."

"Thanks." Taeg headed into the living room to see Keegan playing a bowling game on the Wii. Brynn and Maya watched him with amused expressions, no doubt due to how much he was sucking. Keegan had bought the gaming system after Brynn had gotten pregnant and they'd ended up staying in more, but bowling was the one game he couldn't seem to master. Not that he didn't keep trying.

"Damn it," Keegan cursed into the screen.

"Do I need to give you another lesson?" Taeg half-joked.

They all turned to look at him.

"Taeg!" Maya flew off the couch and launched herself into his arms. Damn did that feel good. "You're okay."

"Of course I am." Taeg closed his arms around her and buried his face in her hair, drinking in her scent. He hadn't realized until this very moment how much he'd been missing the aroma of honeysuckle.

"How'd it go?" Keegan asked him.

Taeg broke away, keeping an arm around Maya's shoulder. He tried to muster up the enthusiasm he should be feeling. "Got the coordinates."

"Sweet!" Keegan approached and gave him a high-five. "What did you have to do?"

His brother's innocent question was like a swift kick to the gut. But Taeg couldn't tell him. Not yet. Knowing Keegan, he would feel guilty about it.

He shrugged. "Some trials of courage. Climbing a scary mountain and shit like that. No biggie."

Keegan's eyes narrowed in on him, as if he could sense something was wrong. But in the end he just asked, "So where is it? When are you gonna go get it?"

"In Wales. I figure we'll fly out tomorrow."

"Wales?" Maya said, her voice tinged with a note of shock.

"Yup." He winked at her. "What do you say, sugar? A nice

little Welsh vacation? You, me…and Dagan."

Her brow wrinkled. "Dagan?"

"The sword is at the bottom of a lake."

Keegan whistled. "Thank the devil we've got a brother who can breathe underwater."

"My sentiments exactly."

Maya placed her hand on his stomach, rubbing in a slow circle. It didn't look like she noticed what she was doing, but he sure as hell did. Made him think of what other body parts she could be stroking right about now. He knew with sudden certainty they weren't going to make it back to his apartment. Not when there was a perfectly good bed here.

Taeg let out an exaggerated yawn. "It's been a long day. I'm pretty beat. If you two don't mind, we'll sleep in the guest room tonight."

"Of course not," Brynn said from her spot on the couch.

Keegan no doubt sensed his train of thought, because he smirked. "No problem."

"Good night, bro, sis." He grabbed Maya's hand and pulled her out of the room.

"Subtle," she whispered, the corners of her mouth tugging up into a smile.

"That's my middle name," he deadpanned as he led her to the end of the long hallway, where a doorway cut into each side of the corridor. "Hell of a day."

But he knew how he wanted it to end.

It had all been worth it. To keep from having to betray Maya, to hopefully keep Brynn safe, it had been worth the loss.

Impatience spiked his blood pressure. He wanted to be inside her. *Now.* Pushing the door to the guest room open, he led the way inside.

ᔆᕔᕐ

Maya felt a sudden bout of relief as she followed Taeg into the bedroom. It had been a long day, one filled with worry over him. She was glad he'd talked her into staying here, though. Spending time shopping and chatting with Brynn had calmed her like going to school never would have. And now, everything was all right. *He* was all right.

And they were going to *Wales* tomorrow.

She turned to him, anticipation sparking in her stomach when she read the naughty expression on his face.

"Guess you're exhausted," she teased. "You probably want to go straight to sleep, huh?"

Taeg slammed the door shut behind him. He grinned and pulled her into his body. "Not exactly what I had in mind."

She slid her hands up his chest, then around to his ass. Lord, he was delicious. And right now he was all hers. "You have a little stress you need to work out?"

"Mm-hm," he murmured against her ears, sending a shiver through her. "Working it out was exactly what I had in mind."

Her, too.

"I have an idea." She undid his jeans and slid them down his thighs, along with his boxers. Dropping to her knees, she guided his erection to her mouth. She spent the next several moments simply enjoying him, alternating teasing licks with deep swallows, where she worked as much of him into her mouth as possible. Finally he emitted a low groan and wound his hands around the back of her head, pumping hard into her mouth. This what was she wanted. What she needed.

"Yes." His body arched as his release overtook him.

She swallowed his salty essence, squeezing her legs together. He tasted so good she was on the verge of her own orgasm.

"Come here." He pulled her up and stepped out of his jeans, sliding off his shirt before leading her to the bed. "Turn around."

Heart pounding, she did as he asked. He moved behind her, sliding her shirt up until it rested over her breasts, and tugging the cups down so he could palm her nipples. She gasped when he pressed against her. He was already hard again, the thick length of his erection nudging her bare skin.

Lord, she'd never been so turned on before. How did he manage to do that to her every time?

His nimble fingers undid her jeans and he slid them down to her thighs before bringing one hand up to knead first one breast, then the other. His free hand slid down between her thighs, expertly parting the slick folds of her sex before he buried two fingers deep inside her.

"You're driving me crazy," she panted.

He let out a hoarse laugh. His thumb flicked against her clit. "That's the goal."

After a few more minutes of mind-numbing pleasure, he stepped back to pull her jeans all the way off. "Get on the bed. On your hands and knees."

Why did he always want her at her most vulnerable? And why did she find that so hot? Legs trembling, she climbed onto the bed.

"Spread your legs," he ordered in a hoarse voice.

Desire warred with the primitive instinct to flee. Biting her lip, she did as he asked.

He let out a groan. "You are so fucking beautiful."

His fingers ran along her parted folds before he slipped them inside her once again, sliding them in and out. She moaned and bucked beneath him. The feel of his fingers inside her threatened to drive her over the edge.

"No," she whimpered when he withdrew his fingers. She had almost been *there*.

"Patience." He grinned at her before lowering to the floor and lifting his hands to the globes of her ass. Parting them, he rewarded her with a long, thorough lick along her center.

She let out a soft cry.

His tongue was magic, flicking along her sensitized clit, working its way inside her. When he thrust two fingers into her again, it was enough to push her over the edge. She shoved her face against the mattress to muffle her yell as her hips jerked up to meet him. Tides of pleasure washed over her, sending electric waves throughout her body. It was amazing. She felt sated...but not complete. She still wanted him inside her.

"Maya," he whispered behind her. "You are so incredibly delicious. Do you know how much I want you?"

"Yes," she confessed. "I want you just the same."

"Do you?"

She was dimly aware of him standing, then kneeling behind her on the bed. His hand grabbed onto the backs of her thighs, pushing her ass higher in the air.

"I wonder how far you'll let me go, little slayer?"

"What do you mean?" She moaned when he pressed forward, sliding his thick, long erection along her wet folds without seeking entrance.

"Do you want to know what I really want right now?"

"Ah...yes."

"This." His moistened cock slid along her crease again before he lifted it, pressing it against the rim of her backside.

She automatically tensed and looked behind her. "You want to—?"

"What do you say, slayer? Are you willing to try it?" His face could have been made of stone, he seemed so in control of himself. But she recognized the fire in his eyes. He wanted this.

"I..." She didn't know how it would be possible to enjoy what he wanted, but if there was anything she now knew, it was that she trusted him. He wouldn't hurt her, no matter what. "Okay."

He made a low growling sound in his throat. On instinct, she tensed again.

"So apprehensive," he said on a laugh. Instead of pressing forward as she'd expected, he backed off and, still gloriously nude, strode toward one of the nightstands at the head of the bed. After opening the top drawer, he rummaged around until he withdrew a small square packet. When he headed back toward her, she realized what it was. A sudden, uncontrollable tide of jealousy washed over her.

"You must bring girls here a lot," she accused. What else could account for him knowing exactly where to find lubricant?

"Calm down," he said with a chuckle. His eyes flashed with amusement as he ripped the packet open with a soft tear. "I left a few things behind when I moved out. It's pure luck that this happened to be one of them."

"Oh." She regarded him with suspicion. But then, he'd never really lied to her before, had he? When he stepped behind her once again, his hands trailing down her back, she returned her gaze forward and arched into his touch. "I guess so."

Taeg made a satisfied sound deep in his throat as his hand slid down her body. Slowly he thrust one, two, then three fingers inside her, moving them in a soft, easy rhythm. Little by little she relaxed, until he'd once again worked her into a frenzy. Only then did he withdraw his fingers. A moment later, when he slid them along the rim of her ass, the increased moisture told her he'd transferred the lube to his fingers. He worked a finger gingerly into her opening..

"Oh..." A hint of pain mixed with the stirrings of pleasure. It felt mostly good, but his finger was a whole lot smaller than a certain other part of him. "I don't know about this."

"I promise, little slayer, you'll like it," he whispered.

When his cock replaced his finger and he slowly inched past the entrance of her rear, she ceased hearing or seeing, or doing anything besides feeling. The sensation of him inside her was almost overwhelming, but he kept his movements slow, building up a steady cadence that he punctuated with the strum of his fingers against her clitoris. Amazingly, she found herself adjusting and relaxing into his touch, until at last she began to arch into him with every pump.

"Ah, just like that." He moaned and pushed harder, focusing all his attention on her throbbing clit. The stroke of his fingers was so intense that in the end she found herself pushing back to meet every thrust, urging him to go harder. Faster. Deeper. Until at last her vision fractured with the blinding force of her climax.

When she could finally think once more, she managed one simple thought: He'd been right. She *had* liked it.

❧❧❧

The sound of snoring woke him. Taeg smiled and turned his head toward Maya. She lay on her side, her hair still damp from the shower they'd taken. Every few breaths a little snort would escape her. It seemed he'd exhausted her.

Devil, but she was freaking gorgeous. He couldn't help but wonder how he got so lucky to have her in his bed.

You lied to her, remember? You told her you were searching for her family's killers when in reality you've done squat about it.

He groaned. *Fuck you, conscience. Go back to sleep.*

But it was right. He couldn't let this go on any further. She needed to know the truth.

He reached his hand out to nudge her awake when he heard a soft scratching at the door. That's when he felt it. Dread pushing against the back of his throat, threatening to choke him. Something was wrong.

Sliding out of the bed, he tugged on his jeans and picked up his shirt before walking to the door. He glanced back at Maya, who was still dead asleep, before opening the door.

Keegan stood on the other side, and his expression was foreboding. Taeg stepped out and closed the door behind him. "What happened? Is something wrong with Brynn?"

"No."

"Oh thank the devil." Taeg relaxed. "For a second I thought—"

"I got a call from Bull."

Bull was a security guard who worked for the Council at its headquarters. There was only one thing there that was of importance to them.

Apprehension clawed its way up his throat once again. "What is it?"

"The *Book of the Dead*." Anger flashed in Keegan's eyes, along with a glimmer of fear. "It's been stolen."

CHAPTER TWENTY-TWO

Taeg sat with Ronin in Keegan's office, waiting for their big brother to rejoin them. Dagan leaned against the wall, looking worn and bleary-eyed. For the first time he noticed Keegan had redecorated. Whereas before the room had been nondescript, with nothing more than an antique cherry desk and bookcases, now a collection of swords and other weapons lined the walls. Not real antiques but replicas, though of the finest kind. Brynn's doing, no doubt.

Crazy how he could notice something so trivial at a time like this.

Just when he thought he was going to explode with anxiety, Keegan walked in.

Taeg cut straight to it. "How is it possible that the book was stolen right from under the Council's nose?"

Keegan sighed and sat in his chair. "It was kept in a locked room at the Council headquarters. They discovered it missing when they did their daily inventory of dangerous artifacts. But there's no sign of Leviathos or anyone suspicious entering."

"What does that mean?" Dagan asked on a yawn.

That really burnt Taeg's ass. "Oh, I'm sorry. Are we keeping you awake, princess?"

"Cut me some slack," Dagan complained. "It's four o'clock in the morning."

He was right. Taeg forced down his misplaced anger. If only he had Leviathos in front of him right now.

"Bull says the only way Leviathos could have gotten it is if he bribed someone to steal it, which isn't likely given that the only recent visitors have been Council members," Keegan continued. "If not that, he must have managed to get into the headquarters without the use of a Council portal."

"Well, that's not possible. Is it?" Ronin asked.

"Headquarters is between planes," Taeg pointed out. "There's no other way to get to there besides using a portal."

"Yeah, but was it a *Council* portal?" Keegan asked.

"What do you mean?" Taeg said.

Keegan pursed his lips. "I've heard a rumor of an undocumented portal in New York."

"*What*?" Taeg asked. "When?"

"And why are you only telling us now?" Ronin added.

Dagan scoffed. "What difference does it make? It's not possible."

"But what if it is?" Keegan leaned forward over his desk. "Listen, we know that the portals were created by Council scientists millennia ago. That means that those scientists knew how to make more."

"Whoa." Ronin hopped up and started pacing the room. "It's theoretically possible that scientists might have created more portals. Ones that the Council wasn't aware of. Hell, there could be thousands. Millions."

Taeg blinked at him, then at Keegan. "Okay, yeah. Theoretically. But we're talking the real world now. Who would be crazy enough to do something like that, and why?"

Keegan shrugged. "Your guess is as good as mine. But there are rumors that such a portal exists."

"Where'd you hear these rumors?" Dagan asked him.

"Heard whispers about it at Eros and Opiate. And I didn't mention it because I didn't think it was true. But now..." Keegan let out a loud, weary sigh. "I don't know. Maybe we're totally off track. All we know for sure is that the book has been stolen."

"Leviathos has it," Taeg said. There was no doubt in his mind. He nodded toward Dagan. "Hope you're ready to travel. Looks like we're going to Wales."

Dagan nodded. "I'll be ready."

Keegan swallowed, appearing sick to his stomach. "I'll stay here with Brynn. Until he's found, we'll have to keep her here. For her own protection."

It was obvious how distasteful Keegan found that thought.

"At least she'll have you here with her," Taeg said.

"Yeah, but she's still not going to like it," was Keegan's grim response. "Not at all."

కావ

"Wales?" Leviathos spoke into his phone. "Are you certain?"

"Positive," Garin replied. "They boarded a flight to Dublin about ten minutes ago. Him, the girl, and one of his brothers. I overheard the attendant confirm they were continuing on to Wales."

What business could they possibly have there?

A warning bell sounded in his head. There was something off about this, and no doubt it involved him. Why else would they be flying to a foreign country right after he'd stolen the *Book of the Dead* out from under those stupid Council members?

"You want me to fly out after 'em?" Garin's voice asked nervously over the phone line. "Because if so, that's gonna double my fee. You know wolves and airplanes don't mix. It ain't natural, sitting in a metal box thirty thousand feet in the air."

"No. Stand by. I'll let you know once I need you again."

Leviathos hung up and set his phone down on his small living room table. The window ahead provided a view of the southeast corner of Gramercy Park. He blindly took in the scenery while he considered his options. What he should do was find a way to get Brynn, his key to raising the undead. Now that he had the book, nothing was stopping him from using her to command the army. To rule the world.

Yes, that was what he should do. But his gut told him to keep an eye on Taeg and his oh-so-interesting human. They were up to something. And now that he knew who had murdered her family so many years ago, she might be more than willing to come to his side. Revenge was such a useful negotiation tool.

And wouldn't he know?

Funny, he barely thought about Ana anymore, the woman who'd caused him to sever his friendship with Taeg. But he never stopped thinking about the man who used to be his friend. Although Ana's betrayal had cut him deep, Taeg's had nearly killed him, had driven him to where he was today.

After so many years, perhaps he'd finally get his revenge.

Leviathos stared at the book, lying unobtrusively on the table. It looked like nothing more than a book, albeit one of unusual construction, with its gold- and silver-toned metal and intricate scrolling. But in truth it was so much more. He slid his hand over the cool metal. Taeg no doubt knew it was he who'd taken the book. In fact, it wouldn't surprise him if Taeg had men trying to track him down at this very moment.

He would have to keep the book with him at all times. It wouldn't do to have it stolen now that he'd finally gotten his hands on it. Or worse, have Belpheg figure out a way to take it from him. No, the book would remain with him, keeping him safe.

Once he knew what Taeg was up to, he would be able to formulate a plan for Taeg's destruction. And for his rule of Earth.

"Have patience," he whispered. "Soon."

Very soon.

A current of unexpected energy ran through the room, causing him to shiver.

Shit. Belpheg.

Now was the time to put that spell he'd bought to use. Hiding the book under the table, just in case the spell failed, he recited the words given to him by the witch. The air shimmered, and for one moment Leviathos feared he saw Belpheg's figure forming. But then it dissipated, taking the electricity zooming throughout the room with it.

That was easy.

Grinning in satisfaction, he withdrew the book so he could admire it once more. Who was the smart one now?

He'd bet Belpheg wouldn't even have a clue what had happened.

One pesky presence in his life down...one more to go.

"Watch out, Taeg," he whispered.

I'm coming for you.

∾∾

Belpheg's essence snapped back into his body, leaving him gasping for a painful breath. Dumbfounded, he stared blankly at his dark meditation room.

What the hell had just happened?

Perhaps his body had begun to fail him so badly that he'd lost the ability to project his spirit.

But no, his body didn't feel any weaker. No stronger, either, but then his physical form couldn't be what caused the spiritual link to break.

Leviathos. With sneaking suspicion, he placed his hands on his knees, resuming the meditative pose he used to astrally project. He shut his eyes and concentrated on establishing a link to Horster, the junkie who had his ear in just about every shady dealing going on in New York City.

He found nothing but inky blackness...nothing like when he'd attempted to contact Leviathos. That link he'd found but had somehow been cut off from. No, Horster's spiritual connection was gone altogether. Which could only mean one thing...

The junkie was dead.

Damn it. What were the odds of the man dying shortly after Belpheg had connected him with Leviathos for the purpose of finding a way to the book? Granted, he was a *score* addict, so it could happen. But still…

Something smelled wrong about this.

Good thing he knew of another way to go about getting the information he needed.

Eyes remaining closed, Belpheg concentrated on stroking the cord that bound his soul to Leviathos. The stupid fool didn't even know about it, didn't realize that when he'd bargained to join forces with him, Leviathos had irrevocably bound himself to Belpheg.

Once he received the answering hum of Leviathos's soul, Belpheg projected his spirit into the astral realm he'd specially created. A dark, barren wasteland, it was the perfect representation of his rage over the genocide of his family. And thanks to the knowledge he'd gained from his scrolls, here he could do all manner of things, from spiritually connecting to others…to even causing harm to the bodies of those who projected their spirits here.

Now he would use the soul bond he'd created with Leviathos to download the lackey's memories…see what Leviathos had been holding back.

A lightning bolt zigzagged across the darkened sky as Belpheg's spirit-body knelt on the rocky ground and concentrated on pulling memories from Leviathos's essence. Like inky tendrils of smoke, they wafted toward him, floating into his mind on a series of images.

He saw Leviathos procuring a blocking spell… Later, with Horster…a piece of paper was exchanged…coordinates… Leviathos sneaking into the Council headquarters and nabbing the book.

That sneaky little pest! How dare Leviathos try to cut him out of the deal?

Belpheg read the coordinates, then broke the link, snapping back into his body with an agonizing *pop*. He let the pain wash through him, drinking it in until it faded and he was able to stand.

Fury coursed through his veins as he tromped out of his meditation room and into the library of the dank, dark cavern he called his home. Buried deep in one of the rocky mountains in the Asrai region of Faelan, home to goblins and gnomes, the cavern had served as his place of refuge throughout the years he'd remained hidden, building his abilities in preparation for destroying the Council. It had all the comforts of home, including an enchanted globe of this world. Feeding the globe the coordinates he'd stolen from Leviathos's memories, Belpheg watched as the globe swirled and swiveled, at last coming to a stop at the location.

Damn, it couldn't have been just down the street, could it? The portal was several days' journey from here, if he were to travel without drawing attention to himself.

The thought of leaving this cavern in his actual physical form, of journeying to another dimension, was more than a bit daunting, but what choice did he have? He wasn't about to let that snake Leviathos make off with the spoils. The fool probably thought he was invincible now that he had the book. Little did he know just how wrong he was. If the idiot tried to send an army of reanimated corpses after Belpheg, he would simply gobble them all up, absorbing their energy and making his body that much stronger. Then…then would come his payback.

Leviathos couldn't attempt to double-cross Belpheg and expect to live.

CHAPTER TWENTY-THREE

"I can't believe I'm in Wales," Maya said to no one in particular.

With the stop in Dublin, it had taken over a day to get here. Since that meant there was no way she'd be showing up to work, she had called in sick for the first time ever. To say that her boss had been shocked had been an understatement. She clearly hadn't bought the sick excuse, but what was Maya going to tell her—the truth? That would've earned her a one-way ticket to the insane asylum.

Lush greenery bounded them on both sides as they drove out of Cardiff and headed toward Gwynedd, the location given to them by the Vivi sisters. It was so different here from New York City. Green rolling hills and rocky mountains replaced skyscrapers of steel and glass. The sweet scent of fresh air instead of car fumes.

Taeg grabbed her hand from his spot in the driver's seat, rubbing a slow circle along her palm that made her shiver. He seemed relieved to be back on land. Earlier, he'd admitted that given his ability to flash, he'd never flown in a plane before. And he hadn't seemed to like it very much.

"First time here, I'm guessing," he said to her.

"First time anywhere," she admitted, "other than Mexico and New York City. Thankfully, Helen insisted I renew my passport in case I ever decided to go back to Mexico for a visit."

He turned to her, the corners of his mouth ticking up. "When this is over, we'll take a nice, long vacation. Travel the world."

Her breath gave an inadvertent catch in her throat. This was the first time he'd made mention of the two of them with regard to the future. And she had to admit, it sounded nice. "You mean after we find my family's killers, right?"

The red glow of his eyes flattened a bit. "Right."

If she didn't know any better, she'd say the expression on his face was one of guilt. But that couldn't be the case. If there was anything she'd learned about Taeg in the past few days, it was that he was a straightforward guy. Trustworthy. "Have your contacts found anything yet?"

He opened his mouth to respond, but before he could say anything Dagan yelled from the backseat. "Eyes on the road!"

She swallowed a squeal as Taeg braked and yanked hard on the wheel to avoid going off the road.

"*Son of a bitch*." Taeg cleared his throat. "Sorry. Guess I need to get used to driving on the left."

There was a moment of silence before Dagan spoke up again, his tone biting. "Considering you just started driving a couple days ago, I'd say you're doing pretty damn good."

"How long until we get there?" Her voice came out as a squeak.

"Four hours or so." Taeg gave her hair an affectionate tousle. "Get some sleep if you can."

Easier said than done. But eventually she found herself relaxing into her seat. She preoccupied herself with looking over at Taeg. He was so handsome, now that she allowed herself to see him for who he truly was. The angelic glow of his skin was like a beacon of light, drawing her to him. She wriggled her hand out of his and ran her fingers across his palm, much like he'd earlier done to her. Then up his wrist, marveling at the silky heat of his flesh. His long fingers splayed out, and she couldn't help remember what they'd done to her. How they'd memorized every curve of her body. Brought her to ecstasy countless times. She was beginning to realize she would never get enough of him.

He noticed her staring and gave her a look so heated she felt an answering pulse between her thighs. "Stop that," he said hoarsely. "You're far too distracting."

"Yeah, stop it," Dagan said. "If you two keep up like that, *I'm* gonna need a cold shower."

Maya pressed her lips together to hold back the embarrassed laugh that longed to tumble out. "Sorry."

When they finally arrived in Gwynedd, Dagan had fallen asleep but she was still wide awake, mostly thanks to Dagan's loud snoring from the backseat. With its mountains covered in lush greenery, Gwynedd was easily the most spectacular sight she'd ever seen. Cottages and pretty stone houses dotted the landscape, though the area was close to deserted. It was a far cry from back home.

"That's part of the lake where the sword is supposed to be located. Llyn Ogwen." Taeg pointed to the right, where a long body of water paralleled the small highway they rode in on. It looked rather unremarkable from this vantage point.

"So what are we supposed to do, stop right here?" Maya asked.

He laughed. "I'm willing to bet we need to be on the water to have a chance at spotting anything."

Taeg drove until they reached a large marina where a fair number of sailboats were moored, their tall masts seeming to pierce the thick, white clouds above. He pulled in and parked. "According to the GPS this spot is about a twenty-minute boat ride from the lake."

Dagan's snoring stopped. "What do we do now?"

"Now we commandeer a boat."

"I love that word," Dagan replied. "Sounds much better than stealing."

Taeg's fingers tapped along the steering wheel. "It's not stealing if you return it."

"You're not actually planning on taking one of these, are you?" Maya asked him. "I really wouldn't like spending my first night here in jail."

He laughed and pulled her in for a quick kiss. "Course not, sweetheart. I don't have to."

"Huh?"

"He can charm someone into lending him their boat," Dagan explained.

"Oh yeah." She'd almost forgotten about that ability. Easy, since it didn't work on her.

"There's just one problem," Taeg said.

"Problem?" Maya asked him. "What problem?"

"Sun's going down in about an hour. Does that give us enough time to get out there and find the sword before we lose visibility?"

Good point.

"We could spend the night and get an early start tomorrow," Dagan suggested.

They could. But now that they were here, she was itching to get out there and see what she found. They were so close.

Taeg must have felt the same way, because he said, "Let's chance it."

He slid out of the car and gave her an easy grin, poking his head inside the open window. "Back in a flash."

Sure enough, within minutes he'd reappeared. He grinned triumphantly and wiggled the strange-looking key in his hand. "Our ride awaits."

Taeg led them to a medium-sized boat packed full of fishing rods. An older man with a salt-and-pepper beard watched as they hopped on, giving them a bemused wave.

"Is he going to be okay?" she whispered to Taeg.

He spared the man no more than a quick glance. "Fine. He's just a bit confused, which is typical. But don't worry, he won't say anything."

She gave the old man one more concerned look. He looked more like he'd gotten his brains scrambled than his mind charmed. "I'm *so* glad that doesn't work on me."

Taeg turned the boat on and maneuvered it out of its berth as if he'd been on boats his whole life.

"Nice moves," Dagan said.

"Thanks. In my next life I want to be a boat captain."

She rolled her eyes. Even now he couldn't help but joke.

As they headed down the canal leading to the lake, frigid wind whipped out over the water, making her glad she'd thought to pack her heavy winter coat. She shivered and dug her hands into the pockets.

"Come here." Taeg pulled her in front of him and reached his arms around her sides to steer the boat. She leaned back against him. With his elevated body temperature she felt warmer in no time. A little too warm, maybe. She couldn't help but remember all the things they'd done the last time they were in bed together—a few of them in positions quite similar to this one.

Less than half an hour later, the canal opened up to the lake. It appeared completely different from this angle, with no highway to distract from its beauty. The scenery was dramatic and breathtaking, resembling a scene from a movie based in medieval times. The blue water was clearer than any she'd ever seen back in the United States. They were also the only ones out here, probably because of the frigid autumn weather.

"Be careful." Dagan pointed to a craggy shape rising out of the water ahead. "The lake is shallow and it's littered with rocks."

Taeg slowed the boat to idling speed so that Maya could survey their surroundings. Jagged rocks spiked out of the water at irregular intervals, casting spooky shadows along the water. She slipped out from between his arms and peered over one edge of the boat. The blue-gray water roiled as the boat displaced it, but she couldn't see any farther than a few inches below the surface.

Something about their surroundings lent an aura of mystique to the lake. She could practically imagine some mythical water serpent leaping out to frighten the ever-living crap out of her.

For all I know, sea serpents might actually be real.

That thought made her flesh prickle with unease. But after what seemed like half an hour of searching, nothing struck her as being out of the ordinary. She held back a frustrated sigh. "I've got nothing."

"Let's keep going," Taeg said, his voice clipped.

They putted forward to where the lake opened further. It was larger than she had imagined, a lot of ground to cover. *Too much ground.* She tried to force back the worry of impending failure and moved around the boat, searching for something—*anything*—unusual. When the sun started sinking low on the horizon, lending an orange cast to the water, Taeg flipped on the navigation light on the front of the boat. Still, nothing.

Crap. They were running out of time. What if they couldn't find it? Panic set in, lending a frantic edge to her movements. If only she had the strength and speed of a demon. Maybe that would make things easier.

"How big is this lake?" she asked Taeg.

"Runs about a mile long."

"That's a hell of a lot of water to search," Dagan said.

After half an hour, it was full dark and still she'd seen nothing. Light filtered down from a three-quarter moon, illuminating little slivers of water, which danced in eerie reflection to the light. The temperature had steadily dropped to just short of freezing. Maya pressed her hands to her face to warm her frigid cheeks. Disappointment settled like a bitter pill in the pit of her stomach. Time to admit defeat. "I'm sorry, but I don't see anything."

"Let's head back and find a place to sleep. Maybe we'll have better luck tomorrow." Taeg sounded as frustrated as she felt, and she couldn't blame him. They were so close. They'd come so far. What if they never found it?

He turned the boat around, when she caught a shimmer

of something in the water.

She blinked and it disappeared. "Wait."

Taeg immediately cut off the boat, throwing her a hopeful glance. "What is it?"

"I don't know." She crossed to the edge of the boat and stared at the spot, directly ahead. Nothing there. "I thought I saw…"

Shit. There was nothing there. Swallowing the heavy lump in her throat, she turned away. "I guess it was wishful thinking."

But when he turned the boat back on, the navigation light cut off momentarily.

"Wait!"

"What is it?" he bit out, clearly impatient now.

She rushed back to the side of the boat, her heart thrumming against her rib cage. "Cut the lights."

The moment he flipped the switch she saw it.

"Oh my God." She covered her mouth with her hands, only dimly aware of Taeg and Dagan rushing up beside her.

"What is it?" Taeg asked, at the same time Dagan said, "I don't see anything."

Well, he wouldn't, would he?

"It's there." Her hand shook when she pointed to the spot, about twenty yards from them.

Taeg moved behind her, closing his arms around her front, steadying her with his touch. "What do you see?"

"The air is shimmering, and the water directly below it is glowing blue." What a difficult thing to describe to people who couldn't see it. "Have you ever seen any pictures of bioluminescent bays?"

"I've seen one in person."

She swiveled her head back to look at him. "Really?"

"Mm-hm."

"Well, it's like that." She turned back to the glowing water.

"Amazing. I see nothing but moonlight and dark water," Taeg said. "How big is the area?"

Maya did some rough measurements. "About twenty feet."

He stood behind her for several long minutes, as if letting her absorb the scenery, before finally breaking away. "I'm going to try to drive us over there. Can you call out when we get close?"

She nodded, and when Taeg left to start the boat up, Dagan fell into place beside her. "It's pretty amazing, what you can do. You know that, right?"

"I'm starting to figure that out."

Taeg turned on the lights. "Can you still see it?"

"No." When he flipped the lights off again, she called out, "It's back."

"Interesting," Dagan murmured. "You can only see it in the dark."

"I'd say that's the least interesting thing about it," she retorted. A soft laugh escaped her. This had been the craziest. Week. Ever.

"Keep me posted. I'm flying blind here." Taeg started forward, taking it slow as he edged the boat closer and closer. When they were less than ten feet away, he started to swerve.

"No, keep it steady," she called. What was he doing?

"I am," he bit out.

She exhaled, exasperated. "No, you're going around it."

"I could have sworn I was going straight." He shifted the wheel until she told him to stop, then started forward again.

Like before, he edged past the spot.

"You're doing it again." She tried to keep the sharpness out of her voice, but failed miserably.

"I'm going straight." His voice was no less sharp than hers.

Dagan stiffened beside her and turned to shoot Taeg a meaningful glance.

Uh-oh.

"What is it?" Maya asked Dagan.

"Sounds like a repellent force field."

"That would explain the blue glow only you can see, and why no one has ever stumbled upon it before," Taeg called out. "No one can get close."

A force field. "Ok-a-a-ay. What are we going to do?"

Dagan bit his lip as he looked out over the water. "How far from the spot are we?"

"About fifteen feet now."

Dagan shed his jacket. He turned to Taeg and shouted, "Cut the engine."

Maya blinked at him. "What are you doing?"

He gave her a mischievous grin. "Going swimming, apparently."

"Uh, it's freezing out there."

Taeg took one look at Dagan, who was now peeling off his shirt, and shook his head. "Guess I need to put the anchor down."

She watched him grab the anchor before turning back to Dagan, now in the process of tugging his jeans down over his thighs. Her gaze inadvertently dropped to the dark cotton boxer briefs hugging his lean, muscular body. He noticed it, too, because he winked at her. "Like what you see?"

Heat rushed through her body. Well, at least that was one

way to warm her cheeks.

"Stop fucking around." Taeg spoke with the confidence of a man who knew he had nothing to fear. And he was right. As deliciously handsome as Dagan was—and oh, he was—he was no match for his brother in her eyes.

Dagan laughed and stepped out of his jeans, leaving him clad in his boxer-briefs and nothing else. He stared out onto the horizon again. "Where is it now?"

"Straight ahead," she choked out. "But you're going to freeze out there."

"Don't worry, I'm hot-blooded." With a final smirk, he jumped overboard.

"Smartass," Taeg grumbled as he moved behind her and hugged her, lending her his warmth.

The moonlight barely illuminated Dagan, who expertly swam toward the light. But a few feet before he hit the glowing water, he swerved and started to swim around it.

"Damn it," she cursed. "You're going around it!"

"No shit," Taeg marveled behind her. "Looks like he's going straight to me."

Dagan treaded water as he called out, "Which way did I turn?"

"Right."

He immediately adjusted to the left. Still it took several tries before he managed to swim directly into the glowing pool.

"You're in," she called. "Starts where you are and goes ahead of you for about twenty feet."

Dagan gave them a double thumbs-up sign before diving forward and disappearing into the water. Three, four, five minutes passed. She grew edgier with every minute.

"Relax." Taeg nuzzled into her neck. "He can breathe underwater, remember?"

True. But they didn't have any idea what was down there.

Finally, half an hour had passed with no sign from Dagan. Now even Taeg couldn't restrain his nerves. He released her and began to pace back and forth on the boat. "Maybe I should go in after him."

"That's insane," she argued. "You can't breathe underwater, *plus* you can't see the spot."

"Still, I can—"

She took a deep breath. "I'll go."

That stopped him in mid-stride. His mouth dropped open. "Are you out of your mind?"

"At least I could see what's down there."

"There's no fucking way I'm letting you go down there," he practically spat out. "You'll freeze within seconds of landing in the water."

Two could play the overprotective card. "Well, I'm not letting you go by yourself, either."

"You don't have a choice."

"Um, when you two are done fighting, maybe you could help me out?" Dagan's voice sounded from somewhere beside the boat.

"Dagan!" Relief tore through her, making her feel half-drunk with giddiness. She ran to the side of the boat while Taeg rushed to the console to flip on the navigation lights.

Dagan treaded water at the rear of the boat. He clung to the ladder with one hand while holding onto something with the other. His teeth were chattering, and he panted hard.

Maya lifted her brows. "I thought you were hot-blooded."

"Even demons get c-c-cold."

"Shit, bro." Taeg appeared at her side. "Get the hell out of that water before you freeze your ass off."

"Take this." Dagan hefted the object in his hand onto the deck.

She paid it no more than a cursory glance, enough to see that it was a sword and scabbard, before rising and scavenging around until she found a heavy wool blanket. "Here, dry off with this."

Crawling onto the boat, Dagan accepted it and wrapped it around himself. Still, he shook so badly she could practically hear his bones creaking.

"Damn it, Dagan," Taeg snapped, his eyes flashing in anger. "Why did you stay down there so long?"

"I—I was blind out there. Just kept swimming 'til my hand grazed something."

"Idiot," Taeg croaked. He reached out and yanked Dagan toward him, closing his arms around him and holding on tight.

Dagan attempted to pull away. "Hey, hands off the merchandise."

She moved behind Dagan and circled her arms around him, too, trapping him between their bodies. "Oh please, stop with the whole macho act, will you?"

After a while he'd apparently warmed up more than enough, because he stopped shivering and drawled, "Are you two pervs gunning for a threesome, or should I get dressed again?"

Mortification lent her speed. She retreated before he finished his sentence, averting her eyes when he dropped the blanket to slip off his soaked boxers. She shifted her focus to the sword lying on the boat deck. For the first time it registered what she was looking at.

"Whoa." She knelt so she could run her fingers along the sword and its scabbard. It looked so...so...*ordinary*.

Taeg dropped to one knee beside her. "This is it? Sort of anticlimactic, isn't it?"

"It looks like a plain old sword, even to me," she said. This couldn't be right.

With a swish of his clothes, Dagan squatted down next to them. "The thing has survived at the bottom of a lake for over a thousand years without getting any rust or shit on it. Must be *something* magical about it."

Taeg shrugged and rose to his feet, holding one hand out to Maya so she could stand. He flashed her a brilliant smile. "Have I told you lately how awesome you are?"

She was, wasn't she? After all, she'd managed to find something that had been hidden for over a thousand years. "Not nearly enough."

The corners of his mouth quirked up and he tugged her to him, covering her lips with his. When she made an involuntary sound in the back of her throat, he coaxed her lips apart, sliding his tongue inside. He tasted like chocolate and sin, and victory.

Maya lifted to her toes and ran her fingers through his short, silky hair, memorizing the feel of it on her fingertips. She couldn't wait to find a place for the night. There they could celebrate in their own private manner.

Dagan cleared his throat. "Get a room, you guys."

Taeg laughed against her lips, pulling back long enough to throw his brother a grin. "You drive." Then he brought her in for another kiss, and she forgot about everything else.

CHAPTER TWENTY-FOUR

"About fucking time." The breath Taeg had been holding had escaped in one big rush as soon as the wheels of the plane touched down at JFK in the late afternoon. The thought that from now on he'd have to travel this way whenever he wanted to leave the country made him want to cry.

Later, while they made their way through the crowded airport, Dagan said, "I'm glad we made it past airport security. Close call there, big brother."

"Hey, you try charming your way through three separate airports with a sword in your carry-on bag." Especially given the unusual size and shape of the bag. Damn, but he hated flying.

"Come on, boys." Maya took his hand, the tone of her voice making it clear she found their constant bickering amusing. She'd have to get used to it, though.

The deeper meaning behind that thought hit him so hard he halted in mid-step.

Well, fuck a duck.

Somewhere along the line he'd come to take it for granted she was going to be sticking around. He couldn't fathom the thought of her not being with him.

You went and did it, shithead.

He'd fallen in love.

"What's wrong?" Maya came to a stop and swiveled to face him. She gave him a tentative smile and brushed a stray strand of hair off his forehead. The simple beauty of her hit him hard, tightening his chest until he could hardly breathe.

Sweet devil, he loved her. He was totally batshit about her. The urge to confess his feelings was overpowering.

"What is it?" she asked, her smile wavering.

He opened his mouth to speak when he remembered. Her family. The only reason she'd agreed to help him. He hadn't yet lifted a finger to find the evil demons who murdered them. How could he confess he loved her with that on his chest?

Simple. He couldn't.

Once he'd done something for her, then—*maybe then*—he'd be worthy of her love. Until that moment, he was just a lying sack of shit who was using her for his own selfish purposes.

"Nothing," he muttered.

She looked dubious, and once again the urge to confess tore through him.

"Are you guys coming?" Dagan called from up ahead, where he'd paused to wait for them.

Right. Now wasn't the time. Not yet.

"Come on. We'd better get back to the apartment." Taeg tugged her back to his side and hurried to catch up with Dagan.

❧⚬❧

Keegan greeted them inside his apartment, looking worn and haggard. His hair stuck up in sections and he had deep, dark circles under his eyes.

"When's the last time you slept, bro?" Taeg asked.

"Not since you left. Did you find it?"

Taeg followed him to the living room before yanking the bag off his shoulder and removing the sword. Keegan took it and examined it before setting it down on the coffee table.

"Great," he said in a monotone voice.

"How's Brynn?" Dagan asked their big brother from across the room.

"Okay, considering. Pissed as hell about being on lockdown, but she knows it's for the best. She's in the kitchen fixing a snack."

"Ooh, *snack*. You said the magic word." Dagan turned and headed for the kitchen.

"I'll go, too, and say hi to Brynn." Maya smiled at him before leaving the room.

Taeg waited until they were well and gone before addressing Keegan. "What's the word on Leviathos?"

Keegan sighed and walked over to the bar. He flipped over two highball glasses and filled them with whiskey. "Didn't you once say you think better when you're drunk?"

"True story." Taeg accepted the glass and knocked half of the liquid back with one fiery swallow. "Damn, that burns. I take it the search for him hasn't gone so well?"

"Not a thing. People have seen someone matching his description around town, but no one seems to know anything about him or where he lives. And one more thing."

Taeg arched a brow at the gloom-and-doom in his voice. "What?"

"Horster's dead. They found him in an abandoned building a few blocks from Eros. Head severed from his body."

The only sure-fire way to kill a demon.

Stifling a sympathetic shudder, Taeg knocked back the rest of his drink. "His days were numbered, anyway. He was addicted to *score*."

"Maybe, but one of the bartenders at Eros says she saw Horster with a man matching Leviathos's description a few days ago." Keegan took a healthy swig of his own drink.

"What?" Taeg's fingers tightened on the glass. "That sneaky piece of shit. He was double-crossing us?"

Keegan shrugged. "You said it yourself. He was an addict. I know demons addicted to *score* who'd sell their own mother for another hit."

"You just can't get good help these days." Taeg headed to the bar and refilled his glass. "So now what?"

"Now?" Keegan's lips morphed into a grim smile. "We keep looking. I've got this building guarded, at least. If Leviathos is stupid enough to try coming here, Bram or Reiver can have a team of men on his ass by the time he lands on this floor."

Taeg took another big swallow. "This can't go on forever."

"I hope not." Keegan downed the remainder of his whiskey. "This is no kind of life for Brynn. Or our baby."

No. The baby wouldn't be forced to live like this. It wouldn't take that long for them to find Leviathos. On his life, it wouldn't.

"We'll find him," Taeg promised. Even if it killed him.

∂∞∂

Hours later, Taeg led Maya to the guest bedroom in his brother's apartment. Only made sense for him to stay here until Leviathos was captured. The more manpower surrounding Brynn, the better. He set the bag holding the sword under the foot of the bed, giving a silent moment of thanks that Maya had agreed to stay with him. At least for tonight.

One day at a time, bucko. One day at a time.

"Taeg, what's wrong?"

He turned and she draped her arms around his neck, rubbing her cheek along his chest like a cat seeking comfort.

"You seem so quiet," she said.

"Just tired, I guess." But with her chest pressed against his, he could feel her nipples hardening. His cock followed in response.

"Too tired?"

Tell her now, his conscience screamed at him. *Admit you were lying to her at first. Apologize. Grovel if you have to, shithead. Beg for her forgiveness.*

Maya pulled away with a teasing glance. She grabbed his hand and led him to the bed, pushing him down so he sat on the edge.

Now. He opened his mouth to speak, to explain, but what came out was, "I'm never too tired for you, sweetheart."

Laughing, she dropped to her knees in front of him. Her hands worked on the button of his jeans while she gazed up at him. Warmth and desire filled her eyes, along with another emotion he couldn't classify. "Have I told you how proud I am of you? I mean, it's amazing how you'll go to any lengths to protect your family."

Yeah, right. He'd do anything. Even betray the innocent.

Tell her.

"Maya, I—" He cut off with a gasp when she closed her hands around his cock and drew it into her mouth. "Oh... *fuck*."

She made a sexy noise deep in her throat while she alternated deep sucks with light, teasing licks. Damn, but she knew how to drive him insane. Soon enough he was lost in his need, lost in the desire to forget about everything in the world but the two of them, and the way they could make each other feel.

Tomorrow. I'll tell her first thing tomorrow. Tonight, he simply wanted to lose himself in her.

"Come here." He pulled her to standing and made short work of her jeans before urging her to stand on the bed with her legs on either side of him.

"This is weird," she said, looking down at him uncertainly.

"Shush." Leaning forward, he slid his tongue along the crease of her entrance. Her honey and spice essence enveloped him, making him ache with the need to bury himself inside her.

She let out a little scream that was like an aphrodisiac, making him harder than he already was. He drove his tongue into her, drinking in her flavor until he was ready to explode. Finally, with a low cry, she pressed his head into her, holding him while she ground herself against his tongue.

Even in lovemaking, she didn't wait idly around for someone to give her what she wanted. She took it, and that more than anything was what made her so fucking right for him.

"I want you," she panted.

Those three words called to him like a siren song. She wanted him, and he wanted her. More than anything. Right now, that was all that mattered.

"Then come. Ride me." He leaned back, supporting her as she straddled him and placed the tip of his erection at her entrance. One easy slide and he buried himself in her welcoming heat. An involuntary groan tore out of his mouth. "Take me in deeper."

She arched her back, pressing her hips forward until they were joined as much as could be. Then she bent down to press sucking kisses to his neck and chest. Nothing mattered but the deep, wet glide of their bodies. The eager, pounding rhythm they set. "I want you so much, Taeg."

"So take me," he whispered. "Take me."

Hips pumping and gliding, she did. Harder, faster, until her body was nothing but a blinding blur of passion and ecstasy. When his release overtook him, he finally realized what she was to him. His own little taste of heaven.

CHAPTER TWENTY-FIVE

In the span of one instant, Maya slipped from a pleasant, dreamless sleep into an old, familiar nightmare.

Clomp… Clomp… Clomp.

"Donde estas, niñita? Te encontraré."

"No," she whispered. "Not again."

She willed her feet to move, but nothing happened. Once again she was that helpless child, hiding in the shadows.

And then the screaming started.

"No." She shook her head, plastering her hands over ears. No use. Those screams would never stop. "No!"

A pair of scuffed shoes appeared in front of her, startling her out of her panicked frenzy. Then a strange man knelt down in front of her. No, not a man. A demon. The one from her dream that night at Elain's house, she knew with sudden clarity.

"What do you want?" she asked, dropping her hands from her ears.

He tilted his head to the side, as if drinking in the pained screams of the dying. When he returned his gaze to hers, his eyes flashed green. "Same thing as you. Vengeance."

"Vengeance? Who *are* you?"

The stranger gave her a smile, one full of promise and wickedness. "What if I told you I have the names of the demons who savaged your family, who ate them as if they were nothing more than a cheap meal at a fast food stop?"

A sense of dread and foreboding wound through Maya. She sat up and realized she was no longer that lost little girl, but herself.

"Who are you?" she repeated.

"I only want a trade. Small price to pay for justice, isn't it?" His eyes sparked once again. "I can tell you where to find them. At this very moment."

"How?"

"Taeg can't help you. He doesn't know where they are. Who they are." He studied her with a look of pity on his face, his handsome features darkening. "He never made a single inquiry on your behalf."

Just then, she knew who this man was. Knew without a doubt.

"Leviathos."

He grinned and inclined his head in a gesture of acknowledgment.

"How is this possible?" She shook her head, as if clearing away the evil surrounding her. "It's just a dream."

"He's never told you about dreamscaping, has he?"

"Dreamscaping?"

"Demons can communicate telepathically with humans in their sleep. Tell me, Maya, how many times have you dreamt of Taeg since meeting him?"

A series of memories flashed through her mind—the first dream she'd had the night Taeg had kidnapped her, and how guilty she'd felt about it. Her pulse raced. "You mean…"

"He was using you, Maya. Planting dreams in your head. Making you want him. Recruiting your aid for his fool's mission, when he never planned on assisting you in return. He lied to you. Used you."

"You lie." She shook her head in denial. But why had Taeg never told her about dreamscaping? "He'll find out who they are."

He laughed. "Don't you understand? He doesn't care. Now that he got what he wanted from you, how much longer do you think he'll stand your presence? How many more nights will he put up with fucking the same woman, when he has his pick of so many?"

She winced at his crude language, still unwilling to admit he might speak the truth. Unbidden, a thought of Elain popped into her head. Of Nadia, the siren from Opiate. "No."

Leviathos couldn't be right. Could he?

"He betrayed you, Maya," Leviathos said, his green eyes boring into her, all but telling her how stupid she was for believing Taeg. "You'll get nothing from him but heartache. But me, I can give you vengeance. For a price."

Like hell. "If you think I'm going to trick Brynn into running to your arms, you're insane."

"Brynn?" He scoffed, shaking his head. "I don't want the heir. I could care less about her now. I want what you recovered from Wales."

Wales? How did he know about Wales? "I don't know what you're talking about."

"The sword. Excalibur. Ring a bell?"

Her mouth dropped open. "How did you know that?"

He grinned at her. "It was a guess. I knew Taeg would be hell-bent on destroying the book, and there's only one object rumored to be able to do it."

And she'd revealed all their cards by confirming his guess. *Great job, genius.*

"The sword in exchange for the names and whereabouts of the demons," he said. "Your parents would be so proud if you were the one who avenged their deaths."

Who did he think he was? "Fuck. Off."

He stared at her as if taking her measure. "Are you really going to give up your quest for vengeance just because of a man? Did their lives mean so little to you?"

Much as she tried to deny it, his words struck a chord. Finding the killers had been her only focus for so many years. Was she really this close, and if so, could she just walk away?

Dios, this couldn't be happening.

Leviathos laughed and rose to his feet. "Here are your choices. You can sneak the sword out of the apartment and meet me in Central Park, where I'll give you the information you seek in exchange for the sword. Or you can refuse, and my army of men will storm that lovely, exclusive penthouse where you and your lover are currently sleeping and kill everyone inside. Including the heir. Then I'll simply take the sword."

Penthouse? Could he know where they were? He had to be bluffing.

She shook her head. "Not going to happen."

"Do you truly think I don't know where you're staying? I've known for ages. Just like I know the heir is pregnant. I could easily walk in there and take it now, but I'd like to avoid a bloodbath if at all possible. I'm not like Taeg's father. Unnecessary violence holds no thrill for me. Now, do you really want all their deaths on your hands?"

Fear and uncertainty ate at her. What if he spoke the truth?

"Tell me, Maya, do you know of blood bonds?"

She blinked at him. "No."

"Has your lover informed you at all about demons?" He shook his head. "Demons are bound to oaths they make. And I swear by my blood that if you deliver the sword to me, I'll leave your lover and those he cares for alive. However, should you fail to deliver it, or should you notify anyone at all before doing so, I will kill them all. This I swear."

She stared at him, anger making her blood boil. "You son of a bitch."

"That I don't deny. Now, meet me at Bow Bridge in Central Park. Come alone and I promise you safe passage."

"Come alone? What about you?"

"I will be alone as well." He inclined his head. "You have one hour. After that, the deal is off."

One hour? "That's not enough time."

"One hour," he repeated with a grim smile. "Ticktock. Ticktock."

"But—"

Just like that she awoke, nestled beside Taeg on the bed. He slept on his stomach, one long arm thrown protectively across her hips.

Oh shit. Oh shit. What was she going to do?

She eased Taeg's arm off her and sat up inch-by-inch. He looked peaceful, sleeping like that. Content, even. He seemed so happy. Could he have betrayed her the way Leviathos said he had?

The sudden memory of Taeg in their rented car in Wales replayed in her mind. The way his eyes had dulled when she'd mentioned searching for her family's killers. The way he'd put it off whenever she tried to question him about it. And when had he taken the time to search for them?

Son of a bitch.

Leviathos was right. Taeg hadn't done a thing about her mission. That was why he looked so damned guilty whenever she brought it up.

Fury and betrayal churned in her gut. Had he ever meant to help her, or had he been stringing her along the whole while? Oh God, had sleeping with her been part of his whole ruse? Maya doubled over, clutching her stomach. She felt sick at the thought he might have used her in that way. But she couldn't lose it now. She had a decision to make.

What if she woke Taeg up and explained what had happened? What could the possible consequences be? Knowing him, he'd insist on rushing to meet Leviathos. But assuming Leviathos was telling the truth, she couldn't take that chance. Not with Brynn. Not with the life she had growing inside her.

The hardwood floor cooled her feet as she hunted for her clothes in the dark. She struggled to put them on. Leviathos could be lying about meeting her alone. What if he had men with him at the park? They could easily overpower her and take the sword. Kill her before she learned who the evil demons were. She might never get the vengeance she desperately craved. No, *needed*. On top of that, she couldn't risk Leviathos getting his hands on Excalibur. It was too dangerous.

Shit! What was she going to do?

A thought hit her just as she located her boots and daggers. She'd seen an office in the apartment. Antique swords hung on the walls. The sword they'd found looked similar to some of those in the office. It might not fool Leviathos forever, but she didn't need forever. If she could get him to believe it was the real deal, it might buy her some time. Or, if he didn't expect it, maybe kill him herself.

And she'd have the names of the demons she'd been seeking for over a decade.

That was the bottom line. She was willing to risk this if it would give her those names. If that meant she might be able to avenge her family's death and finally put the past behind her. No more nightmares, no more guilt. Their souls would finally be at peace.

She would make sure those demons never hurt anybody again.

Oh man, she was actually going to do this.

Her stomach flip-flopped as she tiptoed back to the bed and slid the bag holding the sword out from under it. She underestimated its length and its tip rapped against the bottom of the footboard with a low *ding*. Heart in her mouth, she froze in place as Taeg mumbled and turned onto his back. But when he didn't move again after that, she let out a relieved breath.

That was close.

Hefting the bag over her shoulder, she crept to the door and—boots in hand—opened it wide enough that she could slip out. She closed it behind her and paused. Things were quiet as a tomb out here. Good. She hadn't been sure everyone else would be asleep.

She made it all the way down the corridor without incident. The office was the final door on the end, right before the hallway led out to the foyer. The door was closed but there was no light visible from under the crack.

What if Keegan was in there? He would know something was up. But then, what was her alternative? Biting her lip, she turned the knob and pushed the door open. Moonlight filtered in through the window and illuminated the space. *Empty.*

"Thank God," she whispered as she snuck inside. She slipped the bag off her shoulder and onto the desk, unzipping it before she removed the sword. Then, after scanning the room, she dragged one of the chairs behind the desk to the sword on the wall closest resembling Excalibur. Sliding it from its scabbard, she examined its sharp blade. It wasn't an exact match, of course.

"But it'll do."

After hastily packing it in her bag and tugging on her boots, she lifted the bag over her shoulder and made her way to the front door. *Oh shit.* She froze in place when Bram—or was it Reiver?—looked up at her from where he sat on the chair in the foyer, holding an e-reader. How could she have forgotten about him?

He cast her a questioning glance.

Maya forced herself to stand up straight and tilted her head toward the door, motioning for the both of them to go outside. She didn't want to risk waking someone by speaking with him inside the apartment. He rose and unlocked the door, then stepped aside for her to walk out, and she quietly waited for him to shut it.

"What are you doing?" he asked her.

She did some hasty thinking. "I have to be at work early today."

"You have to leave at four in the morning?" Reiver asked, glancing at his watch.

"Well, I need to go home and change first."

He cast her a dubious frown. "By yourself? Does Taeg know about this?"

"Of course." She forced a reassuring smile to her face. "We discussed it. I'd better go. See you later, okay?"

"Okay." He let her leave, though he still wore a frown.

Maya kept her steps slow as she walked to the elevator, praying he wouldn't comment about the bag on her shoulder. Had he seen Taeg bring it in earlier? She made it all the way to the elevator and, once the doors opened, stepped inside. Sighing with relief, she pressed the button for the ground floor.

"Wait, Maya," Reiver called out from down the hall.

Shit! Reaching up, she jammed on the button that closed the elevator doors.

His footsteps grew louder as he raced toward her. "Hey!"

The door slid shut seconds before he came into view.

Whoa, that was too close, and she hadn't even exited the building yet. It would be a miracle if she made it to Central Park without dying of a heart attack. But when she cleared the building without any commotion, she became all too aware of another fact.

She was about to meet with an evil demon and try to pull one over on him.

Lord help her.

CHAPTER TWENTY-SIX

Terror and uncertainty gnawed at Maya, rolling around in her stomach like a flesh-devouring parasite. Too late to back down now. She was already here. There was a time when she would have welcomed facing down a demon. Just a few days ago, in fact. She would never have been foolish enough to be obvious about it, but, oh yes, she would have relished the chance to destroy him.

But then she'd met Taeg. He'd made her feel alive for the first time in so many years. Had made her dream of a future. With him. Maybe it had all been a lie, but he had changed her forever. She no longer wanted to live that reckless existence. She just wanted to live.

Dew-covered grass crunched under her feet as she made her way through Central Park, until finally Bow Bridge loomed in the distance. The city lights illuminated the trees and foliage, etching the stark figure of a man who stood along the edge of the bridge. The figure turned to face her, his emerald green eyes flashing in the dark. The temptation to retreat was almost overwhelming, but she fought it, continuing forward until she was about twenty feet away from him.

Revenge. She focused on that, used it to feed her emotions. To turn her into the mindless demon-killing machine she'd once been.

Show no weakness.

"You came." His lips curved into a smile. "And alone, as we agreed."

"The way I see it, we didn't agree on much of anything." She scanned the dark, looking for the figures of other men he might have brought with him. But she found nothing. "What about you? Are you alone?"

Leviathos's gaze flitted from her face to the strap on her shoulder. "Is that the sword?"

She ignored the clenching of her stomach. "Yes."

An unholy light glazed his eyes. He held out his hand. "Give it to me."

Maya let out a snort. "I wasn't born yesterday. The names first."

"So smart, are we?" He grinned. "Let me see the sword first, then you'll have the names."

That wasn't anything she hadn't expected. She held her breath and dropped the bag, keeping her eyes on him the entire time she unzipped it. When she held up the sword and scabbard, he looked at it for a long moment.

He sneered, his disbelief obvious. "That's it?"

"What did you expect, for it to glow?" she countered. "It's a sword."

"*This* is the famed Excalibur?"

"Yes." *Please, oh please, don't be able to tell I'm lying.*

Leviathos stared at the sword as if enthralled. She held her ground, prepared for anything, but after a long moment he whispered, "They are called Vestin and Neros. Two maliki demons who were in Mexico at the time of your family's slaying. They have admitted to slaughtering several families while there."

Vestin and Neros. Maya sucked in her breath. After all these years of pointless research, she now knew *something* about the evil demons who slaughtered her family. *Finally.*

"You know, a little bit of research and Taeg could have found this out, too."

"Enough." She gritted her teeth. "I get it."

He let out a laugh and raised his hand again. "Now, give me the sword."

This was it. The deciding moment. What should she do?

She stared at the sword in her hands as if it could give her the answer she sought. Should she surrender the sword to Leviathos and hope he bought the ruse long enough for her to report back to Taeg? Or should she try to kill him herself? True, she was no match for a demon's strength. The demons she'd killed had all been unsuspecting. But would Leviathos expect her to attack him? It might work.

Undecided, she edged closer to him. The fingers of one hand crept up to the scabbard, readying to take the sword out. Her heart pounded in her throat, so loud she feared it would give her away. She was close, a few feet away from him now.

A familiar voice cut through the relative still of the night. "Maya, no!"

What the hell?

She swiveled to see Reiver running toward them, his

phone up to his ear.

"You lying bitch," Leviathos snarled behind her. "You brought someone with you."

Before she could turn to face him, Leviathos snatched the sword out of her hands. "Garin," he yelled toward a patch of bushes. "Get him."

Something that looked like a wolf leapt out of the shadows and ran toward Reiver, drool dripping from its lips as it snapped and snarled. Reiver dropped the phone and began to shift, his flesh and bone popping and reforming itself in grotesque angles. In less than three seconds he changed from man to panther, but he had time to yell out one last warning before he fully shifted. "Maya, behind you!"

She whirled to face Leviathos, just in time to see that he'd ripped the sword from its sheath. The sharp blade sliced downward, headed straight for her neck.

"No!"

Amazing what thoughts flashed through one's mind when facing imminent death. When she was younger and the demons had come for her, it was that her parents would be so angry with her for drawing the killers there. Now, it was that she still wore yesterday's underwear. She didn't want to die wearing day-old underwear.

No.

She wasn't going to go down. Not like this. Not now, after she'd learned the names of the demons she'd sought for so long.

You can do this. For your family.

With the sword mere inches from her flesh, she made her legs collapse underneath her while arching her body backward. Instead of striking her, the sword made a whirring sound as it cleaved through the air above her head. A long lock of her hair floated down to the ground in front of her, proof of how sharp the blade was.

The ground in front of Leviathos wasn't the most advantageous spot to be, but then he didn't know much about her and he probably wouldn't be expecting *this*.

She snuck her dagger out of her right boot, jabbing it into the side of the demon's leg. The weapon sliced through his flesh with a sickening *thwack* that confirmed she'd hit the bone. Leviathos screamed and dropped the sword, bending forward to yank the dagger out. That gave her enough time to hop to her feet and kick the sword farther away from him.

"You bitch!"

He gritted his teeth, gripping her dagger in his hand. Blood dripped down the tip, falling in heavy drops at his feet. The wild look in his eyes told her he'd gladly return the favor, if given the chance. "You'll pay for that with a pound of flesh."

She'd truly pissed him off now, hadn't she? She edged around Leviathos, pausing long enough to retrieve the dagger from her other boot.

He noted it and smiled. "You came prepared. How many more of those do you have in there?"

"I won't need any more than this," she said, unable to help herself from taunting him. He didn't need to know about the dagger strapped to her waist.

"True," he agreed easily. "Since you'll be dead."

With those words he lunged at her, aiming the dagger toward her stomach. She edged to the right, then spun around in a reverse roundhouse kick that caught him on the side, sending him flying.

Leviathos straightened and, with a muffled groan, whirled back around to face her. Rather than the rage she expected to see, his expression was thoughtful. "You surprise me. You've got a lot of spirit for a human."

That calculating look was a hundred times more frightening than seeing him angry. It made her skin crawl. She fought back an involuntary shudder and braced her weight on both feet. "Want to see what else I can do, demon?"

Before he could reply, she leapt toward him, pointing the dagger at his jugular. But he was ready for her this time. He reached out with his empty hand, swatting the side of her head with a loosely closed fist.

Madre de Dios, *that hurt.*

She staggered back and shook her head, trying to clear the shrill ringing from her ears.

"Give it up. You know you're no match for me," Leviathos said with a laugh. He punctuated his words with a lunge and she spun to the side, barely avoiding his grasp. Just as she prepared to strike again, she heard footsteps pounding across the bridge.

"Maya!" The familiar sound of Taeg's voice echoed in the night, coming from the same direction from which Reiver had approached.

Taeg? What on earth was he doing here? Distracted, she swiveled her head in his direction. Before she could process it, something knocked the dagger out of her hand and a rough tug at her wrist jerked her backward. She slammed against Leviathos's chest. There was no time to react when his arm jerked around her throat, cutting off her circulation. He lifted the hand holding her dagger to her sternum, digging the tip between her breasts without breaking the surface of her skin.

Stars blurred her vision and she desperately tried to suck in a breath.

"No," she heard Taeg cry, closer this time.

"Relax," Leviathos called. "She'll be fine as long as you *stop right there.*"

The pressure eased around her throat. After several blinks her vision cleared enough to see Taeg. He stood no more than thirty feet away. Clad in nothing more than jeans that hadn't been buttoned properly, with his cell phone hanging limply from his fingers, he seemed impervious to the cold. The look of abject horror on his face made her throat constrict and a curious pain hit her chest.

"Try flashing and she's dead," Leviathos said in a tone cold as steel.

Taeg ignored him. "Why, Maya?"

"I'm sorry," she choked out, willing him to understand. "I didn't think I had a choice."

"I can't believe you gave it to him."

The sword? He thought she'd brought Leviathos the actual sword? Oh Lord, he believed she'd betrayed him and his family.

Taeg turned to Leviathos, his face contorting into an expression of pain. "Let her go."

Suddenly she knew. Maybe he hadn't kept his promises. Maybe he had deceived her. But Taeg cared for her. The desperation on his face was proof enough.

"I don't think so," Leviathos spat, tightening his grip on her neck.

"Please." Taeg's voice cracked a little.

There was a moment of marked silence before Leviathos chortled. "You know, I thought you were using her to get to the sword, but now I realize it's another thing entirely."

"I don't know what you mean," Taeg replied.

"Don't you?"

Taeg's eyes narrowed in on Leviathos. "We used to be best friends. We grew up together. Isn't there any shred of decency left in you?"

"Decency?" Leviathos let loose a disbelieving chuckle. "I lost my decency right about the time you *fucked the woman I loved*. Don't talk to me about friendship and decency. I trusted you, and you betrayed me."

Taeg pressed his lips together. "I tried to apologize to you a million times. My actions that day are one of my biggest regrets. I was stupid and careless, and I'm sorry I hurt you, man. I loved you like a brother."

Leviathos laughed. "I know all about you and your fucked-up family. If that's the way you would treat a brother, it's no wonder your father used to beat the shit out of all of you."

Taeg stiffened, anger flickering in his eyes. "Okay, let's put the past aside. Why are you doing this, Leviathos? You know it's a fool's mission. If we don't stop you, the Council will."

Leviathos shifted behind her, increasing the pressure on her throat. "Not once I use the book to resurrect an army. Now that I have the sword, nothing can stop me."

Taeg gave Maya a pained look before turning to Leviathos. "Fine. You have the sword. Take it and leave. Just let Maya go."

She couldn't stop the gasp that tore from her throat. Had he really said that?

Leviathos laughed, his voice silky. "You'd give the sword up for her? How human you've become."

Taeg pressed his lips together, not bothering with a response. *Oh God. Oh God.*

Taeg cared enough about her to give up everything he'd been fighting for.

Tears overwhelmed her vision. If he was willing to give everything up for her, then she could do the same for him. She was going to end this. *Now.* She poured all of her emotion into making Taeg understand. *I love you.*

For the second time today, she was about to do something very stupid. Slowly, she moved her hand to her front and slid it under her shirt.

Taeg noticed. His eyes widened and he shook his head almost imperceptibly. *We'll find another way to defeat him*, his eyes seemed to say to her.

No. They were going to stop Leviathos once and for all.

Maya closed her fingers around the hilt of her dagger.

Here goes everything.

CHAPTER TWENTY-SEVEN

Taeg watched in silent horror as Maya slid her hand toward her dagger. *No, slayer, don't risk your life.* The bastard held a knife to her chest, for devil's sake. So close to her heart. And damn it, he couldn't even flash over there to stop him. The one time in his life when he really could have used that ability and it was gone. Just his fucking luck.

But of course, Maya didn't listen to him. She kept digging her hand under her shirt.

"Let her go," he repeated to Leviathos. "You have everything you wanted. You don't need her anymore."

Leviathos grinned, and a crazed look crept into his eyes. When had he become so mentally unhinged? Or had he always been that way, and Taeg had never noticed?

"I don't think so. See, there's one more thing I want. Revenge."

Taeg's breath hitched in his throat. "Take me. I'm the one you have beef with."

"That's funny. Hilarious. I don't want you." Leviathos slid

the dagger toward Maya's face, running it across her cheek. Not hard enough to cut, but it was still terrifying to see how fragile her life had become. "Your human, on the other hand, is far more intriguing than I'd originally thought. I'll take her with me—"

Taeg read Maya's intent in the narrowing of her eyes, a split second before she yanked the dagger out of its hidden compartment. "No!"

The words choked out of him involuntarily. What if Leviathos rammed the dagger into her throat, or the side of her face? But he needn't have worried. Before Leviathos knew what hit him, she'd slammed the dagger into his side, then taken advantage of his shock and pain by grabbing the wrist that held the dagger and twisting it, wriggling underneath his arm.

In the span of a heartbeat, Taeg raced over to Leviathos. He pushed Maya to the side, yanking and jamming the dagger farther into Leviathos's body.

Leviathos screamed, falling to the ground. Taeg followed, keeping a death grip on the dagger.

"Where's the book?" He punctuated his question with another turn of the dagger.

Leviathos shrieked. "Stop...*stop*." He panted, looking up at Maya. A calculating expression crossed his face. "If you want to know the location of the demons who killed your family, you'll convince him to let me go."

Taeg turned toward Maya. "What?"

She ignored him, glaring down at Leviathos with a look of seething hatred. "Screw you, asshole. I'll find them myself."

Leviathos sputtered, appearing genuinely surprised. Yeah, definitely unhinged.

Taeg gripped the handle tight and twisted again. "Where's the book?" He shouted so Leviathos would be able to hear him over his own pained screams.

"It's...it's in the urn," he cried, lifting a shaking hand toward one of the large ornamental urns that decorated the bridge. The base of the cast-iron urn was built into the top of the railing, and it extended about three feet up, with several kinds of plants stuffed inside. The perfect place to hide something.

"I'll go look." Maya raced over to it.

"Be careful," Taeg said as she hoisted herself onto the railing.

"I am." She stood on her toes so she could dig through the plants. "What does it look like?"

"A book," Taeg snapped. When she let out an angry curse, he elaborated. "Two-toned metal."

One, two, three seconds passed. Finally, he lost his patience. He swiveled his head toward her. "Anything there?"

"No," she called. "Wait!"

"What?" He craned his neck, trying to peer through the thick plants in the urn.

"It's a satchel," she called out, drawing back with a dark brown bag.

Something punched into his gut with a flash of searing pain. Grunting, he turned around to see Leviathos holding onto another knife, this one spearing his stomach. Shit. Where had it come from?

Leviathos laughed and a thin stream of blood dribbled out of his mouth. "Doesn't feel so good when it's you, does it?"

Damn straight, it didn't.

Leviathos jiggled the knife, tearing a jagged gouge in his

gut. It felt like his insides were being ripped out. Taeg cried out and doubled over, loosening his hold on the knife in Leviathos's side.

"No," Maya screamed. She jumped down off the railing. Her boots pounded hard on the bridge as she ran toward them.

Laughing, Leviathos slid the dagger from his own flesh. "I'm going to kill you now."

With a shrill cry, Maya was on them. Every inch the warrior, she moved with more speed than he thought possible for a human, closing her hand around the discarded sword and racing toward Leviathos. One long slice and his head detached from his body. It rolled to the ground, the maniacal smile still on his face.

She kicked it away and fell to her knees beside Taeg, grasping his face in her heads. "Taeg, are you okay?"

He let out a short laugh and agony melted his insides. Damn, that hurt. "Just peachy, sweetheart."

She had never looked more beautiful than she did now, with those tears running down her face. Damn, but he loved her.

"Do me a favor, will you?" he gasped.

"Anything," she said fervently.

"Pull the knife out."

Anxiously biting her lip, she obeyed.

He let out a pained cry. "Aw, damn…shit. *Shit.*"

Where were Keegan and Ronin when you needed them? He'd heal, but not nearly as quickly as he would if one of them worked his mojo on him.

"Jesus, Taeg, are you going to be all right?"

"You know I am, slayer." When she didn't look the least

bit reassured by his words, he tried for distraction. "Thank the devil you brought that sword with you, huh?"

She laughed through her tears. "It's not Excalibur, you idiot. I traded the real thing for one of the swords in your brother's office."

"Oh." *Oh.* He had to hand it to his little slayer, she was full of surprises. "You've got some explaining to do."

Maya had the grace to look ashamed. "How did you know I was here?"

"Reiver called me as soon as he noticed you left with the sword. He gave me directions while he tracked you here." He shook his head. "I can't for the life of me figure out why you left without waking me."

"He told me that—"

"It's not important right now." Nothing mattered more than the fact that Maya and Brynn were both safe. An overwhelming sense of relief made him feel dizzy and high. Or maybe that was the loss of blood. "Help me up, will you? I need to call Keegan and tell him to get his ass over here. My stomach is fucking *killing* me. While he's here, maybe he can save us the trouble of walking and fly us back to his place."

With a strangled laugh, she helped him to his feet. Her brow creased into a frown. "Leviathos is dead now. We have the book, and I'm safe. Why don't you flash over to your brother so he can heal you? I'll wait right here for you. Promise."

"Can't." He gave her a pained smile. "Long story."

❧❦

After taking the interdimensional portal to the strange,

terrifying world that was called Earth, Belpheg had glamoured his image into the humanoid form he presented to Leviathos, then followed the threads of the invisible cord binding his soul to Leviathos's. Finally he'd arrived here, at a giant park in the midst of a concrete jungle. He made it just in time to see a dragon-shifter, in hybrid form, flying off with a man and a woman. Another one of Mammon's sons, if he wasn't mistaken. And in the spot where they'd taken off from, Leviathos's body lying on the ground, several feet from his severed head.

No!

Oh, he didn't care in the slightest that Leviathos was dead, but the book. Where the fuck was the book?

Belpheg stalked over to Leviathos's corpse and, gritting his teeth, bent to examine the body.

No, it wasn't there, and he didn't have any hope of recovering it from Leviathos's apartment. He could sense it already…

The book was gone.

Hopelessness and rage fueled his body, sending adrenaline coursing through his veins. Feeding him temporary strength. But he didn't kid himself—it wouldn't last. If he didn't find an energy source to replace what he'd hoped to gain from the reanimated corpses—and soon— he would have no chance. His years of amassing power, of readying himself to annihilate the Council members, would have been for naught.

Thanks to the fury that bled through his pores, he felt no pain when he stood.

A building wave of energy warned him that someone was approaching. Stiffening, he turned his head to the side.

A woman stumbled out of the shadows, her long, thin legs wobbling in spiky high heels. Her essence emanated from her like a cheap perfume, identifying her more clearly to him than if she'd told him what she was.

A succubus.

That would explain why she dared to wander in this deserted park so late at night. A succubus didn't have much to fear from humans.

And he didn't have much to fear from her.

He relaxed and started to turn away, dismissing her from his mind, but the clueless succubus didn't get the hint.

"Hey, you." She slurred her words as she spoke. "Where you going, handsome?"

Oh, great. Distaste wrinkled his nose. She was an addict, either liquor or, more likely, *score*.

She drew close enough to spot Leviathos's headless corpse and stopped cold, staring down in awe. "Wow, you sure got him, baby."

"I did nothing," he said coldly.

"Whatever." She shrugged and glanced over at him. A sly expression crossed her face, as if she judged what she might be able to get out of him. She inched closer. "Look at you, so handsome. Wanna have a good time, baby? It'll only cost you fifty."

From her words, it was clear she was more than just a *score* addict. She was a whore who most likely earned her cash by seducing unsuspecting johns, then robbing them once she'd managed to kill them off with her special succubus brand of loving.

"Get lost." He turned away, intending to leave the scene, when she grabbed his arm.

Her long, ragged nails raked into his skin. "Wait, baby—"

"Don't touch me!" Furious, he yanked his arm from her and cast her a deadly glare. Intending to push her away, he lifted his hands. But in his rage, something unexpected happened. White ribbons of light shot out from each of his fingers, all zooming toward her. She screamed and arched her back, and to his surprise streams of energy began to pour out of her body, winding their way toward him and slamming into him. He started to lower his hands when he felt it…

The energy he drained from her was strengthening him.

Yes. Oh, yes.

Her essence cascaded into him like a drug. Repositioning his hands, he allowed it to continue siphoning out of her and into him, taking more and more and more…until at last, she collapsed before him, her body a lifeless husk. The essence he'd absorbed fueled his body and his mind. But that wasn't all. He sensed something else.

A troll. She'd fed off one earlier, and he could feel traces of the troll's essence running through his own bloodstream, strengthening his weakened cells.

Unbelievable.

Though he hadn't known it was possible, he'd somehow managed to siphon the succubus's life essence, and along with it, the essence she'd earlier absorbed.

Well, what do you know?

Turned out he could use energy from the living just as easily as he could have used that of the reanimated corpses. Which made the book useless to him.

He let out a hoarse chuckle. Very, very interesting revelation.

But then his eyes met the lifeless ones of the succubus, and his heart twisted in regret. She might have been a drug-addicted whore, but she was an innocent, and he'd killed her. Worse, as her essence wound through his body, he knew it wouldn't last. Even now, it slowly seeped from his pores, returning to the very earth. Eventually it would all be gone, and he would have to kill again if he wanted more energy.

If he used people like her, killed them for his own purposes, was he really any better than the Council members who'd decimated his parents?

No. No, you cannot think like that.

Desperate times called for desperate measures. If he didn't gain some strength, however he could take it, he wouldn't be strong enough to take on the Council. After a lifetime of dreaming of its eventual defeat, he would allow nothing to get in his way...not even a few innocents.

Steeling his back, Belpheg turned away from Leviathos. Away from the dead succubus. As he walked through the park, his steps springy from the energy he'd just gained, he recalled something he'd run across while reading his scrolls. Something he'd never quite understood. The fact that he'd been able to absorb some of the troll's essence through the succubus brought it to mind...

Perhaps if he read the passage with his newfound knowledge, he could find a way to permanently cure himself—and to destroy the Council—once and for all.

CHAPTER TWENTY-EIGHT

Taeg stood on the balcony of Keegan's apartment with Ronin. Dagan walked out, clad in nothing more than a T-shirt and a pair of boxer shorts. "I ran into Reiver on my way to the kitchen, and he told me about Leviathos. Is it true?"

"It's true." Taeg filled him in on the events of the past few hours. "Keegan made it to the scene and healed me, then flew Maya and me here before calling a cleanup crew to dispose of Leviathos's body."

"And the book?" Dagan asked.

"Hidden in one of the urns on the bridge. Can you believe the bastard took it with him?"

"He was probably scared that if he left it at his apartment, we'd steal it back. That was a valid concern, actually." Dagan laughed and rubbed his eyes. "So fucking glad this is all over."

"Huge relief," Ronin agreed.

"Yeah."

Brynn didn't have to live in fear any longer. She and the baby were safe. He should have been bouncing off the walls with excitement, but the tight knot in his gut was still there. He had one more thing to do.

"It's been a long night. I'm gonna head in." Clapping Ronin on the back, Taeg went inside and searched Keegan out. He found his big brother in his study, pensively staring at the sword lying across his desk. "S'up, bro?"

"Come in. Have a drink." Keegan motioned him toward the sidebar he'd set up in a corner of the room.

Taeg poured two glasses of whiskey, then set one on Keegan's desk, next to the half-filled glass he already sipped from. He took a seat on one of the chairs set up across from the desk. "Where's the book?"

Keegan nodded his head toward the floor next to him. Rising, Taeg saw the shattered pieces of two-toned metal all over the floor. "Huh. Well that's that, I suppose."

Thank the devil.

"Yeah, no more book," Keegan intoned dully.

Taeg surveyed his brother. "Then why the long face, sourpuss?"

Keegan sighed and finished off the liquid in his glass. After setting it down, he picked up the glass Taeg had brought him. "Brynn just confided to me that the words contained in the book are embedded in her memory."

Taeg blinked at that surprising bit of news. "That means—"

"Book or no, she still has the ability to call forth the zombies."

"Wow." Taeg whistled. "That's some powerful backup to have on her side."

"Yeah," Keegan agreed. "I just…fear for her. If anybody ever discovered what she could do, especially the Council…"

"Nobody knows but us, right?"

"Right."

"Then we're good."

"I suppose you're right." Keegan took a breath and lifted his eyes to Taeg. "Why didn't you tell me you'd lost your ability to flash?"

Taeg winced. "It wasn't important."

"It *is* important," Keegan said. "That was a big thing you gave up. Huge."

"And it was worth it, one hundred percent."

Something deep and heavy flashed over Keegan's face. "Thank you, little brother. Thank you."

Aw, hell. Taeg blinked past the sudden stinging in his eyes. If they didn't stop now, things were going to get mushy. He hated mushy. He cleared his throat and nodded toward the sword. "Now that Leviathos is gone, what should we do with it?"

"Take it back," they said simultaneously.

Taeg laughed. "I'll make sure it goes back to the right spot. It's too dangerous."

"Agreed," Keegan said. "Taking Maya with you?"

That was a good question. He hadn't gotten to spend much alone time with her since she killed Leviathos. She'd disappeared with Brynn as soon as they'd gotten back to the apartment. But he needed to find her. There was something he had to tell her, and it couldn't wait any longer.

"Don't know," Taeg said to Keegan. "Have you seen her?"

"In the master bedroom room with Brynn, last time I saw her."

With a nod, he rose to his feet and left the office.

The door to Keegan's bedroom was open. He poked his

head in and saw Maya sitting on one end of the king-size, four-poster bed. She faced Brynn, who lay on her side. The two spoke intently, their voices so hushed he couldn't hear them.

Damn, but she was breathtaking. Her face was so expressive, so animated. She was just so right for him.

I hope I didn't fuck it up between us.

Devil, he hoped not. He couldn't imagine living one more minute of his life without her.

The truth was, she deserved better than him. Someone who wouldn't lie to her, who'd move heaven and earth to make her happy. If she let him, he would be that man for her. He couldn't change the past, but at least he could put things right.

Taeg stepped inside. "Hey, ladies."

Maya stopped mid-sentence and both women turned their attention to him.

"I…" He cleared his throat. "Maya, can I talk to you for a minute? Alone?"

Brynn sat up. "You know, I'm hungry. Why don't you guys talk in here? I'm going to the kitchen."

With those words she rose and headed toward the door.

"Thanks," Taeg murmured as she walked by.

She gave him a reassuring pat on the arm and left.

Maya rose and stalked toward him, a shuttered expression on her face. "Taeg, I—"

"Wait," he said before she could say another word. "There's something I need to say to you. Something I should have said a long time ago."

She closed her mouth and stared at him expectantly.

He shifted in place. *Here goes nothing.*

"Maya, I never did anything to find your family's killers."

When she lifted a brow, he let the rest of his words out in a desperate rush. "I'll admit it, when I first agreed to our bargain, I was…using you. I told myself my mission was more important than yours. I…I was an asshole. I realize now I was wrong. I know you may never forgive me, but if you do, I swear I'll do anything in my power to make up for it."

She was silent for so long he wondered if she'd heard anything past his first few words. Then, when he was just about to ask her, she balled her fist and punched him on the shoulder. Hard.

"Ow." He rubbed the spot, scowling.

"I know that, you idiot."

What? "You do?"

She nodded and closed the distance between them. When she wrapped her arms around his neck, his whole body loosened.

"I was mad at first, but I can't say I don't understand," she said. "You were trying to save lives. To save Brynn. My family was already dead. I'm not saying I'm happy about it, but I get it."

He closed his eyes and crushed her to him. "Thank the devil. I was so worried." He stepped away from her, still holding her arms as he stared into her eyes. "I love you, Maya. More than I've ever loved anyone in my life. You're strong and bold and stubborn and…and absolutely right for me."

Her lips curved into a slow smile. "That's good, because you're stuck with me now. I'm finding a certain demon has grown on me."

A low laugh bubbled in his throat. He lifted her into his arms and kissed her senseless. He couldn't have asked for a better ending to this crappy day. Leviathos was dead and Maya was his. Who could ask for more than that?

She finally broke away for a gasp of air, throwing him a stern look. "You know, just because I forgave you for lying once doesn't mean you have free rein. Lie to me again and I'll kick your ass."

"I wouldn't expect anything else, my little slayer," he rumbled.

Later—much, much later—when they were back in their own bed, tired and sated, Maya turned to him with a teasing look on her face. "So in the past week we've fought demons, left the country, and maybe saved the world. What do we do now?"

"Now?" Taeg ran his hand down the silky expanse of Maya's naked hip. "I have to bring the sword back to Wales. Want to go with me?"

She grinned. "Hell yeah."

"Mmm…" He moved in for a slow, heated kiss. "After that, we go hunting."

She gave him a confused look. "Hunting?"

"Yup. I know a couple of maliki demons whose days are numbered."

The crease between her brows flattened and she let out a soft laugh. "Now *that* sounds just about perfect."

ACKNOWLEDGMENTS

It takes so many people to make a good story shine. Lucky for me, I've got an amazing team over at Entangled Publishing. Heather Howland, Libby Murphy, and Suzanne Johnson, thank you for helping me make Taeg's story into one kickass book. And thanks to my publicist, Cathy Yardley, for working to get my name out there so more people will actually read it!

I hear so many horror stories about terrible in-laws. I'm so glad I don't know what that's like. I want to thank my husband's family for being so freaking cool. If you weren't around to help with the little tyrant, aka my son, I don't know how I'd be able to pull this writing thing off. I'm so glad to be a part of this family.

I also want to thank my parents, sisters, nieces, nephews, and everyone else in my wild and crazy family. You're sometimes crazier than one would hope, but there's never a dull moment.

And don't forget to check out these dangerously delicious titles, exclusively from Entangled Select

Devil May Care by **Patricia Eimer**

Being the Crown Princess of Hell has its drawbacks. For one, it makes falling in love with an angel named Matt a teensy bit tricky. It's even more complicated if his heavenly ex and devious, haloed mother are hell-bent on breaking up the new couple. When the matriarch of Heaven declares war on Satan's royal family and kidnaps Faith's brother, there's nothing Faith can do but risk it all—including her heart—to restore peace between Heaven and Hell.

Out in Blue by **Sarah Gilman**

In a violent world where fallen archangels are hunted for their valuable plumage, Wren knows one thing for certain: the human woman who saved him from a poacher attack will die if she stays with him. The demon responsible for his parents' gruesome deaths pines for the chance to rip apart any woman who stands under Wren's wing. And when Ginger reveals a unique talent of her own and discovers the truth about Wren's father's disappearance, Wren must confront his demons to save his father—and the most courageous woman he's ever known.

Kiss of the Betrayer by **Boone Brux**

For fifteen years, mix-blooded Bringer Luc Le Daun has blamed himself for the death of his beloved. But he isn't the only one who carries hatred deep down in his soul. Jade Kendell has been seeking revenge on him for years and is finally armed with a plan. But when her plot goes awry, Luc and Jade must plunge together into the dangerous world of the demon Bane, and as the peril of their journey grows, so does the fire between them.